CHARMING
THE
RECLUSE

ALSO BY MINDY BURBIDGE STRUNK

CHARMING THE RECLUSE

Castles & Courtship Series

MINDY BURBIDGE STRUNK

Copyright © 2023 by Mindy Burbidge Strunk
Cover Design: Ashtyn Newbold
First print edition: October 2023

Library of Congress Number:
ISBN 978-1-953054-33-3
FiveJoys Press
Taylorsville, UT

PRONOUNCIATIONS

While there is not space to provide pronunciation of all of the Welsh in this book, it might be helpful to know the pronunciations of a few characters.

Arawn= rhymes with lawn

Ane= said like Ain

Dafydd= Like David, only the dd is pronounced as a th

Mathias= Math-i-as

Havard=Hafard

Garath= Gar-e-th

Alwyn=Al-win

Seren=Ser-en

Baglan=Bag-lan

CHAPTER ONE

ANGLE, WALES

Marjorie Fitzroy's excitement built with every turn of the carriage wheel. She had visited a fair number of great houses in her lifetime. But this time was different. This was the first time she was attending as an invited guest. And the first time she was going to a genuine, centuries-old castle.

Castles were something she had only read about in gothic novels, with their great turrets, looming keeps, and imposing stone walls. And their dungeons. Any castle worth its weight had a dungeon. A shiver ran up her spine just thinking about it.

They passed through the archway in the wall surrounding the fortified village. Much to Marjie's chagrin, there were no soldiers or knights guarding the entrance. Indeed, the driver did not even have to stop to open the gate. The town was completely open to anyone who might wish to pillage or seize control of it at any given moment. It was a pity for such a notable fortification to be serving no purpose at all. Except perhaps for providing a rather picturesque setting.

The old shops fluttered past her window and transported her back to a time long ago when knights competed in tournaments simply for the chance of a kiss from a fair maiden. Oh, how she would like to be a fair maiden someday. She lifted her shoulder. Not that it would ever happen. But it was enjoyable to daydream about.

She studied each shop, or as much as she could as they quickly rolled past her window. Would she have a chance to explore the village, even if she could not have her leave in the castle?

"Mama, who is it we are visiting again?"

"Lord and Lady Angle, poppet."

She shifted her gaze from the window to her mother. "And do they know?"

"Know what?" her mother asked, even though Marjie was quite certain she knew.

"Do they know that until recently you worked as a modiste?" She hated to bring it up, but Marjie preferred to know what expectations she should have.

Her mother sat a little taller, but Marjie could see the vulnerability in her eyes. "Lady Angle knows. We have been friends since before both of us married. We stayed in contact over the years. Indeed, Lady Angle was one of the few friends who stayed in touch after I married your father." Her hands tightened around the ribbons of her reticule. "What Lord Angle knows, I have no notion."

Marjie sighed. They were to visit a stuffy old marquess and his wife. She could not imagine there would be much fun to be had, but perhaps she could find something to amuse her for the next fortnight. She was staying in a castle after all.

She leaned her head to the side, looking dreamily out the

window. It had been just over a year since their entry into society. A re-entry of sorts for her mother. And a rather rocky entry for Marjie.

While her mother had been born Lady Mariane, Marjie's grandfather, the late Duke of Yarm, had disinherited her mother upon marriage to her father. Indeed, he had denied her —even though it was not within his rights—the use of her title. But since his death, everything had been put to rights, thrusting the two of them into several advantageous, if not awkward, social situations.

"Then she doesn't care about our past?" Marjie continued to look out the window, wondering when Hywel Castle would come into view.

"If she cared, I should not think she would have invited us to be her guests." Her mother's words said she was certain, but her face did not show the same confidence. She patted Marjie on the arm, but it seemed for her own comfort more than for Marjie's.

Her mother had a not-so-secret desire to find Marjie a match. And not just any match. But one among the elite of English society. How her mother thought to find such a match when so many thought of them as no better than servants, Marjorie did not know.

What she did know was that she was not sought after among those of the *ton*. She was the daughter of a merchant and a modiste. Or at least she had been. Now she was introduced as just the daughter of the daughter of a duke. But even still, it was not a pedigree that most of England's *beau monde* were looking for. And then there was the matter of her personality, which many seemed to find lacking. Or that is what the girls at school had said. Miss Kindrick mentioned that gentlemen did not like it when a lady spoke her mind, especially when it was done with nary a thought beforehand. If the lady had a fair dowry, then a gentleman could overlook such things. But when the dowry was slight, the prospects did not look favorable.

Miss Kindrick had inferred the slight was intended to help, but Marjie had yet to understand how such a comment could be considered kind, let alone helpful. Merely telling someone they were lacking did little more than hurt feelings. Would it not be more helpful to teach Marjie how to not be lacking?

The carriage started across the bridge connecting the castle island with the rest of the village. Marjie pressed her back against the bench, feeling the vibrations of each wheel as it crawled toward the castle. Her heartbeat picked up and she felt an overwhelming desire to squeal like a piglet she'd seen on the Musgraves' farm as her excitement about the castle warred with her fears of plummeting into the water below.

She craned her neck to peer out the window on the other side of the carriage to see if she could discern if the bridge was safe. Surely it was. They could not be the first carriage to cross. But such thoughts could not bring her to the edge of her seat to see what lay below them.

"Poppet, what is the matter?" Her mother looked at her with concern.

Marjie gave a tentative smile. "I am well enough. I simply was not expecting the bridge to be so...rickety."

Her mother chuckled. "I am certain there is nothing rickety about this bridge. The Marquess of Angle is nothing if not particular. He would never allow an unsafe bridge."

"Then you know the marquess well?" Marjorie pierced her mother with a probing gaze. She had been rather closed lipped about this visit. "You have said little about him."

Her mother shrugged. "I do not know him well. As I told you, I am more acquainted with Lady Angle."

There was something she was not telling her. Marjie

squinted at her mother, trying to wheedle out whatever it was she was hiding. But it was for naught. She remained just as closed lipped as before.

The carriage moved onto cobblestone and Marjie moved back to her view out the window. She supposed she would just have to wait until they reached the castle. Perhaps then she would know what it was her mother was about.

The carriage crossed over the drawbridge and through the main gate that loomed large overhead. Was there a gargoyle? She stretched and contorted but was unable to see the arch above them. Hang it all, she would just have to walk down and look once they were settled.

The carriage turned for a moment and Marjie let out a quiet gasp as the castle came into view. But before she could study any part of it closely, the carriage turned again, and the castle was gone.

But she only had to wait a moment before the driver brought the carriage to a stop in front of a set of massive stone steps. There were not many of them, only four or five, but what they lacked in number, they made up for in bulk and presence. Her heart continued to thump quickly in her chest. They were finally there. After more than a week of travel and daydreaming, she was finally at the castle.

Her mother sat primly, waiting for the footman to open the door to their handed-down carriage. It was not the best sprung, nor was the interior fresh and new. But it was nice enough. It was another present from her uncle and a necessity for those trying to ingratiate themselves with the *ton*.

Marjorie glanced at her mother one more time, hoping her mother's uncertainty might cause her to give away her secret, but still she sat quietly. Marjie pushed out her lips in thought. Could it be that the uncertainty was the secret?

Hmmm. That was something to think on.

Marjie watched with interest as her mother scooted off the bench and moved toward the open door. She stepped from the carriage and waited on the pebble ground for Marjorie to join her.

Stepping down, Marjie got her first intimate look at the castle walls. The stones looked much larger when seen up close. Indeed, everything looked much bigger. The doors, the stairs, the walls. It all left her feeling dwarfed and inconsequential. She squared her shoulders. Thankfully, she had felt that before and knew how to deal with it.

The doors to the castle keep opened and a slight woman, about the same age as Marjorie's mother, stepped out onto the landing. The glimmer in her eyes and the easy smile on her lips offset the severity of the knot at the crown of her head. She clapped her hands in front of her chest and smiled widely. "Lady Mariane, welcome to Hywel."

Marjorie's mother walked up the steps and dipped into a curtsy. "Lady Angle, thank you for your invitation." She waved Marjie forward. "I do not believe you have met my daughter, Miss Marjorie Fitzroy."

Marjie hurried to her mother's side. She dipped a curtsy, but mostly so she could catch a discreet glimpse of the marchioness. This was her first time meeting one. "It is an honor to meet you, my lady."

Lady Angle smiled down at her. "You are just as your mother described in her letters. I am very happy to make your acquaintance at last."

Marjie ducked her head, uneasy under the appraising gaze.

The crunch of gravel sounded behind them, and they all turned to see a man approach. He was a young man. Or rather a younger man. He was decades from the school room and even many years from his university days. But from the looks of his firm jaw and his broad shoulders, Marjie would not have put him as older than one and thirty.

She sucked in a breath. Her mother had not told her Lord and Lady Angle had a son. A very handsome and very tall son. Perhaps that was the secret her mother had been hiding.

"Ah, just in time." Lady Angle smiled, although it did not reach her eyes. Perhaps it was not her son. "Arawn, please, come and meet our guests."

Marjie flinched at the designation, still unused to it.

Her mother shot her a warning glance.

Guests. It remained to be seen if they would be treated as such. In the eyes of much of society, once a modiste, always a modiste. Her mother's use of the title made little difference. But the irony of it all was that it did matter to those of the lower class. Where once Marjie had fit in—unfortunately, her mother never had—those people now saw them as too high in society. Any previous friendships had gone by the wayside.

She and her mother were ladies without any society.

The man made it to his mother's side in only two large steps. He was not quite as tall as she had originally thought, but still the top of her head would not reach much higher than his shoulder. Now that he was closer, she could see him in more detail. And they were very handsome details. His chin was neither angular nor pointed, but rather perfectly curved. And from the wrinkle visible at the left of his mouth, she guessed he had a rather deep dimple when he smiled. But as he currently only frowned, she could only speculate.

Her mother nudged her, and she dipped into a curtsy. Where was Lord Angle? Gads, they would have to go through introductions all over again once he joined them. Or perhaps, he did not intend to join them until much later.

"Lady Mariane, Miss Fitzroy, I would like to introduce you

to my son, Lord Angle." She smiled over at him. "They are to be our guests for the next fortnight. Is that not agreeable?"

Marjie's mouth dropped open. *He* was Lord Angle? "But you are not old," she blurted.

Her mother's sudden coughing fit pulled her attention away from Lord Angle. Although the cough seemed rather forced, she patted her mother on the back. "Are you unwell, Mama?"

"No, Poppet, I am well. A sudden tickle is all." Her wide eyes motioned to Lord Angle.

"I beg your pardon for my greeting, my lord. I was simply expecting someone much older than you."

Marjie puffed out her breath. If her mother's secret involved Lord Angle, she was sure to be disappointed. This man did not look like someone who would condescend to socialize with her, let alone form an attachment.

"I am supposed to be old? I am sorry, but no one told me, else I should have attempted to alter my appearance." While his words seemed to make light of the situation, his voice held no such levity. Indeed, his face also looked even more dissolute than it had before. Which she would not have thought possible. "But as I was not told we were expecting guests, I made no special plans for my appearance." He cast a stoney glance at his mother.

It seemed both their mothers had kept a secret or two. Perhaps she and this man had more in common than it had first appeared. She gave him another appraising look. He did not look like a man who would care if he had something in common with someone like her.

Marjie lifted a single shoulder. It was not as if she was surprised by the reaction.

"Please excuse Arawn. I had not yet spoken to him on this matter. But I am certain he is honored to make your acquaintance." Lady Angle said the last part through gritted teeth. "Be polite," she mumbled as she turned toward her son.

Marjie looked at the ground, trying to hide the smile tugging at her lips. She was gratified to know that she was not the only one to receive lectures through gritted teeth.

"Havard will show you to your rooms, and Garath will bring up your trunks shortly. I'm certain you are both fatigued after your long journey. Why do you not rest for the afternoon? Dinner will be served at seven." Lady Angle motioned them inside and Marjie forgot she was supposed to be listening as she looked around at the tall walls and timbered ceilings.

It was just as she had imagined a castle would look, minus the suits of armor that should line the walls. Perhaps they were in the Great Hall. But even without the metal guardians, it was impressive. Rocks and stones formed all the walls. Tall pillars held up the carved arched buttresses of the roof timbers. It reminded her a bit of the nave in the cathedral in York. Although, the cathedral did not have long tapestries hanging down from ceiling to floor as she saw here.

Marjie swallowed hard. It was all quite unbelievable. The only thing missing was a dungeon. Because everyone knows a castle isn't really a castle without a dungeon.

She glanced over at Lord Angle's scowling face. And from the looks of him, he likely already had *guests* staying there.

She grinned to herself. Even if there was no dungeon, she was quite certain this was the most excitement she'd had in her entire life. And she planned to enjoy every second of it. Even with Lord Angle glowering down at her.

CHAPTER TWO

Guests? His mother had invited guests to the castle and not even mentioned it to him? He had not made himself accessible for the last few weeks, perhaps more, on purpose. But that, it seemed, had been a mistake. He had simply not wished to speak with her because he knew exactly what she wanted to speak to him about. And he wasn't ready for it.

He sighed and ran a hand through his hair. Or he had thought he knew what she wished to discuss with him. He'd thought she wished to discuss putting off her mourning clothes. But it seemed there'd been more to the conversation than he had suspected. Much more. And it had intense pale green eyes and the most beautiful red hair he had ever seen. Not that he was paying her any mind. Because he wasn't. But he'd have to be blind not to notice those things.

Lud, he had jumped from the frying pan directly into the fire.

He would be having words with his mother. Inviting people to the castle without even consulting him? And then to add insult to injury, she had not muttered her order for politeness nearly as quietly as she had thought. Miss Fitzwilliam's—or whatever her name was—averted eyes and slightly shaking shoulders were confirmation of that.

Either that or the young woman had keen hearing that he would need to remember while she stayed within the castle walls.

She glanced over at him, and he pasted a smile on his face.

She was a pretty sort of girl. Even he could admit that. Indeed, her red hair almost made him wonder if she wasn't Welsh. He'd been mistaken to say her eyes were simply pale green. Upon closer inspection, the outer border of the iris was green, however, nearer to the pupil they were almost golden. He had never seen such eyes in his life, and they captivated him. Reluctantly, he pulled his gaze away, noting she did not return his smile. Perhaps she was no more convinced of its genuineness than he was.

"You will be staying in the Southwest Tower. Lady Mariane, I thought it best if Miss Fitzroy has the top room and you stay in the lower room. The two of you may share the sitting room in the middle. They are all adjoined by a staircase. I believe you will have plenty of space." His mother motioned toward the tower. "However, if you find it is not to your liking, please do not hesitate to mention it."

Lady Mariane smiled and dipped a slight curtsy. "Thank you, my lady. I am certain it will more than meet our expectations." She cleared her throat. "Is that not right, Marjorie?"

The young lady nodded.

His mother smiled and patted the woman on the arm. "Relax, Mariane. You are among friends, here."

Mariane? Just how did his mother know these women and what was their relationship?

Lady Mariane's shoulders slackened, and she took a deep

breath. "Thank you, Sable. I know my position is tenuous at best. But your greeting is greatly appreciated." She lifted her chin and gave a nervous laugh. "Not everyone has been so kind."

His mother leaned in and embraced Lady Mariane lightly. "I have never stopped being your friend."

Lady Mariane nodded. "I know. And it has meant more to me than you'll ever know."

"We shall have plenty of time to catch up once you both are rested." His mother patted Lady Mariane on the arm and glanced at Arawn. "I have some business to discuss with my son. He was out riding this morning before we had a chance to speak."

Arawn clasped his hands behind his back to keep from clenching them at his side. *Now* she planned to speak to him? That bell had already rung. Nothing she said could change that.

He ran a hand through his hair. "I will meet you in my study, Mother."

She nodded but turned her attention back to their guests. "I will have tea delivered to your chambers. Please do not hesitate to ask for anything you need."

"Thank you, Sable." Lady Mariane motioned her daughter to follow the butler and then fell into step behind her.

When they disappeared through the arched doorway, his mother turned on him. "How could you have been so rude?"

"Me?" Arawn reared back. "She is the one at fault. Telling me I am not old, as if that is a fault in my character." He straightened. "And what about you? Telling me to be polite in front of them. I am not a child, Mother."

She released a huff. "Sometimes I wonder." She walked toward the lesser hall door leading to the Great Hall but stopped and looked over her shoulder. "Did you not say you were headed to your study?"

He nodded. "Yes. I have some accounts I need to settle."

She swished her hand in front of her. "Then hurry up about it. I have something I need to discuss with you before you set to work."

Arawn swallowed. He knew what was coming. Perhaps if he trudged a little slower, she would forget about the conversation and leave him to his ledgers. He grunted. Never had he desired to spend time with the ledgers.

He moved toward the door leading to the outer bailey.

"Why are you not using the corridors inside?" His mother hurried along beside him, struggling to keep up with his long stride. He knew he should slow down for her, but he could not seem to make his legs heed the command. "The autumn nip is already in the air."

"I needed the fresh air, Mother. You are welcome to take the corridors and meet me there."

She huffed beside him. "No, I am out here now. I may as well just follow you. But for the love of all that is holy, please slow down."

He released a sigh but made a conscious effort to shorten his gait. Perhaps this was not so bad. The slower they walked, the longer it would take for them to have the *conversation*. But all too soon, they reached the inner bailey and his study door.

The room, when the castle had functioned as a defensive stronghold, had served as the king's cellar. But it had been several centuries since that had been its primary function.

He held the door open, and his mother glided past him, settling in the chair opposite his desk. He found it telling she had chosen that chair, rather than one by the fireplace. Did she feel their conversation was to be of a business nature? Or perhaps she felt a battle was on the horizon and was preparing for it.

He took his seat. Perhaps the seating arrangement was for the best. She would not be able to see his fists clench beneath his desk.

She looked at him. Her elbows rested on the chair's arms, and she interlaced her fingers in front of her chin. "It has been nearly six months since your sister died."

Could they not at least have a bit of meaningless small talk before she jumped into the conversation? "Yes, Mother, I am painfully aware of how long it has been."

"Most would not expect you to mourn more than three or four months. Especially not Angharad. Your sister would want you to live and be happy—"

"I am happy," Arawn growled.

One side of his mother's mouth turned up in a sort of half smile. "Yes, you seem particularly overjoyed this afternoon."

"Perhaps that is because I was ambushed within my own home." He smirked at her as he leaned back in his chair and interlaced his hands behind his head. "Besides, Mother, Ane always claimed I was grumpy, even when I was not."

His mother smiled softly. "Yes, that was her way."

They both remained quiet, absorbed in their own memories. A breeze shuffled several of the papers on his desk. Arawn put a firm hand over them, looking for the open door. But he discovered nothing. He shook his head. One of the disadvantages to living in a castle was they were often drafty.

His mother lifted her chin, a determined look on her face. "I have decided to put off my mourning clothes. I know you are not yet ready, but I believe it is time, son."

"I've known this was coming," he sighed. "And I can do nothing to stop you." He crossed his arms over his chest, but then they dropped to his side and his mouth gaped in realization. "That is why they are here. You have planned a house party to celebrate?"

She shook her head slowly. "I had thought to have a house party. Although not as a celebration." She scowled at him. "You make it seem as though I am happy to stop mourning Ane. I will have you know I shall never stop mourning her. But I also cannot stay locked away in this drafty old castle for the rest of my life. I need people around me, Arawn."

"I find I'm perfectly content to stay within the castle walls."

"But you at least go out for a ride every day. I do not have even that."

He flinched. "It is your choice not to ride anymore, Mother."

"It is hardly a choice, and you know it."

Arawn stared at her. "How many people have you invited?"

"To stay? Just Lady Mariane and her daughter."

He narrowed his eyes at her. He knew there was more to this.

"But I have invited friends from the neighborhood to join us for dinner. Perhaps an evening of cards or games?" She raised a brow. "An evening of amusements."

He sighed heavily. "And how long are they to be here?"

"A fortnight at least. But perhaps longer. We have not yet settled on the date of their departure." There was a challenge in her voice, as if she was daring him to object.

"A fortnight? I am not to have peace for a fortnight?" His voice exploded as he leaned forward, his hands on his desktop.

She scowled at him, surely unhappy with his reaction. "I am certain you will survive, Son. But after your earlier exchange, I feel I must again remind you to be proper. And by proper I mean that you are not to scowl and mope about the house the entire time they are here."

"I offered her a smile. Two, in fact, if I remember correctly." He cocked a brow.

"Two whole smiles? I am surprised you have not had to retire to your bed from the fatigue of it all." His mother gave him a blank stare. "Surely you can muster a bit of genuine joy while they are here."

Genuine joy? She acted as if it was something he could turn on or off. "Lud, Mother. Do you know how much you are asking of me?" His tone came out biting, and he knew he should regret it, but he found he could not. His whole world had been turned upside down in a matter of only an hour.

"It is almost as if I lost both my children that day." Her eyes glistened with unshed tears and a tug of guilt pulled in his chest. He had been so consumed in his own guilt and loss, he had not thought much on his mother and her anguish. "*Hir yw'r dydd*, Arawn. How long must I wait for you?"

Hir yw'r dydd. Long is the day. His mother had been using that phrase on him since the day he was born. Long is the day she must wait for him to quit teasing Ane. Long is the day she must wait for him to return from Parliament. Long is the day she must wait for him to marry. Long is the day she must wait for grandchildren. The list of waiting his mother had to endure was lengthy, or so she would have him believe.

"It seems you have planned this all very well, Mother. I have no choice but to allow them to stay. And it seems I am to put off my mourning as well."

"You act as if I'm being unreasonable. It's been six months."

He leaned back in his chair and stretched his legs out under the desk.

The glisten in her eyes formed into full-fledged tears that hovered in the bottom of her lids. "I'm doing it for you. You need to move on, Arawn. We both do."

He glanced down at his hands. What did she want him to say? "And the only way for me to move on was to invite strangers to stay in my home?"

"It is my home also." She shifted angrily in her seat, the tears all but dried up. He would need to remember that for the future. If he made her angry enough, she would cease crying. "Do not place all the blame on me." She shook her finger at him. "You were the one avoiding me for weeks. Not the other way around."

Arawn lifted a hand to his black armband. The feel of it around his muscle had become an anchor. It tied him to Ane. Indeed, he did not know if he could go without it. "Why have I never heard of them? Surely, I would have seen them at a few events in London."

His mother folded her arms in her lap. "Lady Mariane has only just recently returned to society. And I do not believe her daughter has been to London, yet." She sucked in a deep breath. "But I am certain you know of her late father, the Duke of Yarm? And her brother, the current duke."

Arawn's brow creased. "Yes, I do know of them. But I did not know Yarm had a sister."

His mother tipped her head to the side. "Yes, well, her father disowned her when she married. He was not pleased with the match."

"What was wrong with the gentleman?"

She smiled sadly. "That was just it. He was not a gentleman but a merchant. Theirs was a love match, but her father refused his blessing. When she went through with the wedding, the duke cut her off without a penny. And he refused to let her use her title."

Arawn frowned. "That isn't his right. Only Parliament could take that from her."

His mother shrugged. "Regardless, as long as he lived, she did not use it."

"If she was disowned, how did she return to society? Did her husband make his fortune?"

"No, I'm afraid he never saw great success before he died. But when Lady Mariane's father died last year and her brother became duke, he restored her inheritance and title." His mother pushed out her lips in thought. "I believe I even heard he bestowed a small dowry on Miss Fitzroy. Although, I do not know the particulars of that."

Of all the people in the *ton* of his mother's acquaintance, why had she chosen these ladies to be her guests? They could barely be considered gentry, let alone nobility.

"You must have been very close to Lady Mariane if you singled her out to be your guest."

"Indeed. She was one of my dearest friends. Although, once she married, we never saw each other. But we did continue to correspond. When I learned she was back among society, I could hardly wait to see her. But then Ane died, and we went into mourning before I could extend an invitation." She pierced him with a stern look. "But regardless of their situation, I insist you treat them with respect."

He sucked in a slow, deep breath. It pained him that she thought he needed the reminder. "I promise you, Mother. I will be a perfect gentleman when I see Lady Mariane. You have my word."

"And what of Miss Fitzroy?"

"Yes. Her as well."

His mother released a breath.

Had she really thought he would not treat the ladies with respect? Did she think him so changed since Ane's death that she worried he would treat them ill?

"Thank you, Arawn. I should not have doubted you."

He stared hard at his mother. She had changed in the last few months since Ane's death. He could not say exactly how, only that she was different somehow. But why should that surprise him? Had he not been altered by Ane's death also?

Arawn pushed out from his desk, suddenly needing air that he could not seem to get in the castle. "If you'll excuse me, Mother." He moved out from his desk and opened the door, waiting for his mother to leave.

"I thought you had ledgers to review." His mother stood slowly.

"I do." He shoved a hand through his hair. "They can wait. I'm going for a ride."

"But did you not just return?"

"I'm in need of another one." He growled and hurried from the room, heading straight for the stables.

If his mother made further comments, he did not hear them. Indeed, he did not rightly care if she had. He had too much on his mind to worry over such things.

The urge to mount was too great to wait for Dafydd or Mathias to come and help him. He needed to have his thoughts pounded from his mind and blown away by the wind.

Swinging up onto the saddle, he walked his mare, Taran, out of the stable.

Few people understood why he was still mourning after so long. Indeed, even his mother did not know. But then, how did he tell her that he was the one who had killed Ane?

CHAPTER THREE

Arawn paused outside the door to the parlor. He knew his mother was likely already inside, and he did not wish to arrive too early before dinner was announced. She would surely have more muttered commands and pointed looks to give him.

He did not understand why she was so concerned. It was not as if he treated their servants poorly. Why should he treat the daughter of a duke worse? What had he done to make her think he would?

Pulling on his waistcoat, he took a long, deep breath, building up the patience he was certain he would need to survive the evening.

"Good evening, Mo—" He stepped inside the parlor and the greeting froze on his lips.

Miss Fitzpatrick? No, that did not sound right. Miss Fitz-something sat on the settee across from his mother, her hair piled high on her crown with thin ribbons bundled with the hair. He sucked in a breath and shook out his hand at his side. Why had she been the first person he sought out in the room?

Arawn recovered his senses and dipped his head toward the ladies. "Good evening, Lady Mariane, Miss—" Lud, why had he not paid more attention to her name? "Fitzrawm—," he mumbled the last letters together as he turned and dipped his head, hoping they would simply think they did not hear him fully.

He glanced at his mother's disapproving face. Obviously, she had not been fooled. "Good evening, Mother."

She raised a brow. "I was beginning to wonder if you were going to join us."

"And why would I not?"

She glanced at the mantle clock. "I did say dinner was at seven. You are cutting it rather close, are you not?"

Had she mentioned the time? Arawn could not fully remember the conversation from this afternoon. He had been too caught off guard by the ladies' arrival. How was he supposed to remember the entire conversation when he had been reeling for most of it?

"I must have missed that part." He put a false smile on his face, lest his mother try to use that against him later. He settled into a chair opposite the ladies. "I am pleased you are joining us. It has been far too long since we've had guests. It will be nice to have others participate in the conversation." He shot a pointed look at his mother.

Others participating in the conversation. His head nodded. Indeed, he had not readily realized what a benefit the newcomers could be at the dinner table. If the fates were on his side, he might not have to utter a single word the whole of the evening. Especially considering how long it had been since his mother and Lady Mariane had spoken to each other in person.

The situation may not be so wholly undesirable. Besides, it may give Arawn some insight into the guests who had invaded his home.

"Your face looks far less pleased than your words," Miss Fitz- looked at him, her brow furrowed.

"Marjie!" Her mother scowled at her.

She looked down at her hands. "Please excuse me, my lord. I did not mean to speak that aloud."

"I do not believe that is any better," her mother chided her under her breath. But in such a close seating arrangement, it was not difficult for Arawn to make out the words.

What was it with this woman? He had never met someone so completely unconcerned about her disrespect of a gentleman. And a noble gentleman at that. Where did she get the temerity?

Arawn leaned back, uncertain how to respond. She was not incorrect.

He had never been good at hiding his true feelings. His mother often said he wore his emotions on his face. It was something his father had thought a weakness. But his mother had always told him it was a strength.

Arawn had yet to discover how it served him in the least.

He released his breath. "I am the one who should apologize. My manners have been very poor since your arrival. I hope you will forgive me. It is not your fault my mother and I have not communicated well of late." He smiled, trying for a more convincing one this time.

His gaze rested on his mother. "However, I'm certain by the time dinner is over, we will be as old friends." It was doubtful, but what else was he to say?

Lady Mariane returned his smile, putting him slightly at ease. "You need not apologize, my lord. I can only imagine my discomfort at learning I was to receive guests, only after they had arrived."

Arawn relaxed. It was not difficult to like this woman. She

was gracious and tried to put him at ease, even if he did not deserve it.

She glanced over at his mother, likely trying to discover if she had offended her while trying to smooth things over with him. It was as if he was making her choose to whom she would stay on pleasant terms with. Perhaps his mother had reason to worry about him after all. So far, he'd done little to set Lady Mariane's mind at ease.

"Perhaps being surprised with such lovely guests is what made me uneasy. It has been some time since the castle has had guests. And for them to be as beautiful as you and your daughter—" He stopped, not knowing where else to go with that train of thought.

"Dinner is served, my lord."

Oh, thank the heavens! He had little else to say. And the more that came out of his mouth, the more he seemed to lie. Not that Lady Mariane was not a pretty lady. She was quite beautiful. Especially for one her age. And the daughter—how was he going to discover her name? His mother would likely toss him from the castle should he ask her.

But he did not wish to think on the daughter and her impertinent comments. He knew their beauty was not the root of all his problems since their arrival. No, he blamed most of his current troubles on his mother.

Linking her arm with Lady Mariane, his mother left Arawn to offer his arm to Miss Fitz-.

He smiled at her as an idea came to mind. "We seemed to have started our acquaintance on the rocky side of the road. Perhaps we might start over with introductions?"

She tipped her head to the side, and he wondered if she might have figured him out. But then she nodded, and he thought with relief that maybe she hadn't. "I would like that very much, my lord," she murmured.

"I'm very pleased to meet you, Miss?" He drew out the word, and winked, as if he were just playing along with the game of starting over.

She smiled and dipped into a curtsy. "Miss Marjorie Fitzroy, my lord. And the pleasure is all mine."

Fitzroy! That was it. How had he not remembered something so simple? He grinned down at her, and only partly because of his cleverness to learn her name.

He lifted his arm to her. "Miss Fitzroy, may I escort you into dinner?"

"Thank you, my lord." She beamed up at him and his breath caught in his throat. He tried to clear the obstruction, but it would not have it. Strange.

They walked down the corridor, and he led her into the dining room. His mother was already seated in the chair to the left of his seat, with Lady Mariane on her other side. That left the chair on his right for Miss Fitzroy.

He was not completely certain if this was good or bad. He slipped into his chair as a footman helped her into hers.

She shook out her napkin and draped it across her lap. "Are you always so grumpy? Or is it simply because my mother and I arrived today?" Ah, it was to be bad, then. Her voice did not seem to hold any censure. But what kind of lady asked such a question?

He wanted to tell her to keep her impertinent comments to herself.

But then she looked at him and her eyes widened. "Oh, I'm sorry, my lord. Sometimes things come out of my mouth before I even realize I've had the thought." She frowned. "It can make for some awkwardness at times. It's something I'm trying to change, but when I am nervous, it just seems to increase."

"Why are you nervous?" He knew what it was like to be nervous. And while he rarely spoke without first thinking about his words, Ane had not had such restraint. Much to his mother's chagrin. Could it be this young lady was not so different from his sister? The thought both tightened his chest and lifted his spirits.

Miss Fitzroy darted a look at her mother. "As you likely already figured out, I have not been to a...." Her brow creased. "I don't know what to call this. I have never been to a home where the lord did not even know we were coming." She leaned toward him. "It was not something that was covered in my time away at school."

She had been to a girl's school? That was interesting. Arawn smiled. It was not often people within the *ton* were so honest and open. It was rather refreshing, even if it was rather blunt and directed at him.

Miss Fitzroy looked over at him from beneath her lashes as a footman ladled out her soup. "I could not help but notice that you did not answer my question."

His smile grew. And while his first instinct was to push it down, he resisted.

Who was this young woman? She was like no one he had ever encountered before. He cleared his throat. "I suppose it depends on who you ask. I would say the answer is I am not grumpy; I am simply thoughtful. But my sister, Angahard, often said grumpy is just my nature."

Miss Fitzroy's lips quirked up. "That does not surprise me of a sister. While I have never had one, I've heard that brothers and sisters often tease one another."

"Am I to assume you have not a brother either?"

She shook her head. "No. It was just Papa, Mama, and me. But then we lost Papa. Now it is just Mama and me."

The familiar pang squeezed his chest. "I am sorry to hear about your father."

She shook her head. "It should not affect me so. It has been nearly a decade since Papa died. But I miss him deeply even still." She glanced up at him. "If you are the marquess, I can only assume you know something about losing a parent." Her eyes flicked over to the black armband.

He reached up and rubbed his fingers along it. "Yes, I do."

She was obviously under the impression that it was his father whom they were mourning. He should correct the assumption, but he could not bring himself to do it. It would bring up emotions that he did not feel comfortable exposing to these relative strangers.

She smiled softly at him and his heart lurched. "You may be as grumpy as you wish, my lord. I believe you have earned it."

He rubbed his earlobe. When she said things like that, it made it deuced difficult to stay grumpy. Did she know it had that effect? Did she know it made his heart lurch and constrict and all kinds of other things that it surely should not be doing?

CHAPTER FOUR

Marjorie stepped out onto the small landing outside her bedroom door. She could not hear any movement from her mother's room below. It was rather early in the morning. The sun had only just begun to crest the horizon. Even her mother did not usually rise that early.

She looked down the staircase, even though her mother's door was not in view. Should she see if her mother was awake and wanted to join her? Marjie shook her head. Making this trip had been stressful for them both, but more so for her mother. She was keenly aware that many still did not accept them as one of their own, and every invitation brought with it anxiousness. Marjie understood all too well the desire to be accepted. She had longed for it for most of her life.

She glanced back down the stairs. Her mother surely needed sleep more than the view of a sunrise.

The door opposite her bed chamber begged her to open it and explore whatever was on the other side. If she had her bearings correct, the door should lead to the castle allure.

However, if her bearings were wrong? She pulled her hand back slightly. She hoped it did not lead to a terrace or staircase that had long since been removed. She would simply need to be cautious.

She placed her hand on the smooth wood. It was hard to imagine this door could have been there for nearly five hundred years. Or was this a newer castle? She did not know the history of it. Perhaps Lord Angle would offer to take her on a tour and tell her about it. He did realize this was her first time in a castle, did he not? When they had arrived, she had not thought him the sort to offer. But after dinner last evening, she wondered if it might not be a possibility. But she needed to accept that if she wanted a tour, she may simply have to ask.

Although Lord Angle was still in a state of mourning for his father. He may not be up to such an activity. Maybe it would be best if she asked the butler or the housekeeper. They were surely more accustomed to giving tours.

Marjie placed her ear next to her hand on the wood, listening to see if there was anyone on the other side. The last thing she wanted was to barge in on someone. The door was obviously as thick as the one leading to the stairwell because she heard nothing.

Sucking in a deep breath, she pushed. It creaked and then a low moan sounded as the door swung open. To her great relief, a breeze lifted her side curl gently. She had been correct. A walkway stretched out before her.

Stepping out onto the allure—she had read in a book that was what it was called—she turned in a small circle, taking in the view around her. It was a crisp, cool morning. She moved to the outer wall and leaned against it, watching as the sun's reflection moved out across the water in Angle Bay.

Sometimes she wished she knew what a sunrise or sunset really looked like. Her mother had described it to her, but having never had the ability to see color, the description had been completely lost. Although, even in the varying shades of gray visible to her, she could appreciate the sun as it reflected off the water. A sigh pushed out her lips. It was the perfect start to the day.

Her gaze dropped and she let out a small gasp, taking a step back. The rocky ground sprawled out an intimidating distance below.

"Are you afraid of heights?" A deep voice sounded next to her, and Marjie looked to see Lord Angle standing only a few feet away from her. The man either had the gait of a cat, or she had been completely immersed in her surroundings.

"I never thought I was. But looking down there makes me wonder." She glanced down at the rocky shoreline where the water lapped up over the craggy stones. "I was watching the sunrise and did not notice how far down it was until just now."

He looked out at the bay. "Yes, it is beautiful, is it not?" They remained silent for a moment as they both watched the sun move lazily across the water. "That is the intent, you realize?" His voice cut into the silence.

"The intent of what?" She pulled her gaze from the horizon and glanced at him.

"Of the walls. One of the main objectives of a castle is to look so imposing that no one dares attack it. If it fails on that front, then the other defenses must be used. But if you can make the enemy believe there is no reason to even try, that is the best outcome."

She turned back to the view. "But if one must be on the wall to be intimidated, have you not already lost the castle?"

He grinned. "If you think the view down is daunting, you should look up at it from the ground below. It looks far worse, I promise."

"I had not considered that." She gave him a side glance. Did she dare ask him for a tour? It seemed rather untoward. But would a moment of embarrassment not be worth it if she was shown the whole castle? "Although, I do not think I shall fully believe you until I have seen it for myself. Perhaps I will inquire of the housekeeper to give me a tour." She tilted her head. "Do you think that view would be included?"

He stared at her for a long moment, his brow creasing and then smoothing. His mouth opened several times, only to snap shut. Finally, he gave a little shrug and grinned. It was just as she had thought. He did have a rather deep dimple when he smiled. Perhaps before she left he would bestow a full, genuine smile upon her, and she might see just how deep it was.

"We need not bother Mrs. Prosser. I'm perfectly capable of giving you a tour." He lifted a proud brow. "Do not tell Mrs. Prosser I said so, but I believe I am even more capable than she."

Marjie bit back her own smile. While she had hoped he might agree to give her a tour himself, she had not really believed he would.

She clapped her hands together in front of her chest. "Oh, would you? Thank you. I should love to hear the stories you know of the castle." She put a finger to her lips. "But you need not fear. I shall not breathe a word of it to Mrs. Prosser."

She turned back to the view of the sun, which had fully crested the horizon. "This is my first time visiting a castle." She ran her fingers along the edge of the wall and looked up at him with hopeful eyes. "I had hopes of seeing a dungeon."

When he did not respond, she frowned. "You do have a dungeon here, do you not?"

"There was a dungeon, but I'm afraid it was repurposed centuries ago." He gave her a look that said he might be questioning her sanity. "They are not the most uplifting of places. Pray, why should you wish to see one?"

Her shoulders dropped. "I have read about them. They sound rather intriguing." She reached out toward him but stopped short of touching his arm. "Not that I wish to discover what it is like to be confined to one. But looking at it could not be so terrible, could it?"

He clicked his tongue. "I am sorry, but I'm afraid you will have to learn that someplace else. The Dungeon Tower is now guest chambers."

Marjie released a disappointed sigh.

"Do you still desire a tour, or was your only wish to see the dungeon?" He folded his arms across his chest.

She hurriedly turned toward him. "Gracious, no. I should like to learn about everything. For example, I read somewhere that this walkway is called an allure. Is that correct? Because I have learned that not everything I read is accurate. Sometimes people make things up just to create a better story." She shook her head. "Although, why they would do it, I know not."

"Very well, we shall plan a tour. I have a meeting with my steward this morning. And a meeting with the constable and overseer of the poor this afternoon." He looked out over the water. "But I am available tomorrow."

Marjie grinned. "That is perfect." She leaned over the castle wall, slightly. She may be enthralled with the castle and all it offered, but that did not mean she did not have a healthy respect for its heights as well. "Will you teach me all the castle terms too? Was I correct about the allure?"

He nodded. "Yes. Although it is also correct to call it a wall-wall."

"And what is this called?" She patted her hand on the tall part of the wall that came nearly to her chest.

"That is called a merlon, while the gap you are leaning on is called a crenel."

Her eyes widened. "The tour has not even started and

already I am learning so much." Lord Angle's life must be fascinating. How could it not be living in a castle? He surely looked like he belonged there with his broad shoulders and tall form. She opened her mouth, but he lifted a hand and stopped her.

"If I tell you everything now, what will I have to say on the tour?" He tilted his head as if he were challenging her.

She clamped her mouth shut, but still managed to offer him a closed-lipped smile.

He pulled a watch from his pocket. "I must go meet with my steward. Thank you, Miss Fitzroy."

"Thank you?" Her brow creased. "For what, pray tell?"

"For allowing me to see the sunrise with you. It has been some time since I last had the pleasure of watching one. Or perhaps I just have not allowed myself the opportunity."

"But why?" Why would someone purposely avoid something so beautiful?

He shrugged. "It seemed selfish."

"How is enjoying the sunrise selfish?" Her brow creased.

He did not respond immediately. Instead, he stared out at the brightening water. "It seemed selfish that I should enjoy something so beautiful when—" His voice fell off, but he lifted a hand to the black band around his arm.

"But why should it be selfish? I tend to think that Papa sees the sunrise and sunset every day, just as he did when he was alive. Indeed, I have often felt that he is standing beside me, and we are watching it together."

"You really believe that?"

She shrugged. "Why should I not? My Papa was a good man. I have no reason to believe he landed himself in Hell. So why should he not be allowed to join me in watching the sunrise?"

Lord Angle was quiet again, his brow creased. "I like your

belief. It is much more comforting than what Mr. Brown, our vicar, taught."

"Was your father a good man, my lord?"

Arawn swallowed. "My father was a hard man. But I believe he did what he thought was right."

She leaned a little closer. "Then I think you can believe he is still watching sunrises too," she whispered.

He took a deep breath and nodded slowly, as if he were still thinking on her words. "I think I shall. Thank you again, Miss Fitzroy." He dipped his head and walked in the opposite direction from her room.

Marjie watched his back as he left. Perhaps she had misjudged him and there was more to his demeanor than just sadness. Could it be there was a degree of guilt that he was still living—enjoying everything life had to offer—while his father could not?

CHAPTER FIVE

Arawn sat at the breakfast table alone. The silence was both welcomed and dreaded. There had been a time when Ane ate breakfast with him almost every morning. She had rattled on through the entirety of the meal, often leaving him in desperate need of quiet. But now, he would do almost anything to have those days back. To have Ane back. Even at the expense of his peace.

He glanced out the window, wondering how high the sun had risen into the sky. Since his discussion with Miss Fitzroy the morning before, he had thought of little else. Was she correct that his father—but more importantly Ane—could still see the sunrise or the sunset? It had been one of Ane's favorite things in the world. And the thought that she might still have that pleasure left Arawn feeling hopeful. Hopeful that one day his guilt would ease. Hopeful that eventually he could move past her death and enjoy life. Unfortunately, he had difficulty believing any of that could happen. He didn't deserve to be happy.

The curtain fluttered once then settled softly back in place.

Arawn shook his head. The castle seemed to get draftier by the day.

"Good morning, my lord," Miss Fitzroy walked into the breakfast room, and for a split second, Arawn hoped she might fill the silence as Ane had done. But it would not be the same. How could it be? He did not have the same easy rapport with this woman as he'd had with his sister. Hers would simply be noise that shattered his quiet. It would bring no peace.

But still, perhaps a little conversation would not be unwelcome.

He smiled at her. "*Bore da.*"

"Excuse me?" She looked around as if she thought he might be speaking to someone else.

"*Bore da* is how you say 'Good Morning' in Welsh." He raised a brow. How would she respond? He had already discovered that she rarely responded in the way he thought she would. But would she in this case? If she were like most of his acquaintances outside of Wales, she would not respond favorably.

There had been a time when he was younger when he thought everyone wished to hear Welsh. While it was not considered their native tongue anymore, most true Welshmen knew how to speak it as well as they did English. However, it only took one day at Eton to realize he was quite mistaken. Although even that did not prepare him for the reactions he received from several of the ladies he had thought to pursue. Most English ladies he knew turned up their noses when he would utter even a word of Welsh. Indeed, Lady Olivia had asked him not to ever use such a vulgar-sounding tongue around her again.

There had been a few women, Lady Sofia and Miss deLong, who had seemed to tolerate it. But he later realized their toleration would only last until the nuptials were said.

He looked at Miss Fitzroy with raised brows. How would this young lady react?

She smiled and her eyes widened with excitement. "I am to receive language lessons as well as history lessons? It is more than I could have hoped for." She clapped her hands together.

He had not realized he had offered to teach her Welsh. But he found he did not hate the idea.

She moved around the table to the sideboard and Arawn nearly coughed on his eggs. What was she wearing? Her morning dress was a deep red, with fine gray feathers. The gown itself was lovely enough. But the bright yellow fichu and the bright pink shawl made his eyes hurt. His mother would never wear something so gaudy.

"I hope you slept well." He tried not to stare at the clothing, but it was difficult to pull his gaze away.

"I did." She glanced over her shoulder at him and frowned. "Is something the matter? Do I have a spot on my dress?"

Arawn shook his head. "No, no. There is no spot. I was simply...admiring your gown."

"Oh, thank you." She turned back to the side table and continued to fill her plate. "My mother made it."

"Your mother made your gown?" Why would the daughter of a duke make her daughter's clothes?

She tilted her head to the side and gave a sort of wince. "You do not know?"

He shook his head. "Know what?"

She pulled her bottom lip between her teeth and bit down for a moment as if trying to decide if she should tell him or not.

Breathing deeply, she placed her plate on the sideboard and clasped her hands tightly in front of her. "When my father died, he left us very little in the way of financial support. While he was a wonderful father, he was not so great of a businessman. Mama had done some sewing to help support us while father lived, so after he died, she began offering her sewing services to members of the *ton* she'd once associated with."

"Your mother was a seamstress?" he asked with incredulity. He had not expected that. When Miss Fitzroy's face fell, he wished he had not reacted so haughtily.

She nodded. "A very proficient one too. She sewed for many within the *ton*. And while they would not acknowledge their past friendships, they were happy to have her make them fine gowns." She looked down at her dress. "Why should we pay someone when my mother could make a finer gown and for less than half the cost? Just because we are not paupers anymore does not mean it could not happen again."

Arawn was not sure what to think. If he was being honest, he was impressed by Lady Mariane. It was not easy to survive when left in those circumstances. But from the sounds of it, they had not just survived, but thrived. At least as much as one could in their position.

"Good morning, my lord." As if her ears were burning, Lady Mariane stepped into the breakfast room.

Arawn's face heated, even though he knew she could not possibly know his thoughts.

"*Bore da*, Mama." Miss Fitzroy cast a knowing grin at Arawn, and he could not help but smile back. "It means 'Good Morning' in Welsh. Is that not simply perfect and on only our second morning here."

Lady Mariane smiled kindly at him. "You are having quite an influence on my daughter, my lord. She told me yesterday that you offered to give her a tour of the castle this afternoon?"

Arawn nodded. "I am happy to do it. It is not often I find someone as excited about Hywel as I am."

"No, I would guess not. Marjie has been looking forward to our visit here since I received your mother's letter. She has quite romanticized it. I blame it on those gothic novels she reads."

Miss Fitzroy turned from the sideboard and her mother's eyes went wide. "Marjie, what are you wearing? Did not Susanna help you dress this morning?"

Miss Fitzroy waved her mother's concerns away. "No, I dressed myself. I awakened early, and I did not wish to put Susanna to any trouble. And I did not wish to wake you."

Her mother flicked her glance from Miss Fitzroy to Arawn. "But—" She let the thought die on her lips. Arawn guessed it was because she was at a loss for words.

Marjie looked down at herself. "I do not know what the matter is, Mama. Lord Angle was just complimenting my gown before you walked in."

Lady Mariane's eyes widened even more, which Arawn found a rather remarkable feat. "It is an older gown, my lord. Not what the current fashion plates are showing."

"It is not out of fashion, Mama. You only made it in the spring." Miss Fitzroy sat down and slathered butter on her bread.

Lady Mariane's mouth dropped open, and she gawked at him. "Did you not look at the collars, Poppet?"

Miss Fitzroy glanced at her mother's face, and her whole body sagged in a look of defeat. "No, Mama. I did not. It was not yet light enough to see."

This breakfast was quickly descending into awkwardness.

"You do fine work, my lady. I had no idea you were so talented." Had he sounded sincere enough? From what his mother had said, they had not had an easy time entering society, which made even more sense knowing the lady had lowered herself into service, but he did not wish to add to their unease.

Perhaps it was not the notion that he knew she had been a

seamstress that put her on edge as much as she was aware of her daughter's rather appalling choices but was trying not to embarrass her in front of Arawn.

It seemed both these ladies would continue to surprise him.

Perhaps it would be best to change the subject and put both women more at ease. "What are your plans today, my lady?" Arawn leaned back in his chair. "Do you wish to join us on our tour?"

Lady Mariane shook her head. "While I am certain you would prove a very knowledgeable and amiable guide, I told your mother we could spend the afternoon chatting. I believe we will be working on some stitcheries."

"Are you certain, Mama? I'm sure you will have plenty of time to do stitcheries later."

"No, Poppet. I am content to visit with Lady Angle. You go with Lord Angle and enjoy your tour. Then you may tell me all about it when it is finished."

"I will leave the decision up to you, madam. Please do not feel any obligation. But should you change your mind and decide you wish to join us, the invitation remains open. And I will take the full weight of my mother's displeasure."

She smiled demurely, her cheeks pinking slightly. "You are too kind, my lord."

How had this woman ever fit in among the working class? She exuded grace and nobility. He turned his attention back to the younger Fitzroy lady. "Shall we meet in the outer bailey at two?"

Marjie nodded with bright eyed excitement. "The outer bailey at two." Her smile dimmed slightly. "Where is the outer bailey again?"

"I should have thought you would know from your extensive reading." He gave her a side look. "The outer bailey is the main courtyard."

Her brow furrowed. "Why do they not just call it that?"

"I think the better question is why did they start to call it a courtyard? The term 'bailey' has been in use for more than four hundred years. Much longer than 'courtyard.' But courtyards are for abbeys and monasteries. I should think if I used 'court-yard' regularly, those who came before might actually haunt me." He lifted his brows in an exaggerated look of fear. He tipped his head to the side. "And did you not say you wished to learn all the terms, Miss Fitzroy? Or did you mean only those terms that you are already familiar with?"

Her lips pursed but he could see it was feigned indignation. But then she grinned. "I suppose you are correct. You need not simplify things on my account."

A hint of a grin pulled at the corners of his lips. It still felt odd to exercise those muscles again.

"I thought that would be the case. I am pleased to know I will not be disappointed." He pushed his chair back and stood up, placing his napkin on the table. "I shall see you at two, Miss Fitzroy." He raised a brow. "In the outer bailey."

"Yes, in the outer bailey." She gave him the same knowing smile as she had given her mother when she greeted her in Welsh. "Perhaps then we may stroll along the allure and near the parapets and the crenels?"

A full smile stretched the ill-used muscles of his face. "Indeed, Miss Fitzroy, we shall."

Her shoulders rose and fell on a wistful sigh. "I can hardly wait, my lord."

"Nor can I, Miss Fitzroy. Nor can I." He was rather surprised to realize he was telling the truth.

Dipping his head to both ladies, he walked around the table and out into the corridor. He had thought to go directly to his study, but changed his mind when his legs carried him toward the stable instead. Indeed, a ride would be a better use of his time. He did, after all, have a tour to plan. And he wanted to ensure he did not miss a single story or piece of history. He did not know how, but he knew if he left something out, Miss Fitzroy would surely discover it. And he did not wish for that young lady to think him lacking in his knowledge of his home.

CHAPTER SIX

Marjie hurried down the tower steps, making certain to hold tightly to the iron handrail lest she trip and tumble down the carved stone. Midway down, a sudden deep chill swept over her. She paused but then decided it was simply that she could hardly wait for the tour Lord Angle was to give her. She knew he was proud of his heritage, and he would surely know things about the castle that she would never learn elsewhere.

She pushed through the door of the anteroom at the bottom of the tower and breathed in the fresh air. The early autumn sunshine warmed her cheeks, and she unconsciously lifted her face toward it. It would not be long before the sun dipped so low that the castle walls would shield its rays.

The outer bailey was empty, save for a few birds. They were different than any bird she had seen in England, and she had no notion what they were named. Perhaps she could look in the library and see if Lord Angle had any books on that subject. Glancing around her, she took a deep breath, hardly able to contain her excitement. Ever since she had read her first gothic novel, *The Castle of Otranto*, she had wished to see a real castle. When her mother told her of their trip to Hywel, Marjorie could barely believe her luck.

The sound of a heavy thud turned her head to the far end of the outer bailey. Lord Angle strode across the pebbled courtyard from the main structure of the castle. Marjie knew it had a name, but she was not certain what it was. This castle did not seem to have a proper keep. He raised his hand in greeting.

She raised one in response.

Her questions were not only about the castle. She was just as curious about him. She'd asked several at their first meeting, but that was not to say there were not other questions swirling about in her mind. What were his hobbies? What did he enjoy doing on a cold, rainy day?

She glanced up at the blue, cloudless sky, and resolved herself to the notion that not all her questions would be answered today. Perhaps not ever.

But those questions were not what weighed heaviest on her mind. What she wished to know more than anything was what he thought about seamstresses' daughters. She released a sigh. Or one seamstress's daughter, in particular. For a reason she could not explain, she desired his good opinion, but she was not certain she would ever have it. That had not been the way of things for her mother and her. She brushed that thought aside. Perhaps some things were best left as a mystery.

She would surely learn other things about him on this tour, because she did not believe a person could give a tour of their home without telling a bit about their own personality.

"*Prynhawn Da*, Miss Fitzroy." Lord Angle dipped his head in greeting.

Marjie was pleasantly surprised to see a smile on his lips when his face drew up to meet hers. It was not large or overly toothy, but it was more than she usually earned from him.

Could that mean they were becoming friends? She paused at the realization of how much she hoped that was true. "Are you ready to begin our tour?"

Marjie nodded quickly. "Indeed, I've had a difficult time sitting still for the whole of the morning. I thought my mother was going to turn me out because I was so restless."

Lord Angle gave a light chuckle, although Marjie did not know if he truly thought her comment funny or if he was simply being polite. Would she be here long enough to discover such things about him?

"I do not have difficulty picturing that in my mind." He partially raised an eyebrow.

"I am not usually one to bounce and fidget. But today my excitement got the better of me."

Lord Angle nodded. "I am pleased to know that you are anticipating seeing my home. I find it the most captivating place in the world." He tilted his head to the side and gave a slight shrug. "However, I've been told that I might be a bit biased."

"I do not think bias has anything to do with it. You live in a castle. What is not magical about that?"

"Magical?" He quirked a brow at her. "Tell me, Miss Fitzroy. Are you of a superstitious nature?"

Marjie lifted her shoulder as they began to walk toward the far wall of the outer bailey. "I would not say I am superstitious. However, I am not opposed to the notion either. I have simply never seen anything to make me believe in specters or fate."

"Then you are the type to believe only those things which you can see with your own eyes?"

"I would not say I have to see something to believe it. But I should think I need some sort of proof. Whether that be through a feeling or sight, it is no matter." She glanced up at him. "And what of you, my lord?"

He looked down at her. "What of me?"

"Are you the superstitious sort?"

Looking at him she could not think that he could be. He seemed too stern and proper for anything so unlikely as fables or lores. But then he was proving to be different than she had believed from their first introduction. His long stride made it difficult for her to keep up with him at her normal walking pace. She felt as if she might need to run just to stay even with him.

"I believe, Miss Fitzroy, that you will find most of the Welsh people rather superstitious. Most believe in ghosts and spirits."

Marjie picked up her skirt and hurried along beside him. "I did not ask about your countrymen, sir. I asked about *you*." Her words puffed out breathlessly.

He came to an abrupt stop and turned towards her. "Yes, but I am Welsh. Should I not include myself in the generalizations I make of my countrymen?"

"Do you always answer a question with a question?" Her hand came to her hips. Not out of any exasperation, but rather to help her catch her breath.

He stared at her for what felt like a full minute at least. What was he studying about her? What did he hope to learn?

She ran her gloved hand over her lips. Perhaps she had not wiped all the preserves off after breakfast. But why had her mother said nothing?

"I would say we might be of the same opinion, Miss. I do not discount the presence of ghosts and such. But I have not witnessed anything to confirm their existence. For the time, I will stay open to whatever I can learn."

A small niggle of triumph fluttered in her chest. She had learned something about him. It was not much, but she thought it might not be something that every one of his acquaintances knew about him. That made her special, did it not?

They made their way toward the north end of the bailey and walked through the large gate. He stopped and looked up, pointing to the gap in the stones. Sharp and rather intimidating-looking claws hung down above them.

Lord Angle motioned with his head. "That is the gate or portcullis that protects the castle from entry. It has not been lowered in more than two centuries." He flicked up his brows. "However, should the need arise—should the castle ever come under attack—with very little effort, the gate could be lowered and the castle secured."

Marjie stared at the metal grate still visible beneath the rock line of the arch. She glanced at Lord Angle from the corner of her eye. He was much like this castle he called home. She suspected that his roughness was just like the walls surrounding the castle and outer bailey. It was meant to protect him from something. Although what he needed protection from, she had yet to discover.

Glancing back at the portcullis, she lifted a brow and watched him sidelong. What would it take to get him to lower the gate? Need she only ask, or would she need to stage a full-scale attack? She pulled her bottom lip between her teeth, thinking of a scenario in which he might find her charming enough to pull up the portcullis blocking the entrance to the wall he hid behind.

They walked out onto a cobblestone area that was decidedly outside the bailey walls. "This is called a barbican. It is part of the gateway of the castle. And there is one on each end. This one would be the entrance for the tradesmen and other servants. However, the master of the castle and any special guests would usually arrive by boat and would enter through the east barbican."

Marjie walked over to the lower wall and looked down at the rocky shoreline below. "I assume the castle is positioned this way so most of it is only accessible by sea?"

Lord Angle nodded. "Yes, exactly." He gave her a small grin. "Perhaps you should give the tour. You seem to know as much as I do."

Marjorie rolled her eyes. "That seems to be common sense, my lord. Do not think you are bowing out of this tour so easily."

Lord Angle shook his head. "I am not trying to bow out. I simply do not wish to bore you with facts you already know."

"Oh, I'm not bored. Although I am wondering when I shall hear stories that are unique only to this castle."

"I was coming to that part." He clasped his hands behind his back as they walked over the drawbridge. He stopped in the middle and rested his arms on the wooden railing. "You are a most impatient lady, Miss Fitzroy." There was no irritation or frustration. Indeed, when she glanced over at him, he grinned down at the water below.

"This railing obviously is not a part of the original drawbridge. It seems to me it would defeat the purpose. How would it draw up and tuck into the castle with these attached?"

She wrapped her hands around the railing and gave it a shake to test its stability.

"There is little need for the drawbridge any longer, but I can't picture the castle without it, even though many have suggested the measure is outdated." Lord Angle nodded. "But that does not mean we should forsake safety. The railings are not the only impediment to drawing it up. They were added once the bridge was permanently attached to the other side."

She pushed out her lips in disappointment. "What if the castle should come under attack? You have ruined your first line of defense."

"I will take your concerns under advisement." He leaned his hip against the railing and folded his arms across his chest. "You seem most concerned about impending attacks. Do you know something I do not, Miss Fitzroy?"

She chuckled but shook her head. "No, my lord. I just like to be prepared for all eventualities."

He gave her one last penetrating glance before pointing to the far side of the castle's exterior wall. "That is the beginning of the wall around the village. It was a great advantage to keep it protected. Many of the tradespeople lived and worked outside the castle walls. If the village fell, the castle would be cut off from many of its most important workers. In the case of Hywel, that would be the smithy. Unlike other fortified castles, Hywel did not have a blacksmith housed within the walls of the castle itself. Although, if the village was captured, it would only be a matter of time before the castle was completely cut off and the inhabitants would be forced to surrender."

She sucked in a deep breath and let it out slowly through her nose. "It is a very pretty scene. It simply begs to be painted."

His body reared back slightly. So slight that she wondered if she might have imagined it. "My sister started a painting, but she never saw it finished." There was an undercurrent of sadness when he spoke of the painting. Or was it his sister that elicited the emotion? Why was it so important that his sister finish the painting?

It was not the first time Lord Angle had mentioned his sister. Marjie wondered about the girl. Was she away at school? Why else would she not have met her yet? Marjie would have enjoyed having another young lady around the castle.

"Then your sister enjoys painting?" Marjorie moved closer to him, feeling as though this might be the first real glimpse she'd had of the real Lord Angle.

"I would not say she enjoyed painting. However, my mother believed it was a pursuit all young ladies should be proficient at, along with the pianoforte and stitchery."

"If she does not enjoy it, I can understand her not having the desire to finish the painting. From my experience, painting cannot be forced. It must be felt, else it will never be a master-piece." She glanced over at him. "Surely there are other pursuits she could learn. And forcing her does not fit with the picture of your mother I have seen thus far."

Arawn frowned. "My mother was only doing what she thought best for my sister." His voice raised in both tone and timbre, but then he released a breath and ran his hand across the back of his neck. "But you are right, it does not fit her now. She has changed much in the last half year."

Marjie leaned slightly away from him. "I'm sorry if I spoke out of turn. I am certain Lady Angle had her reasons." She turned her gaze slightly at the sound of a bird.

He clasped his hands behind his back and frowned down at the ground. "Not all young ladies know what they like until they have tried a variety. I think it's a good policy to introduce young ladies to all kinds of hobbies. Besides, there is much expectation for ladies in the *ton*. Surely you know that better than anyone." Lord Angle's face reddened all the way to the tips of his ears.

Marjie released a mirthless laugh. "More than you know." She looked down at her hands. "Sometimes I wish it was not so. Otherwise, how do I stand a chance of making an accept-able match? I shall never meet society's expectations."

He looked at her intently. Almost as if he were trying to see things from her view. "But if there are no societal expectations, what kind of society will we have? People would do whatever they want, whenever they want. There would be no order."

Marjorie lifted her shoulder. "Perhaps. But perhaps not. I

suppose it is not something we shall ever know, as I do not see society letting go of its control anytime soon. And your sister, it seems, will have to paint whether she enjoys it or not." Her eyes widened slightly as she realized what she had just said. Saints above, why could she not control her mouth? She would be lucky if Lord Angle did not pack her trunks and have the carriage ready before dinner.

A coldness fluttered over her body, nearly causing her to stumble backward.

She released an awkward laugh, hoping perhaps he had not heard her last thoughts nor seen her clumsiness. She pointed to a tower. "What is that tower for?"

Lord Angle stopped in his tracks and stared at her. "My sister will never be forced to paint again." His voice was quiet but ragged.

"Because of the change in your mother you mentioned earlier?"

He shook his head, and a sheen covered his eyes. "No, because she died nearly six months ago."

Marjie put one hand to her middle and the other to her mouth, feeling as if she had just been punched in the stomach. All the careless words she had just spoken bumbled through her mind. Confound it! When would she learn? How was he ever to forgive her?

She bit her lips. What could she say to offer some relief from his current mood?

She shook her head. Perhaps she should remain quiet. She had already said quite enough.

CHAPTER SEVEN

Miss Fitzroy's brow creased deeply.

He knew he should regret his terse words to her, but he could not. She said everything with such surety and conviction.

"Oh, I am so very sorry." She looked down at her feet, suddenly fascinated with the toes of her walking boots.

"Thank you," he choked out. He did not know what else to say.

She shook her fists at her side and mumbled some unintelligible words, then glanced up at him for the briefest of moments. "I'm certain you don't wish to finish the tour after all my thoughtless words." She turned and walked quickly toward the portcullis.

He watched her back for a moment. Should he not let her go? While she had not intended her words to hurt, they had. Her accusations stung his very soul. And not just on his mother's behalf. Had he not forced Ane to do things she did not want to? While he had allowed Miss Fitzroy to believe it was only his mother responsible for his sister's unhappiness, he was just as much to blame. Only his blame did not simply end with some paints and a canvas. His actions had ultimately led to Ane's death.

But that was not Miss Fitzroy's fault. He needed to stop shifting the blame onto others.

"Miss Fitzroy," he called to her.

She stopped but did not turn back around.

He moved toward her. "Please, stay."

Her head shook and her arm moved back around her middle. "You need not continue, sir. I am accustomed to missing out on things because I cannot seem to control my tongue."

Did he wish to continue? He wasn't exactly certain. But if he was intent on taking responsibility for what had happened, perhaps now was as good a time as ever. She had not intended her words to be malicious. Indeed, they only felt that way because of his role in Ane's accident. Miss Fitzroy did not deserve his anger. And in truth, his mother did not either. He swallowed the bitter taste of self-reproach.

He studied her bent head and hunched shoulders. What had she missed out on because of something she had said? He wondered if they would ever become close enough that she would confide such a thing in him. And he was surprised to admit he hoped they did.

He consciously unclenched his fists. "I want to continue." He released a breath. "Perhaps we may speak about something else?"

She turned slowly toward him. "I believe that would be best."

They walked together toward the grassy area at the base of the kitchen tower. "You seemed to know a lot about painting. Does that mean you enjoy the activity?"

She looked up at him, questions evident in her gaze. "Is that not a volatile subject?"

One corner of his mouth quirked up. "I think it a fine subject, as long as we are discussing *you*."

She nodded thoughtfully. "Ironically, I do enjoy painting, even though I am not proficient at it."

He smiled, glad that she would not be one to simper about their earlier disagreement for the whole of the day. "What else do you enjoy? Needlework?"

She shook her head. "I did not mind sewing to help my mother. But embroidery is not to my taste."

That surprised him, knowing her history. Although maybe her distaste was due *to* that history. Perhaps it evoked too many unfavorable memories.

He pointed to a level piece of ground. "That is where King Henry had Gwen Carew and her associates hanged and beheaded."

Miss Fitzroy sucked in a breath. "I beg your pardon? Why would he do such a thing?"

Arawn clasped his hands behind his back, glad they had moved to friendlier terms again. "While most of his enemies were held in the Tower of London, Henry the Eighth did use Hywel's dungeon as a prison."

She clucked her tongue and shook her head. "And you repurposed them? Do you care nothing for history?" She said it in a way that made him feel as if he were being scolded. But in a kindly manner.

"I did not see them repurposed myself. It was done long before I became master." He held his hands up in front of him. "However, the dungeons at Hywel were used quite frequently for nearly three hundred years."

"What did Miss Gwen do to deserve such a fate?" Miss Fitzroy asked as her body shivered. It was a rather unfortunate story, but he did not believe it was chilling. Or not so much so as to bring about shivers. But perhaps Miss Fitzroy was of the overly dramatic type?

"When Gwen was not yet twenty, she fell ill with a terrible fever. While in the throes of that fever, she had visions of great holiness and in rebuke of sin and vice." He spoke as if he were an actor reciting from a pulpit.

"I did not realize such things would bring with it a death sentence." She placed her hands on her hips, her lips pushed out in disgust.

"It was not those visions that placed her in the briars. The local priest believed in Gwen's visions, and he told the Archbishop of Canterbury about them. From that time forward, Gwen's reputation grew. She eventually joined a nunnery where she continued to receive more visions. It was not until she prophesied about King Henry that she sealed her fate."

Miss Fitzroy leaned in close, and a floral note filled his nostrils. He had not noticed before how pleasant she smelled.

"What did she prophecy about him?" Her words were hushed and almost reverent. He was rather disappointed when she leaned away again.

Arawn put his finger to his lips. "Let me see if I remember it all correctly." He took in a breath, deliberately delaying the story a little longer. Miss Fitzroy looked so intrigued, he could not help himself.

She stomped her foot and scowled at him. "Surely it cannot be so hard to remember. Or are you making up the whole story?"

He reared back. "Make it up? Of course not. Why would I do such a thing?"

"Then out with it," she grunted but then quickly added, "my lord."

He grinned at her impatience. It reminded him a bit of Ane.

"Very well. As the tale goes, Miss Gwen claimed she had a vision where she saw King Henry in the cathedral at Calais. In the vision, an angel denied Henry the consecrated host, then took it from the priest's hand and offered it to Gwen instead. She also asserted that God was unhappy with Henry and if he did not stop his divorce from Queen Catherine and forsake Anne Boleyn, that Henry would lose his kingdom within a month and die the death of a villain."

"Saints above!" Miss Fitzroy put her hand to her mouth. "Even I should not think it a wise idea to voice such a thing."

Arawn nodded. "Indeed, she was not the only one affected. Several monks and friars believed in her. When the charges were read, they too were sentenced to death. Gwen tried to take the responsibility, saying it was all her fault. But King Henry would not have it. There apparently was enough evidence in the other men's involvement that she could not save them."

Miss Fitzroy looked down at the ground. "And this is where it happened?"

Arawn nodded. "That is what the legend says."

She took a large step to the side. "Then I should not like to stand there. It feels rather dark and cold."

That was doing it rather brown, was it not? He wondered if maybe she had understated her superstitious beliefs.

He tipped his head to the side and motioned to her new spot on the grass. "For all we know, *that* could be the actual spot. It could be anywhere around this area." He waved his hand around them. His lips twitched slightly at her look of disgust. "Did you not say you wished to know all the dark and scandalous secrets of the castle?"

"I wished to know them, not stand upon them." She looked at the ground as if trying to decide where she should move.

He lifted his arm to her. "Why do we not explore more of the castle itself."

Her shoulders relaxed. "I should like that very much." She smiled up at him with bright eyes. "Can we enter through the east barbican?"

He shook his head. "Not unless you wish to traipse across the rocks and swim for a short distance." He paused. "But if you are very good, perhaps I could take you in a boat before you leave."

"Oh, would you?" She clapped her hands in front of her chest.

He put up a hand. "Before you become too excited, I must warn you it will only be a small rowboat. I do not wish to set your expectations too high."

"I had no expectations. Except that it will be thrilling." And from the look on her face, he believed her.

They walked up close to the tower wall and stopped. "If you look up, you will understand what I was talking about yesterday."

Miss Fitzroy's head fell back, and her mouth dropped open as she gazed up the castle wall. "Oh, yes. I understand now. It almost looks as if it goes on forever from here."

He could not help the proud feeling that swelled inside his chest. There had been guests at Hywel who found the castle impressive. But Arawn could not think of a single person as utterly captivated as Miss Fitzroy.

They walked across the drawbridge and through the outer gate into the north barbican. Neither of them said much, but it was not an uncomfortable silence.

Arawn looked at Miss Fitzroy from the corner of his eyes. It was a shame Ane was not there. He was quite certain his sister would have liked Miss Fitzroy. She and Ane had much in common. Although, as the daughter of a marquess, Ane had to be much more guarded in her speech. Still, he could imagine the ladies being intimate friends.

"We are back in the outer ward." He motioned to the courtyard around him.

"I thought you called it a bailey." She looked at him with suspicion.

"Yes, I did. But you will discover many things inside a castle have several names. Some come from their French or European counterparts. It is rather convenient. If you should forget one of them, you nearly always have a secondary name to fall back on."

She looked around. "This area may be called a courtyard, a bailey, or a ward?"

He nodded. "Indeed."

"That is rather ridiculous." She said matter-of-factly with a look of utter irritation on her face.

"Indeed, it is. But if you wish to live in a castle, it is necessary to know."

She nodded thoughtfully. "I shall take it under advisement if ever the opportunity to live in a castle should present itself."

"A wise decision, miss." He motioned to the area around them with his hand. "Hywel was built from 1283 to 1287 under the orders of King Edward I. It was part of his strategy to keep the Welsh population under control after he conquered in 1277. It was designed by the master builder James of St. George."

"He designed many castles for the king, did he not?" She dropped her head back to look up the walls.

He joined her in gazing up the wall, not feeling such awe for the castle in a long time. He supposed he owed that to Miss Fitzroy. He had lived in it all his life, yet telling her the stories of Hywel's history, reminded him of how lucky he was to live in such a place. How many people could boast such a rich history in their homes?

"If this castle was built as a royal castle, how did your family come to own it?" She ran her fingers over the rough stone as they walked near the kitchen walls.

"During the civil war, the castle was held by Royalists. Once the Parliamentarians gained control, orders were sent to destroy it. My great, great grandfather—horrified at the thought—pledged his loyalty to Cromwell and his government on the condition that they not destroy the castle. I do not know what he said to them, but they agreed and sold it to him. Hywel is one of the few castles in the country to survive that time period. It has been in our family ever since."

"You see? It is not just the castle that has an interesting history. I knew if you told me about this place, sooner or later I would learn something about your family."

He leaned against the outer wall of the kitchen. "You have discovered something about my family. I think it only fair for me to learn something about yours."

She put a finger to her lips and looked heavenward. "It seems we both have a link to Henry the Eighth."

He pushed off the wall and folded his arms across his chest. "Oh?"

She nodded. "Yes. My father was a direct descendant through a natural child."

His brow furrowed. "I did not think Henry Fitzroy sired any children before his early death."

"It was not through Henry Fitzroy. It was through Alexander Fitzroy. While King Henry never publicly acknowledged Alexander as his child, my father had letters from the king to Alexander, acknowledging that he was indeed, his father."

Arawn's eyes widened. "How has this information not come to light? You are a descendant of a king."

"When Alexander presented the papers after the king's

death, Queen Mary and then Queen Elizabeth called the letters forgeries." She lifted a shoulder. "In the eyes of the government, he was never legitimized."

"But you believe it to be true?"

She pulled at the curl at the side of her cheek, and he watched with fascination as it bounced back into place. "I have the red hair, do I not?" She grinned and shrugged. "It does not really matter what I believe. Society does not give it credence and, therefore, it does nothing to improve my situation. Indeed, if anything, the Fitzroy name has only closed doors to us." She sighed. "Although, I do not wish to be regarded merely for my distant relations."

She smirked. "It is not a very clever desire, as I have very little control over it. But there it is."

"What do you want to be regarded for?"

"For me. As flawed as I am, I want to be liked for me not because a very long time ago my relative was naturally born of a king."

"Why, Miss Fitzroy, how very Whiggish of you." He grunt-laughed. "What do you have to recommend yourself?"

She looked at him pensively. "Should you not discover that yourself? It seems rather boastful for me to lay them out before you."

He nodded thoughtfully. "Then I suppose I shall venture to discover them myself."

"That is all I ask, my lord. But few take the time to do it." She smirked and then ducked her head.

One corner of his mouth quirked up. "You realize what this means, do you not?"

She stared at him blankly.

"You not only have a connection to King Henry, but a connection to Hywel also."

Her head dropped slightly to the side with a look of confusion.

"In 1401, during the Glyndŵr uprising, Rhys and Gwilym ap Tudur captured Hywel and held control of it for three months."

Miss Fitzroy still looked baffled.

"Rhys and Gwilym were the uncles of Owen ap Tudur. He later anglicized his name to Owen Tudor, the grandfather of King Henry the Seventh. Your relatives, Miss Fitzroy, lived in Hywel for three months."

Her mouth dropped open, and she gazed around the ward. If she had been impressed before, she now looked positively awestruck. A glassy sheen appeared over her eyes.

Lud, she was crying? What had he said to bring that about?

"Thank you, my lord." She gave him a shaky smile.

"Pray for what? I have done nothing."

She shook her head. "You've done more than you know." She took a deep breath and blinked the tears away. "Now, did you not promise to show me the rest of the castle?"

CHAPTER EIGHT

Marjie straightened her skirt as she stood outside the door to the lesser hall. She had heard the rumble of voices before she even stepped from the anteroom at the bottom of her tower. She chided herself. It wasn't *her* tower, no matter how much she wished it could be. It was simply the tower in which she had been assigned a room.

What had started out as excitement at seeing Lord Angle again now twisted into anxiousness and worry. From the sounds of it, there were dozens of people inside the room. Dozens of conversations for her to make a fool of herself. Dozens of people to look at her in the way that everyone did when speaking with her for any length of time. And dozens more chances for Lord Angle to see how completely improper she was.

She sighed. While she did not expect anything to develop between them, there was always that small glimmer of hope. Or at least there had been. But with every voice that echoed out of the room, that hope grew dimmer.

She clenched her hands at her side. Who was she kidding? He was a marquess, and she was the daughter of a merchant. She should stop pretending there was any hope at all.

"Poppet, what are you waiting for? I am certain we are expected to move into the hall, not simply wait outside the door."

Marjie ran her hand down the sides of her gown, her gloved hands damp with perspiration. "I was just waiting for you, Mama," she lied.

"I am here. Come along." She put her hand on Marjie's back and gave her a little shove toward the door.

They entered the room and Marjie relaxed. No one seemed to pay them any attention, and it seemed she had been wrong about the numbers. There were not as many as she had assumed. There were surely still opportunities for her to play the fool, but not as many as she had thought. Lord Angle stood with two other gentlemen, while another group of four stood on the opposite side of the room.

Lady Angle stood and called out to them. "Lady Mariane and Miss Fitzroy, please come join us." Her smile seemed genuine enough.

All eyes turned toward them, and low murmurs floated to her ears. Not loud enough to hear the words, but enough to know she and her mother were the topic of conversation. Marjie stood rooted to the floor. Her mouth was stone dry, while her hands continued to seep out moisture.

Her mother gave her another little push forward, and her feet finally moved. When she caught Lord Angle's gaze, she released a stuttering breath. She could do this. She could be just like everyone else, could she not? She would just need to concentrate and focus. Think about everything before she spoke.

Lord Angle separated himself from the gentlemen he was

speaking to and made his way over to her. He dipped his head. "Good evening, Lady Mariane. Miss Fitzroy." He watched her from under his lashes and her face warmed.

"Good evening, my lord." She curtsied.

"I believe there is a seat on the settee. May I escort you there?" He lifted his arm to Marjie and her mother.

Marjie nodded and put her hand on his arm. She breathed deeply, allowing his confidence to seep into her.

He helped her sit and then went back to his conversation with the gentlemen she'd seen him with before.

The curtains next to him fluttered wildly, then settled almost as quickly.

"That was odd," said an older lady sitting across the low table from Marjie.

"It is surely ghosts," the lady sitting next to her sniffed, but she did not seem troubled by the thought.

Marjie glanced over at Lord Angle, wondering if he heard the conversation. From the grin on his face, she assumed he must have.

"Do you believe in ghosts then?" she asked the older ladies.

"It is not belief so much as fact, Miss Fitzroy. There are surely ghosts all around us."

Marjie tipped her head to the side, holding back all the thoughts flitting through her mind. Instead of replying, she simply smiled meekly.

She looked toward Lord Angle from the sides of her eyes and a flutter started in her chest when she saw his gaze flick over to her often. She may have been imagining it, but she thought she saw him grin each time he looked her way.

"Where are you from, Miss Fitzroy?" A slightly shrill voice sounded across from her.

Marjie turned toward a fair-haired young lady, likely close

to her same age. She had tranquil, pale blue eyes which seemed to contradict her voice. "We live in Yorkshire."

"I beg your pardon, Miss Fitzroy. Please, let me make introductions." Lady Angle leaned forward in their conversation circle. "On your left is Miss Penry and then her mother, Lady Stimple. Miss Griffiths and Mrs. Griffiths. And lastly, Mrs. Parry and Mrs. Beddoe."

Each of the ladies dipped their heads and mumbled pleasant greetings. Marjie was uplifted by the pleasant looks that accompanied the greetings. The evening was off to a splendid start. Perhaps she could make it through without embarrassing herself and, in turn, Lord Angle.

"What about you, Miss Fitzroy? Do you not believe in ghosts?" Mrs. Griffiths asked.

Marjie smiled and paused. Thinking of an answer before allowing it to spill from her lips. "I have not yet decided. Until I receive some indication one way or the other, I feel I must remain open to the idea but not convinced."

"Then you think us fools for believing?" Mrs. Parry bristled.

Marjie's head shook and her mouth opened but nothing came out. What had happened? She had even thought that response out before speaking.

"I am certain Miss Fitzroy thought nothing of the sort, Mrs. Parry. Surely you have realized our English friends are more tight-lipped about such things than we Welsh are." Lord Angle walked over and leaned toward the woman. "When last I was in London, I did not hear a single story of ghosts for the whole of my stay in Town."

"Not one?" She seemed shocked by the news.

Marjie's gaze bounced back and forth between the two of them. Did they truly speak of ghosts so often it was commonplace?

Lord Angle shook his head with a feigned sadness on his

face. "I think you must excuse our English guests. Perhaps if they are lucky, they will see something before they leave that will change their minds."

Mrs. Parry nodded slowly. "Perhaps if they are very fortunate."

The butler stepped into the room and announced dinner.

Lady Angle stood and clapped her hands until she had everyone's attention. "As this is simply a gathering of friends, I believe we will dispense with formal seating arrangements."

A man with thick, brown hair sidled up next to Marjie. "Miss Fitzroy, may I escort you into dinner?"

Lord Angle slipped between them. "I'm sorry, Alwyn, but I do not believe proper introductions have been made." He smiled down at her. "I shall escort Miss Fitzroy into dinner."

"Could you not introduce us now?" Alwyn asked.

"I could," Lord Angle lifted his arm and Marjie placed her hand on it. "But everyone is waiting for me to go first. It would be terribly rude for me to hold up dinner while I made introductions. Perhaps after port we may take the time to do it properly." He placed his hand on top of hers and pulled her gently forward. "Come along, Miss Fitzroy. We do not want to keep everyone waiting.

Marjie moved out of the room on Lord Angle's arm, but she glanced over her shoulder just as they passed through the doorway.

Alwyn scowled at Lord Angle's back.

Marjie turned back around, wondering what the history was between Lord Angle and Alwyn—she wished she knew his name. She felt completely improper thinking of him by his Christian name.

"Pay him no mind, Miss Fitzroy. The man has a knack for desiring what he can't have." Lord Angle flicked up his brows.

"And why do you assume he couldn't have me?" Her face

flushed as soon as she realized how it sounded. "I mean, would we not match well? I do not know him well enough to know."

He looked down at her with his brow creased. "Trust me Miss Fitzroy, you would not suit."

She pulled her lip between her teeth. Whatever the history, it was obviously turbulent.

Lord Angle helped her into the seat to his left. His mother took the seat to his right.

"Is this seat taken?" A deep voice sounded over her shoulder. She looked up to see one of the men Lord Angle had been speaking with in the lesser hall.

"Ah, Seren, let me introduce you." He nodded to Marjie. "Miss Marjorie Fitzroy, may I introduce my dear friend, Mr. Seren Lloyd."

Marjie dipped her head as she was unable to curtsy while seated at the table. "The seat is not taken, Mr. Lloyd."

He grinned and slid into the chair next to her. "It is a pleasure to make your acquaintance, Miss Fitzroy." He flicked his gaze to Lord Angle. "Arawn says you are visiting for the next fortnight."

She nodded. "Yes, although we have already been here for two days." Her eyes darted between the two men. She did not detect the undertones of dislike between these two men as she had between Lord Angle and that Alwyn fellow.

"It has been an enjoyable two days, has it not, Miss Fitzroy?"

Marjie snickered. "Perhaps recently, but you were not so keen on our visit when we arrived. Or have you already forgotten, my lord?"

His ears pinked slightly, and Marjie cursed her loose lips. "I mean, you were not unkind or anything so terrible. I believe—"

"You need not temper Arawn's greeting for my sake. We have been friends for practically all our lives. I can guess at the reception you received, knowing his mother had not broken the news to him of your arrival." Seren chuckled as if he could, indeed, picture the scene.

Marjie caught a glimpse of Lord Angle's face. She expected him to be scowling and angry, but instead he smirked at Mr. Lloyd. "You know me too well, Seren." He pierced Marjie with a look. "But please, do not share all my poor qualities with Miss Fitzroy yet. I should not like to ruin any good opinion I've gained so far."

"Oh, I'm certain you will do that all on your own." Seren grinned.

"Thank you for your vote of confidence, Seren," Lord Angle raised a brow at his friend.

Marjie smiled. She liked seeing this side of Lord Angle. While she enjoyed any time she had with him, she had enjoyed their disagreement about his sister less so, but still she would not wish that time away. Perhaps just that bit of conversation. But then, had she not received insight into him, even then?

But this side she was seeing now with his friend was different than what she had seen so far. "I am certain if my opinion of Lord Angle changes, it will only be for the better."

Mr. Lloyd nodded, but his brow rose high on his head. "Well done, Arawn, you have the poor woman completely bamboozled."

Lord Angle laughed.

Marjie stared at him in wonderment. It was possible for him to laugh. She had begun to wonder. And this was not just any laugh, but rather the deep, belly-shaking kind.

All the conversations at the table ceased and all eyes turned to them. Lady Angle and Marjie's mother stopped speaking with Mr. Parry and stared at him. Lady Angle looked as if she might cry. Although Marjie could not say that she looked sad. Perhaps more relieved.

"Ah, Seren. Where have you been these past six months? I could have used your erroneous humor."

Marjie's cheeks hurt from smiling so widely. How she wished she knew how to make Lord Angle laugh as Mr. Lloyd did. His whole face scrunched up in a most adorable way. He needed that more in his life. And so did she, if she were being honest.

"It does not matter. I am here now. I will see that you do not take yourself too seriously." Mr. Lloyd looked at Marjie side-eyed and winked. "We can't have Miss Fitzroy thinking you are dull now. Can we?"

Lord Angle looked at her, his eyes still glistening from the tears of his laughter. "No, Seren. That would not do in the least."

CHAPTER NINE

Marjie sat in a chair next to the small window in her room. She lightly ran her fingers along the rough stones where the opening had been expanded to fit a larger window. Unlike the rest of the tall, narrow windows dotting the walls of her room, this window provided a wide view of the outer ward of the castle.

From what she had learned on her tour with Lord Angle, it was not wise—defensively speaking—to put large windows in the towers, or in any exterior wall for that matter. It was too easy for an archer to shoot a flaming arrow through the animal horn windows, setting fire to the wooden structures inside.

She looked down into the bailey, or ward, or courtyard—she had yet to decide which name she preferred—and tried to imagine what it had looked like when Rhys and Gwilym ap Tudor had lived there. She assumed there would be much more activity than what she saw below her then. In the 1400's, according to Lord Angle, the stables would have been just across the ward, next to the kitchens. She wrinkled her nose, not caring to think about those two places in such proximity. The kitchens now took up the entirety of the space.

Her mind could conjure the sight of fires burning in various pits around the bailey as men sharpened their swords and mended their chain mail—preparing for the next battle that would surely come.

A picture of Lord Angle and Mr. Lloyd laughing together as they did their preparations made her smile. Lord Angle had been right, it had been an enjoyable few days. Last evening she had seen a completely different man. And she liked him. Indeed, she liked him more than was prudent. What if that man was only around when Mr. Lloyd was present?

She guffawed and gave herself a little shake. As if that was her biggest concern.

She pulled her knees up and tucked her gown around her. Wrapping her arms around her legs, she leaned her head against the stone wall. Sometimes she was such a ninny. Sometimes she allowed herself to believe that things were different than they really were. And that was dangerous.

A knock sounded at the door and her mother poked her head in. "Poppet, are you awake?"

"Of course, Mama. It is nearly ten o'clock."

"What have you planned to do this morning?" her mother asked as she picked up a ribbon that had fallen from the dressing table.

Marjie's eyes lit. "Lord Angle showed me the stable yesterday. It is outside the castle walls, but it is rather extensive. I thought I might look at the horses. And while he did not give me permission to ride, I thought I might inquire of the stable master. Surely it was just an oversight." She moved over toward her wardrobe. "I am just pleased I thought to pack my riding habit."

Her mother sighed, her shoulders hunching slightly

forward. "Do be careful, Poppet. You have scarcely ridden a handful of times. And you tend towards the fearless whenever you mount a horse."

Marjie rolled her eyes. "Did not Hodges say I was a fast learner? He said I looked as if I had been riding my whole life." Marjie dropped the skirt of her habit.

"Hodges was being kind," she muttered. "But that was nearly a year ago. What if you have forgotten?"

"One does not forget how to ride a horse, Mama. I'm certain if I did not ride for a decade, as soon as I settled in the saddle, it would come back to me as if it were yesterday." She did not know why her mother was acting this way. Her mother had ridden regularly until she left her father's estate when she married.

"Just promise me you will be careful. Perhaps there is a groom that could accompany you if you decide to ride? Or perhaps Lord Angle would be willing. I will feel more comfortable knowing you are not out riding alone."

"I do not need a chaperone on my ride," Marjie whined. She knew it was beneath her, but she could not help it. Sometimes her mother treated her like she was still in the schoolroom and not a grown woman of two and twenty.

At the sight of the strain lines next to her mother's eyes, she dropped her head to the side. "Oh, very well, Mama. I will ask someone to accompany me."

When her mother's worry lines did not disappear, Marjie sighed and put a hand on her mother's arm. "Do not worry, Mama. I will be careful in every aspect."

Her mother nodded and looked down at Marjie's dress. "I will have Susanna lay out an afternoon gown for you. Come see me in my chambers when you return. I wish to hear all about it."

She gave Marjie a hug, as if she worried it might be her last, and moved toward the door. "Now get dressed and enjoy your ride."

Marjie smiled widely. "Thank you, Mama. I am certain I shall."

She turned to the wardrobe and pulled out the deep blue riding habit her mother had made her before their journey to Marjie's uncle's estate last year. It had not been a long visit, only a fortnight, but it had been life changing.

Marjie was still uncertain if it had been completely for the better. She frowned at herself in the dressing table mirror. They owed much to her uncle, and she should not be so dissolute. It was surely his kindness toward them that was responsible for the invitation to Hywel. At least before she had known where she stood within society. But now? She did not belong among the servants nor among the *ton*.

Twisting her hair into a tight knot, she pinned it up before pulling on her habit. It took longer than she wanted to fasten all the buttons up the front, likely because she allowed her excitement to get the better of her. Goodness, why must there be so many buttons?

"May I help you, Miss?" her maid asked.

"I only have a few buttons left," she said as she leaned over to grab the last few.

The maid hurried over and knelt in front of her. "Let me do that."

"Thank you, Susanna."

Grabbing her bonnet from the end of the bed, she nearly skipped down the stairs.

She had seen a pretty black and white horse in the stable when she had visited it on the tour. That was the horse she wished to ride, although she had not actually asked permission, nor had Lord Angle volunteered it. But surely it would not be a problem. He had been so agreeable on many other things.

She glided down the stairs, enjoying the way her habit bounced off her legs and then fluttered up before dropping down and bouncing off again.

She stepped into the anteroom, glancing down at her habit as she pushed through the doors into the bailey.

"Oof," she glanced up, as she fell backward.

"Miss Fitzroy? I did not see you there, else I should have moved out of your way."

CHAPTER TEN

Arawn held Miss Fitzroy's upper arms, trying to keep her on her feet. His heart skittered. At the surprise, no doubt. He dropped his hands once he was certain she was steady. "Where are you off to in such a hurry?" He glanced down at her riding habit and frowned.

"On our tour, I saw some very lovely horses. I thought to visit them. Perhaps one of them might befriend me and allow me a ride."

Arawn's stomach tightened, and his breakfast soured. "You wish to ride? I'm not certain that is the best idea." He glanced at the blue sky. "It looks as if it might storm."

Miss Fitzroy laughed lightly. "I think you are mistaken. I was just looking out my bedroom window, and I saw not a cloud. I think it a wonderful day for a ride."

His palms felt cold and sticky. "I cannot permit you to go alone." His voice came out sterner than he anticipated, and her smile faltered.

"Why do we not schedule a time when I am available to

accompany you?" He rubbed his hand across the back of his neck, knowing he had no intention of that time ever coming available.

"You need not bother yourself. I'm certain I can persuade a stable hand to accompany me. You are surely too busy."

"Do you not want me to go?"

She shook her head. "Oh, no. You mistake my meaning. I only do not wish to be a bother." She looked down at her feet.

He took in a labored breath. Why was it deuced difficult to breathe? He growled low in his throat to displace whatever it was that was prohibiting him from breathing and swallowing correctly. "I'm sorry, but I cannot leave your safety up to a stable hand. What would your mother say if harm should come to you? No, I think it best if we schedule a time." *Sometime next year, perhaps?* He clasped his hands behind his back, his breath coming easier.

"But I have already dressed." She looked down at her habit.

Arawn could not deny she looked the picture of loveliness. But he could not be sidetracked from his present course by the pleasant fit of a riding habit.

She looked up at him with wide eyes, and he nearly growled again. "But when will you have time to accompany me?"

Curse her very expressive eyes. "Oh, very well. I shall clear my schedule and we may go now." He looked down at her gown. "As you are already dressed."

She nodded and he had a sneaking suspicion she knew exactly what she was doing with her expressive eyes. "Please wait here while I change into my riding clothes."

She grinned happily. "Thank you, my lord."

Arawn dressed quickly, afraid if he took too long, she would go without him.

As they walked to the stables, he fell into step beside her, content to slow his gait to match hers. The longer they took to arrive at the stables, the greater the chance that his pleas for rain might come to fruition. "You have ridden before?"

"Yes." Miss Fitzroy nodded. "Do you not remember I told you I had ridden while staying with my uncle? I was told I was a very good student and learned quite quickly."

"Yes, yes. I remember the conversation." But had she not also said it had been a year ago and only for a fortnight? Lud, this was surely a bacon-brained idea.

"I know you said you have ridden before, but that is not the same as riding. Riding infers a certain proficiency." He glanced over at her. "Did you only ride that one time?"

She shook her head. "No. I have not only ridden one time. I rode every day for nearly a fortnight. That is at least twelve times."

He ran a hand through his hair. "But you have not ridden again since?"

She shook her head. "But one does not forget how to ride a horse."

He tipped his head to the side. How could she be so confident in her answer when she had only ridden a few times? Twelve to be precise, but still.

They entered the dim stable and he motioned her toward the row of stalls, each housing a different horse. "That gray horse there is a gelding. I think he would do very well for you." Thank the heavens she had not yet seen Gwyn.

Miss Fitzroy moved without hesitation, down to the stall at the far end. Zounds! He had obviously thought too soon. Miss Fitzroy held out a carrot—which he knew not where she had procured it—to the black and white Icelandic.

Curses. She had discovered Gwyn.

Arawn bit the side of his cheek to keep from yelling for Miss Fitzroy to back up.

He had bought the Icelandic horse because of its reportedly calm nature. However, it had been anything but calm on the day it threw Ane and then trampled over her.

He had thought to rid himself of the horse, but when the time came, he could not do it. He could not be rid of the animal that had brought his sister such joy, even up to the last moments of her life.

He reached out to pull her away from the rails. "I don't believe that horse is right for you, Miss Fitzroy. If you do not want the gray gelding, then perhaps that gray Welsh Mountain over there would be better suited."

Gwyn lipped the carrot off Miss Fitzroy's palm and took a step forward, nuzzling at her arm. She ran a hand down the horse's face and smiled, then looked over her shoulder at him. "That is a pony, my lord. You need not coddle me. I am capable on a horse."

She knew the difference between a pony and a horse. Lud, perhaps she did know something about horse flesh.

"I like this one." She took another carrot from her pocket and held it out to the horse.

Lud, where had she found the carrots? Arawn swallowed. What could he say? It would be rude for him to decline without an explanation. And they had already made an agreement not to speak of Ane. But if he allowed her to ride the horse and something should happen—. He ran a hand through his hair. He was in a situation with no winners.

"I do not think it best for you to ride Gwyn. He is not always predictable." The horse had shown no poor spirit since the accident. And Mathias had said he had never acted up again. But could he take the risk now? Especially with a guest?

She turned those expressive eyes on him once again, and

Arawn knew he was done for. When had a pair of eyes ever had such control over him? "Since Miss Fitzroy's arrival," he grumbled.

"I beg your pardon?" she leaned toward him.

"It was nothing."

She continued to run her hand down Gwyn's neck. "I think he is perfect." She moved into the stall and Arawn held his breath. But Gwyn merely leaned into her. Smelling her hand and sniffing at her pocket.

"He thinks you have more carrots." Arawn stepped in beside her. It was best if he stayed close so he might jerk her out of the way should Gwyn's temperament change.

"I have one more. I got them from the kitchen while you were changing." She pulled it from her pocket and held it out to the horse. "Aren't you a pretty thing? Shall we take a ride, you and I?"

Perhaps it was best that she was bribing the horse with carrots. It might be enough to keep Gwyn in check long enough for their ride.

Arawn pushed aside the knot forming in his stomach. What would she do if he pushed her aside and forbid her from riding Gwyn? After all, this was his stable, not hers.

But he watched as she crooned to the horse, and Gwyn reciprocated by nuzzling her neck. If Arawn did not know better, he might think Gwyn was lonely. Could it be the horse had missed Ane as much as the rest of them did? Maybe he sensed the similarities between Miss Fitzroy and Ane, just as Arawn did.

He released a deep breath. "Very well. But you must promise to take things slow."

She looked at him and rolled her eyes. "You are acting like an old man, my lord."

He narrowed his eyes and she grimaced. "A very kind old man who is taking me riding at great expense to his time."

Arawn's head shook. He must be daft. "Dafydd, will you please fetch my mother's saddle and ready Gwyn for Miss Fitzroy?"

The stable hand frowned. "I beg your pardon, my lord. But we sent her ladyship's saddle out for repairs just last week. It is not yet back." He twisted the cuff of his sleeve between his fingers.

That was it. That was the excuse he needed. Arawn tried to look apologetic, but his grin won out. "I'm sorry, Miss Fitzroy. I was not aware my mother's saddle was missing. Perhaps we will be lucky, and it will return before you take your leave."

She frowned but then brightened.

Why had she perked up?

She pointed to a spot just over his shoulder. "What about that one? It appears to be a sidesaddle."

Both Arawn and Dafydd looked at the saddle and both their eyes widened. "No," they shouted in unison.

Miss Fitzroy backed up, her eyes wide and glassy.

Awe, lud. She was going to cry. That was far worse than her expressive looks.

"But why not?" she asked in a warbling voice.

Arawn shook his head. He would allow her to ride Gwyn, but he could not allow her to use Ane's saddle. He just couldn't.

"But that is the only sidesaddle, is it not?" She tilted her head. "What is wrong with it? Or is it me you do not trust to use it? I promise I will do it no harm."

Arawn closed his eyes, fighting back the memories of Ane falling from the horse. He rubbed at his eyes with his palms.

Why was Miss Fitzroy so insistent? Could she not see that there was a reason he did not wish for her to use it? Although what the reason was—other than the saddle had been Ane's—he could not say. The knot tightened in his throat.

Dafydd stood rooted to the floor darting his eyes between Arawn and Miss Fitzroy.

What was he to do? He could not have Miss Fitzroy think she was the problem. But neither could he explain what the problem was.

Running an unsteady hand through his hair, Arawn finally nodded. "Gwyn does not care for that saddle." It was a necessary lie.

Her lips thinned and her eyes squinted. "What about the gray horse you mentioned earlier? Is he amiable to the saddle?"

The tightness in his chest eased slightly. "He has not seemed to care in the past."

"Then I shall ride him." She gave Gwyn one last longing look and ran her hand down his nose. "Thank you, my lord. I can hardly contain my excitement."

Dafydd stepped forward with the saddle in his hands. "Are you certain that is best, my lord? What if—" He stopped as if realizing how improper the question was. But Arawn understood. He knew exactly how the man was feeling. It spoke to how concerned they all were about this ride.

Except for Miss Fitzroy, who was blissfully unaware of what she had asked.

"No, Dafydd, I am not. But we've never had cause to worry over Arthur's temperament. It will be fine." He sighed. "Besides, I will be right beside her. If something should happen, I will be there to stop it."

Mathias, the stable master, approached. "Ah, you are taking Gwyn for a ride? I am certain he will be pleased. He has missed his daily rides with—"

Arawn coughed. "No. She will be riding Arthur. But she has given Gwyn some attention." While Miss Fitzroy did not know the story of Ane's death, this was surely not the time to share it. He could not imagine it would deter her. It would only cause her to be tentative and scared in the saddle. And that could do nothing but cause problems.

He glanced over at Dafydd. There was doubt in his eyes that mirrored Arawn's.

Please don't let events repeat themselves, he whispered a quiet plea heavenward.

Miss Fitzroy stopped beside him with Arthur's reins held loosely in her fist. "Are you ready?"

Arawn nodded even as a voice in his head shouted, N*o, I will never be ready.* "Let's be on our way."

He led her out of the stables. An old log stood where the mounting block had been—Arwan had ordered it removed after the accident. It wobbled as Miss Fitzroy stepped up. Gah, why had he not left the block? Had he really thought there would never be a need for it?

He gave a grunt. No, he had not. His mother had sworn off riding after the accident. Arawn had no intentions of bringing a wife to Hywel Castle any time soon. And when he did, he didn't intend to let the same thing happen to her as had happened to Ane. He rolled his eyes. Knowing his luck, his wife would be just as stubborn as Miss Fitzroy.

"That log is not very steady. Perhaps it would be best if I assisted you." He took a step toward her.

She cocked her head to one side and stared at him. Then she stood up, placing both feet on the log. It rocked back and forth, and she waved her arms out around her.

"Let me help you else you will break your neck before you even mount the horse." He placed his hands on her waist and instantly realized his error. His fingers molded to the curve of her waist, leaving him in no doubt of the slenderness of her frame. Her hands went to his arms, and for a moment he just held onto her. A sense of peace rested on his shoulders as a rightness seemed to fill his brain. He sucked in a breath.

But when he caught sight of the saddle, the peace fled. What was he doing? Why was he allowing this to happen? It was as if at every turn, fate had told him this was an ill-conceived idea. Why was he not listening? Simply because he did not wish to tell Miss Fitzroy the details surrounding his sister's death? Or should he blame it on her expressive eyes?

"My lord?" Her question brought him back to the present and his hand wrapped tighter around her waist. "I am ready to mount."

He cleared his throat. "Yes, of course. I only wished to make sure you were certain." He flexed his muscles as he lifted her up to the saddle. She was not light as a feather, nor was she heavy. Rather she was just right.

Arthur jerked and then danced several steps side to side as Miss Fitzroy situated herself in the saddle.

Arawn's body went cold, and he nearly pulled her back off again.

Was the horse acting out of sorts?

"You are certain you wish to do this?" He felt it his duty to ask again. Perhaps he would be lucky, and she would decline. Although, seeing her atop Arthur, he knew his hope was in vain. She looked utterly delighted.

"Of course." She looked around. "Where are we to ride?"

Arawn smiled and his shoulders relaxed, if only a fraction, for the first time since they started this little adventure.

Arthur danced again, and she leaned forward and rubbed between his ears.

Arawn drew in a deep breath, allowing the cool autumn air to fill his lungs and calm the tension inside him. All would be well. This would be a pleasant ride. He would make sure it was not challenging, thus ensuring Miss Fitzroy's safety.

He swung up onto his horse and flicked the reins as he clucked his tongue. The horse started off at an easy pace, not walking fast enough to raise a single hair on his head. It was perfect. Just what he wanted. Certainly, no harm could befall Miss Fitzroy at this pace.

They rode across the drawbridge and over the river, giving them access to the village beyond the castle pastures.

"Which direction are we to go?" Miss Fitzroy pulled Arthur to a stop and turned slightly to face him.

"There is a large open field over that way that has been harvested for the winter. We will head through the gate down this street and then you will be able to see it. We can then follow the shoreline." He lifted his hand and pointed off a short distance. "It is lovely this time of year." The shoreline trail was narrow and curvy, leaving little opportunity to give the horses their heads.

"I was hoping you would say that." She smiled and led her horse in the direction he had pointed and flicked her reins.

Arawn held his breath until Arthur set into a slow steady motion across the fields. He held back, allowing Miss Fitzroy to take the lead. If anything were to happen, he would be close and could provide immediate assistance. It would be fine.

They neared the edge of the field and Arawn sat up in his set. Lud, he'd forgotten about the stream. Thankfully it was not very wide or deep.

"Miss Fitzroy, that stream is not deep. Just walk Arthur through it."

Miss Fitzroy stopped and stared at the water. "But surely we may just jump over it."

"I do not advise it." He snapped. "Just walk. It will be better." It occurred to him that she had done little of what he asked of her on this outing, using her expressive eyes to force him to yield to her wishes. Could he hope that this would be the time she did as he asked?

Miss Fitzroy grinned over her shoulder. "Now what is the fun in that?"

The knot in his stomach tightened, and he opened his mouth to object again as she launched the horse over the stream. She landed on the other side, shifting in the seat as she settled.

Arawn leaned forward, pushing out the breath he had been holding, just as Arthur reared up and tossed Miss Fitzroy to the ground.

He stared, stunned for a moment at her crumpled form. Images of Ane flooded his mind. *Oh, merciful heavens, not again.*

Arthur dropped to all fours and tossed his head. His gaze darted about, and his ears laid flat on his head. He was going to bolt, and he would trample Miss Fitzroy, just as Gwyn had trampled Ane.

Arawn jumped from his horse and ran through the water, reaching Miss Fitzroy just as Arthur reared up again.

Grabbing her beneath the arms, he flung them both around, putting his back to Arthur. He stepped out of the water and carefully laid Miss Fitzroy on the ground on the other side before turning back toward the horse. "Woah, now, Arthur. Calm yourself, boy."

The calm, quiet tones seemed to soothe the horse. He dropped down, knickered, and then set off at a gallop along the coastal path.

Arawn shook his head. He could not worry about that now. He turned and kneeled next to Miss Fitzroy. "Miss Fitzroy. Can you hear me?"

There was no answer.

Arawn dropped his forehead down on her chest. Not again? How many must die at his hand? Was this a punishment for something he had done? A sob escaped his lips. Great Caesar's ghost! What would he tell her mother?

His head rose and fell.

He jerked up in surprise. She was breathing? Thank the heavens! Now he just needed to get her back to the castle.

CHAPTER ELEVEN

Arawn gently put one arm behind her shoulders and head while his other snaked under her knees. He started to lift her but paused. What if she had broken something in the fall? Would it not do more damage if he jerked her around while she had a broken bone? He supposed it would be better if he set anything that was broken or at least secured it before they made the long journey back to the castle.

He felt his way along her head and neck and then down each arm. Nothing seemed to be out of place there. He looked at the rest of her body laying still on the ground and shook his head in frustration. Now was not the time to be worried about proprieties. He felt along her legs keeping his focus on the bones within.

Satisfied that there was nothing broken, he gently lifted her up into his arms and looked back toward the castle. It was a very long walk.

Carefully, he lifted her up and draped her over his dappled horse, keeping a hand firmly on her as he swung up onto

Taran's back. Once he was settled into the saddle, Arawn lifted her into his arms, cradling her to him firmly so as not to jostle her more than necessary once he set Taran into a trot. He feared a gallop or even canter would be too rough.

He clucked his tongue and flicked the reins, settling for a faster pace, needing to arrive at the castle in a timely manner without causing more harm to Miss Fitzroy.

Her head dropped to the side and a low moan sounded. He looked down, hoping she had awakened. But no other sound escaped her lips. His arm shifted beneath her, and he noticed, for the first time, a large lump just below the crown of her head.

Their journey back to the castle seemed to take an eternity. Memories of Ane and her accident came flooding back.

"Arawn, wait for me," Ane called out as she and Gwyn stood looking down at the stream. It was higher than normal after a very wet winter. "Gwyn does not wish to cross."

"Then jump it. It is not so very wide." He grinned wickedly at her. "Unless you are too chicken livered."

She glared at him. "You know I am not afraid to jump my horse. We have jumped many fences together, have we not, Gwyn?"

"From where I am seated, I can see nothing of the sort. I am on this side of the stream, while you are not."

Ane pulled her reins to the side, leading Gwyn back the way they had come. "He thinks we are not brave enough, Gwynie. We cannot have him thinking such nonsense."

"You talk to that horse like he is a mare. It is no wonder you have turned him into a coward."

Ane sucked in an offended breath. "Come on, boy." She flicked the reins and dug her heels into his side. "Let's show Ari just how brave we are."

Ane and Gwyn sailed over the stream, landing on the other side with a thud. Ane dropped hard into the saddle and then time stilled.

Slowly, her smiling face turned to fear as Gwyn reared up, throwing her off his back. Arawn watched, stunned as the horse dropped back down and then reared again, only this time he dropped down on top of Ane, stomping on her head several times in his flight to get away.

The memories played over and over until he thought he might go mad.

Finally, they entered the stable yard, his shirt nearly drenched in sweat. Thankfully sweat also ran down his face, hiding many of the tears that had surely fallen as well.

Dafydd and Mathias both looked up, and Mathias hurried over. "Thunder and turf, my lord. What happened?"

"Arthur threw Miss Fitzroy after she jumped the stream. It was just as it happened with Ane." Mathias reached up to take Miss Fitzroy, but Arawn shook his head fiercely. "No. I will see her to the castle. Please follow behind me."

"I will follow you, my lord." Dafydd hurried over and stood next to Mathias.

"No, boy. You stay here and see that the other hands are not distracted by these events. I'll follow his lordship back to the castle." Mathias took the reins.

Dafydd opened his mouth to argue, but Arawn glared down at him. There was no time for argument.

"Yes, father."

Arawn turned Taran toward the castle as Mathias walked quickly behind.

At the gate to the outer ward, Mathias came forward. "I can hold her while you dismount, my lord."

Arawn shook his head. "No. Please just hold Taran steady." He carefully pulled his leg up and brought it over the saddle, shifting to the side. Sliding off the horse and landing on the cobblestone, he cradled Miss Fitzroy to him.

He turned to Mathias. "Arthur ran off toward the coastal path. Please fetch him and bring him back."

Mathias nodded. "Of course, my lord. I'll send someone for him immediately."

"No, Mathias." Arawn's voice came out sharp and gravelly. "I want *you* to fetch him. This is the second horse to act out of character. Something is not right in the stables, and I wish to know what it is immediately. But I do not wish to endanger anyone else. You are the only one with enough experience. I trust you will be fine."

"I don't understand it. Arthur is the gentlest horse in the stables. Something had to have caused him to throw her." The stable master looked pensive, but when he noticed Arawn's stern face, he nodded. "Yes, my lord. I'll see to it."

Arawn shook his head. "Come see me once you have caught him and he is back in the stable. Then we can decide how to proceed."

"Very well, sir."

Arawn nodded and turned toward the large wooden doors leading into the bailey. Mathias hurried forward to open them for him.

As soon as he stepped through, Lady Mariane hurried up to meet him.

"We saw you coming from the sitting room window," his mother came up behind her. "*Hir yw'r dydd,* Arawn. How bad is she?"

"Marjorie!" Lady Mariane looked near apoplexy. "What happened, my lord?"

Arawn bit the inside of his cheek, trying to keep his emotions in check. Although suddenly the weight of Miss Fitzroy in his arms was almost more than he could bear. "She tried to jump the stream and her horse threw her. She is breathing and has moaned a few times, which seems to be a positive thing." What was he rattling on about? "She needs to be in bed and seen by a doctor. Could you please lead the way?"

Lady Mariane shook her head. "I'm not surprised she did something dangerous. That is her way, unfortunately." She turned teary eyes upon him. "I am grateful you were there with her. Thank you, my lord."

Arawn's skin itched and not just from the sweat that covered him. How could he accept her thanks when it was his fault she was in this predicament?

He navigated the circular staircase, making certain he did not hit her head on the railing or any of the stones that jutted out from the wall. She already had one bump on her head.

When they reached the landing to her bedroom, Lady Mariane held the door open as Arawn side-stepped his way into the room and deposited Miss Fitzroy onto her bed. He stared down at her pale face. Thankfully, it did not look as pale as Ane's had. Perhaps that was because Mis Fitzroy was yet alive.

He took a step back, feeling himself collapsing under the weight of his guilt. He needed to get away...needed to be away from her. "I will leave her to you and summon the doctor immediately."

Lady Mariane sat on the edge of the bed and leaned over her daughter, running a tender hand across her brow. She glanced over her shoulder at him. "Thank you, again, my lord."

He shook his head and fled from the room, unable to listen to any more misdirected gratitude. When she discovered the truth—lud, he had no idea how he could apologize enough.

He slipped out of the bedroom door and moved to the doorway directly across from it. Pushing it open, he stepped out onto the allure. He walked quickly through the kitchen tower and the stock house tower, then through the bakehouse tower, and finally into his own chambers.

He shut the door behind him and leaned his back against it. Sinking to the floor, he allowed the heaviness that had been his companion for these last six months to settle once again on his shoulders. Only then did he realize how much the weight had been slowly lifting the last few days.

But the new weight pushed down that much harder, tightening around his chest and stomach. It had hurt more than he could have imagined knowing he was responsible for his sister's death. But now to add the near death of a guest in his home to the list? It was almost too much.

Although, he was beginning to think of her as more than just a guest. She had become his friend. A friend he had almost killed. Someone should lock him away. It was surely what was best for everyone around him.

⁂

Arawn sat at his desk, looking at the ledgers without seeing them. His hand bounced on the desktop next to the open book and he began adding the column of numbers...again.

He itched to go see how Miss Fitzroy was doing, but he didn't dare. What if she had taken a turn for the worst? She had been quite wet from dragging her through the stream. What if she caught a cold on top of her other injuries?

He glanced up at the door. Why had no one come to give him an update? Not even Mathias had come to see him.

"The doctor is come, my lord." Havard stood just inside Arawn's study door. "Shall I show him up to Miss Fitzroy's chambers?"

At last, he had an excuse to go see her. He offered a silent plea that she had only improved since last he saw her. "I will come and take him to her room. I would like to check in on her."

"Very good, my lord. The doctor is waiting in the lesser hall." Havard backed out of the room on a bow.

Arawn gripped the chair's arms and sucked in a deep breath. He could do this. He had been raised to face challenges head on, not cower in his study until they went away.

He tipped his head from side to side, rolling his shoulders and trying fruitlessly to relieve the tension. Knowing he should not keep the doctor waiting any longer, he stood. The man surely had more patients in need of his assistance. He did not have time to spend the entire afternoon at Hywel.

Arawn trudged toward the parlor. "Good afternoon, Doctor Wells. Thank you for coming out so quickly." He glanced at the clock and noticed it had not been quick at all. Arawn had summoned the man nearly two hours earlier.

"Yes, yes. I would have been here sooner, but it was thought Mrs. Gaily was in labor."

Arawn conceded that perhaps the man had not simply dilly-dallied. "I trust the mother and babe are doing well?"

The doctor grunted. "It was a false alarm. I believe she still has several weeks to go. But it is her first, and at any pain she feels, she is certain the baby is coming." He turned bright eyes on Arawn. "Now, what can I do for you, my lord?"

"One of my guests was thrown from a horse while riding this morning."

Doctor Wells looked on with wide eyes. "Another thrown from a horse? I should think you might consider closing your stables, my lord. Simply for the safety of the neighborhood and your future—" He stopped when he looked up and saw Arawn's face. "I did not mean—"

"Yes, I know what you meant, Doctor Wells. But I think I will take the advice of my stable master and steward over that of the parish doctor." Arawn knew his voice was harsh, but he did not care for the doctor's impertinent comments.

"Yes, yes. Perhaps that is advisable." He clasped the handle of his bag a little tighter. "And how is your guest feeling?"

"I do not know. When last I saw her, she was not yet conscious."

"She is unconscious? Why did you not mention that earlier, my lord? Please, show me to her immediately." The doctor tsked and muttered under his breath.

"Right this way," Arawn led the man through the anteroom at the bottom of the south tower where Miss Fitzroy was staying. He waited at the top of the stairs for the doctor who panted up slowly behind him.

"Why can you never put people in the lower rooms of these blasted towers? Is it your intent to kill me?"

Arawn's hand clenched around the iron handrail. He knew the man was jesting, but did he not have enough sense to realize that such a jest was completely inappropriate at present? "Perhaps the problem is that you need more exercise," Arawn grumbled.

Doctor Wells jerked his gaze up but did not stare long as he tripped on a stair. Finally, he arrived at the top and Arawn rapped on the door.

Lady Mariane cracked it open and peered out. Her eyes were red-rimmed but seemed dry. "Please pardon the interruption, madam. Doctor Wells has arrived and wishes to see Miss Fitzroy."

"Thank you, my lord." She opened the door wider.

"Who is there, Mama?" Miss Fitzroy's voice called from inside the chamber.

Arawn's heart thumped, and he released a ragged breath. She was awake.

"It is Lord Angle and the doctor. They have come to check in on you, Poppet."

Doctor Wells slipped past Arawn and stepped into the

room. "Ah, I am pleased to see you are now conscious, Miss." He walked over to the bed while Arawn stayed lingering in the doorway.

Doctor Wells walked around the bed, tilting his head this way and that. "Where does it hurt, child?"

Miss Fitzroy's brow creased. "Why, everywhere, sir."

"Everywhere?"

She nodded. "I suppose you have never been thrown from a horse, else you would know that not more than an inch of my body does not hurt."

He shook his head. "No, I can't say as I have been thrown." He pushed out his lips and hmmed. "Everything hurts. Can you wiggle your fingers?"

Arawn waited with bated breath.

Miss Fitzroy lifted her hands, her fingers dancing in front of her.

"Very good, very good. There is no permanent damage to your arms then." He turned to Lady Mariane. "Would you lift the bottom covers so I might see her toes?"

She did as he requested, pulling the cover up to Miss Fitzroy's ankles.

Arawn knew he should look away. That would be the proper thing to do. But he found his eyes riveted to the toes sticking out from beneath the bedcovers, waiting to watch them dance as her fingers had.

"Can you wiggle your toes?" Dr. Wells asked.

Her toes, much like her fingers, only with less grace, fluttered back and forth. "Capital. There does not seem to be any paralysis. A good thing considering the type of accident."

Arawn stared at Miss Fitzroy's fluttering toes. Who knew they could be so captivating? Or perhaps he was just exhausted and anxious.

Doctor Wells turned toward Arawn. "She seems to be in fine health. Especially considering the accident."

"But you have not even looked at her head. Could that not prove to be troublesome?"

The doctor turned back to Miss Fitzroy. "What is wrong with your head?"

"There is a rather large lump just below the crown." Arawn sighed. Why had Dr. Wells not checked her head to begin with? That seemed like the first thing that should be looked at.

"There is a lump? Why did no one tell me of this lump when I came in?" There was agitation in his voice. But Arawn felt his own irritation rising to an equal level. "You were too busy complaining about the stairs and then rejoicing over her consciousness."

Doctor Wells shrugged. "Yes, well, that is something to rejoice over. But I should have preferred to learn about the lump shortly thereafter."

Arawn gave the man a bland look. "I shall try to remember your advice the next time someone is thrown from a horse."

"Yes," Doctor Wells said absently as he turned back toward the bed. "With the way it happens around here, I should hope you will."

Arawn glanced to Miss Fitzroy but could not meet her gaze. Her brow creased as she looked from him to the doctor and back. But whether her questioning look was due to their disrespectful banter or the off-handed comment Doctor Wells had made, Arawn did not know. But whatever the reason, it stopped Arawn's angry retort. His mouth clenched shut but did not stop working furiously.

"Where is this lump?"

"It is right here, sir." Lady Mariane leaned over the bed and gently pulled her daughter's head toward her. She parted the hair and even from the doorway, Arawn could see the discoloration of the skin.

Doctor Wells leaned over and stared at it. "Does it hurt?"

"Are you daft?" Miss Fitzroy turned and scowled at the man, which brought a grin to Arawn's face. "Of course, it hurts."

Doctor Wells frowned at Miss Fitzroy. "Young lady," his voice held a reprimand.

"Please accept my apologies, doctor. Marjie does not usually speak so freely. I am certain it must be in part to the bump on her head. It is surely causing her to say things she normally would not."

Again, Arawn's lips turned up. What was this bouncer Lady Mariane was saying?

"Yes, yes. I am certain you are correct. I have seen bumps cause many uncharacteristic things in my days." He patted Lady Mariane on the arm. "She looks well enough to me. I should advise her to stay abed for a day or two and rest. I shall leave some laudanum for the pain. And for pity's sake, stay off the horses." He directed the last comment to Arawn.

"Thank you for coming, Doctor Wells." Arawn motioned the man toward the door. "If you will follow me, I will see to your fee."

Lady Mariane jerked her gaze over to Arawn, her brow furrowed.

He smiled tightly at Miss Fitzroy, focusing on her right earlobe. As far as earlobes went, it was rather pleasing. And it kept him from looking her directly in the eye. A win from all angles. "I am pleased to see you are feeling better, Miss Fitzroy. I shall miss seeing you at dinner the next few days." What he said was true, even as a part of him dreaded spending time with her. How could they go back to their easy companionship after this?

"Feeling better? Did you not hear me tell the doctor that I hurt everywhere?" She huffed out a deep breath. "I beg your pardon. I should not have said that," her voice was resigned, and she laid back against the pillows.

Arawn grinned slightly. She looked as exhausted as he felt. "But when compared with unconsciousness, I should think that just hurting everywhere would be considered an improvement. Am I wrong?"

She switched her mouth to the side. "I may have to think on that one for a moment."

CHAPTER TWELVE

Susanna placed Marjie's dinner tray down on the bedside table. "Here is your dinner, Miss."

Marjie wished to scowl at her, but she knew her maid was just following orders. It was not as if Susanna was the one forcing Marjie to stay in her room day after day. Or maybe it had only been two days? It was difficult to know. However long it had been, it felt as if she had been cooped up in this room forever.

Susanna set about straightening the books on the bedside table and rearranging things that did not need rearranging.

Marjie sighed and reached for a slice of bread. She bit the side of her cheek at the pain stretching out her arms still caused. This was the third dinner she had eaten by herself in her room.

She pushed her lips out, and, at the sight of them, she became distracted as she tried to touch them to the tip of her nose. Scrunching up her face, to give the best chance of the two meeting, she contorted until her eyes squeezed shut. But it was for naught. Her hands dropped to her side. Why could nothing go her way?

She looked at the tray of food. If this was the third dinner, it meant she had been stuck in her room for more than two whole days. Other than the sore and stiff muscles, she felt completely fine and did not know why she could not eat with her mother at least, if not with Lord and Lady Angle. Surely the exercise of walking around the castle would help.

She stared at the wall on the other side of the room. There were still fifty-six nearly black stones, forty-three of dark gray, twenty-two of light gray, and ten nearly white stones making up the wall. There was nothing left to count. She had counted the beams in the ceiling—fifteen—and the planks on the floor —forty-four. What else was she supposed to do?

She looked at her door longingly, then glanced at her dinner tray.

Moving as quickly and painlessly as possible, she pulled the tray onto the bed and then onto her lap. She would eat her dinner in her room as she had been instructed. But then she would go down to the drawing room and visit with the others. Surely they would not turn her away.

"Susanna, please ready my dark green gown. I wish to join the others after I eat."

Susanna paused in her task and slowly looked over. "Are you certain that is best, Miss?"

Marjie nodded. "Indeed. I believe the exercise is just what I need."

Her maid stayed still for several heartbeats before she nodded and shuffled toward the wardrobe.

Marjie peered into the drawing room. The ladies were already within and not just Lady Angle and her mother. Miss Penry and Lady Stimple sat nearer the fireplace with Lady Angle, while the Griffith ladies, Mrs. Parry, and Mrs. Beddoe sat near the pianoforte with her mother. And there were other people Marjie had not yet met that milled about the room.

Marjie let out a low growl. She would have to bite back any pain she felt while sitting, especially with all these guests. But at least the men had not returned from drinking their port.

"Miss Fitzroy, I did not think you were coming down tonight." Lord Angle's voice sounded behind her.

Marjie's head jerked around. Botheration. Now she would have to try and sit with everyone looking on.

He hurried toward her and offered his arm to her.

She smiled and took it willingly. "I thought perhaps I might manage a visit this evening." She glanced at the men behind him. "I had not realized you had other guests." She bit down on her cheek as she waited for him to insist she return to bed.

He stared down at her, concern in his eyes. "Are you certain you are well enough?"

Marjie shrugged. "I am fine. A little stiff, perhaps, but nothing that should keep me in bed any longer."

His shoulders relaxed. "I am glad to hear it."

The Alwyn fellow stepped up on her other side. "As am I."

Marjie smiled over at him but quickly turned her attention back to Lord Angle.

He raised a brow and scowled at Alwyn, leading Marjie away. "Let me help you into the drawing room. There looks to be a seat available by your mother. I'm certain she will wish for you to be near her."

"Thank you, my lord."

He walked her to the couch near the pianoforte and carefully helped her as she lowered herself down.

She held her breath as muscles she had not known she had cried out in pain. But once she was settled, she took a long, deep breath, then smiled at the wide-eyed and raised-brow looks around her.

"Marjorie, what are you doing out of bed?" Her mother asked, putting a hand to Marjie's brow.

"I am fine, Mama." She pushed her mother's hand away with more force than she had intended. "He said for a day or two. Not the rest of my life."

Her mother guffawed. "I hardly think two days could be considered the rest of your life."

"But two days it has been." Marjie looked defiantly at her mother. "I simply could not stay in bed a moment longer."

Miss Griffiths studied Marjie closely, though from across the low table, Marjie did not know how much the young lady could really see. Besides, most of the bruises were covered nicely by her gown.

Several people milled about at the far side of the room that Marjie had not yet met. Their attire was altogether strange. A young woman in a dark colored riding habit stood just behind Lady Angle, almost as if she were hanging on every word the older woman said.

Several men in hose and tunics stood speaking to each other in one corner, while a man in full military uniform, albeit not from this century or even the last, spoke with a man in a thick, roughly woven cloth-type tunic that hung down to his knees. It was covered with what looked to be chain mail hauberk.

A woman in a rather strange looking nun's habit walked apart from the other people, talking quietly to herself.

Marjie squinted as she gazed around the room. "Mama," she whispered. "Who are all these people?"

Her mother's brow creased. "Do you not remember meeting the Griffiths and Mrs. Parry the other night?"

Marjie nodded. "Yes, of course I do. But I was not meaning them."

Her mother frowned. "Then who were you meaning, Poppet?"

Marjie motioned to the men in the hose and tunics. "Those men over there in the tunics. And what of those ladies over there in the kirtles with the long, fur-lined sleeves? They all look as though they just stepped out of the pages of a history book. Was tonight to be a costume party and I was not told?"

"Dearest, what are you talking about? There is no one here in costume. And everyone, save Mr. Griffiths, is seated." Her mother placed her hand to Marjie's brow again. "Perhaps you exerted yourself too soon."

Marjie pushed her hand away. "I'm fine, Mama." As if to emphasize her point, Marjie pushed herself off the couch. She closed her eyes to stave off the cry caught in her throat.

Why did her mother insist that those people were not here when it was quite obvious they were? Marjie moved toward the pianoforte where a dozen or more portraits hung on the wall. The portrait closest to her looked familiar.

She glanced over her shoulder seeing the same face on the lady standing behind Lady Angle.

"Miss Fitzroy, is the conversation not to your liking?" Alwyn sidled up beside her and a little chill ran up her spine. She did not know what it was about this man, but she did not like him. Perhaps it was just his persistence in making her acquaintance. But why should that make her uneasy?

"The conversation was very amiable. But I saw this

painting and thought that perhaps I recognized the young lady."

"Alwyn, what are you bothering Miss Fitzroy about now?" Lord Angle came up behind them and relief washed over her.

"If you would introduce us, perhaps I would not need to be a bother." Alwyn smirked.

Lord Angle rolled his eyes. "Miss Marjorie Fitzroy, may I introduce Mr. Alwyn Pugh. His family estate is on the other side of the village." He gave Mr. Pugh an "Are-you-happy" look.

"It's a pleasure to meet you, Mr. Pugh," Marjie lied. Indeed, she thought she could be content if she never made the man's acquaintance. But now that she had, would he leave her alone?

Mr. Pugh bent low and placed a dry, scratchy kiss on Marjie's hand. "The pleasure is all mine, Miss Fitzroy."

Lord Angle did not return to his seat, instead, he moved to stand between Mr. Pugh and Marjie. She couldn't help but grin. And feel very grateful. She did not like the thought of being alone with Mr. Pugh. Even if there were other people in the room. The way he looked at her felt very untoward.

"Mr. Pugh, what are you doing over there?" Miss Penry called from across the room.

"Why does she not walk over and see for herself?" Marjie muttered. Lord Angle's lips pinched tighter. Had she made him angry or was he suppressing laughter?

"Perhaps I will go see what Miss Penry needs. If you'll excuse me," Mr. Pugh smiled and dipped his head to Marjie. He mostly only scowled at Lord Angle.

"Perhaps Miss Penry is of use after all," Lord Angle muttered.

"You do not favor the young lady?" Marjie continued to look at the portraits.

He moved a step closer to her. "She will make a very suitable match." Marjie bit her cheek, only then realizing how much she did not want to know what he thought of Miss Penry. "For someone else."

Her heart skittered for a moment until her brain caught up with his words.

"You seem to have taken a great interest in the portraits." He clasped his hands behind his back.

"Yes, it is diverting to see their portraits and compare them to their actual likeness."

He frowned. "But how are you able to compare? It is not as if you can see their person."

"What do you mean?" Marjie pointed to the nearest painting. "That young lady standing by your mother looks exactly like this young woman here."

Lord Angle's jaw worked. "There is no one standing behind my mother. And that picture is of my sister, Ane."

"But did you not say your sister died?" She lowered her voice. "How could she be standing there if she is dead?"

"There is no one standing there." Lord Angle's voice rose. Several conversations stopped and they turned to look at them. Including the young lady behind the couch.

Marjie looked pointedly at her.

The young woman looked around her, but then motioned to herself.

Marjie nodded. Why did he keep arguing with her? Could he not see the similarities between his guests and the people on the wall? "A soldier dressed like the man in that picture there is standing there by the long table." She motioned to a painting of a man in puffed-out pantaloons. He wore a metal wide-brimmed helmet with a ridge running from front to back.

"But that's the man I told you made a deal with Cromwell not to destroy the castle." His head shook. "Perhaps you should return to bed. I do not think you are seeing things clearly."

The young woman who looked very much like his sister Ane stopped in front of Marjie. She blinked several times. "You are able to see me?"

Marjie looked behind her. Who was she speaking to? But no one was there. Why would she ask if Marjie could see her? And why did Lord Angle think she needed to return to bed? Her vision was clear. She was not *completely* blind. "Of course I can see you. Why should I not?"

"*Mae'n syfrdanol!*" The woman twisted her head and looked at Lord Angle. "Arawn, can you see me?"

Lord Angle made no move to speak, which seemed rather rude.

"Are you not going to answer her? The lady asked you a question."

Lord Angle threw up his hands. "What lady, Miss Fitzroy? You and I are the only two here." He motioned between the two of them.

What was going on? Marjie's hands started to shake but not as badly as her knees. Why did Lord Angle keep insisting that no one was there when there most certainly was someone there?

She reached out to grab hold of the woman and pull her directly in front of the man, but her hand went right through, a coldness seeping into her fingers.

She yanked it back and cradled it against her body. What was happening to her?

"Gwen and Gilford, come over. I believe she can see us," the young lady called to the people across the room. The man in the metal hat and the woman in the nun's habit practically floated over to her.

Marjie put a hand to her head. Maybe she should not have left her room so soon.

"How can you tell she sees us?" The nun asked.

The young lady looked to Marjie. "Can you describe Gilford?"

Marjie licked her lips and looked at Lord Angle. "You are certain it is just the two of us here?"

He nodded, but his brow seemed to crease deeper with every word she said.

"He looks like one of the Royalist soldiers. Like that man," she pointed up to the painting.

"Who are you talking to?" Lord Angle hissed at her, his gaze darting to the other people in the room. The ones he could see.

"You see, Gilford, she can see us." The young woman stood in front of Arawn and drew up to her full height. "*Mae'n syfrdanol.*"

"What does *mae'n syfrdanol*, mean?" Marjie looked from the woman to Lord Angle. She had done a poor imitation of what the woman had said. But from the look of recognition on Lord Angle's face, which could not have come from Marjie's pronunciation, he must have heard the young woman say it.

"*Mae'n syfrdanol?* It is an exclamation of amazement. My sister used to say it often. Where did you hear it?" Lord Angle narrowed his eyes as if he were trying to see what was inside her head. "You are not learning Welsh from someone else, are you?"

Marjie shifted back a step. "It is what the woman said before she asked you if you could see her and then again just now." Could it be—Marjie reached out again to touch her, and again her hand went through her as if she were made of dust. "I don't believe it."

"Don't believe what?" Lord Angle asked.

She chewed on her bottom lip, not certain how she was going to say it. He would never believe it. Lawks, she wasn't sure she believed it herself. "I think I can see your sister," she whispered and then cast a look over her shoulder to make certain no one had heard her.

"What?" There was no whisper to Lord Angle's voice.

Marjie twisted at the tips of her fingers. "Did you not tell me that you had an open mind toward things such as ghosts? That you only lacked belief because you had seen or felt nothing to convince you?"

"And I still have not. Do you expect me to take you at your word?"

The young lady dipped a curtsy. "It seems my brother is not to introduce us properly. I am Lady Angharad Bevan. But please, call me Ane."

Marjie smiled. "I am Marjorie Fitzroy, but you may call me Marjie."

Lord Angle grunted. "I am aware of your name. If I am to call you Marjie, you may call me Arawn."

Ane rolled her eyes. "Tell my brother he will feel a chill run through him on the count of three."

Marjie repeated the instructions.

"Why should I feel a chill?" he asked.

"One, two," Ane looked at Marjie. "If you will say the last number."

"Three," Marjie said just as Ane walked through her brother.

Arawn shuddered from head to toe, rubbing his hands up and down his arms. "What happened? Where did that draft come from, and how did you know when it would happen?"

Marjie swallowed. "It was not a draft. It was your sister, Ane, walking through you." She made a face, scrunching up her nose.

"If it is really my sister, ask her where she hid my toy soldier."

Ane smiled and turned toward her brother. "Tell him I hid

it in the flour barrel at the very bottom. It made me sneeze for nearly a week afterward. Cook was not happy when she discovered it nearly six months later." She smiled fondly. "But she was very nice and scrubbed it up good before returning it to Ari."

Marjie repeated word for word what Ane had said.

"Ari?" Lord Angle slumped against the pianoforte. "Ane is the only person who called me Ari. And only cook and Ane knew about the flour." He ran a hand through his hair, rubbing at the back of his neck. "I do not even know what to think about this." He glanced around them. "Where is she now? Is she still here?"

Marjie nodded. "She is standing right in front of you."

He looked down. "How long has she been here?"

"She was in the room when I came down."

"I don't mean just tonight." He shook his head. "I mean at the castle...in her current state."

Marjie shrugged again. "I don't know. I only just saw her tonight."

"I have never left." Ane clasped her hands in front of her and sighed. "It is all rather frustrating. I cannot imagine this is how it is supposed to be."

"In verity, she is most eager to bid us farewell for eternity." The nun shook her head sadly.

"Is my father here too?" Arawn asked.

Marjie shrugged and looked to Ane. She shook her head. "No, that is what is so vexing. Not everyone leaves, but there does not seem to be any understanding why or who is picked to stay and haunt." She sighed and a breeze fluttered the bottom of Marjie's skirt. "I simply walk about the castle day after day with no one to talk to." She perked up. "Until today."

"The miss regards us as naught," Gilford raised his nose high into the air.

"She says she has never left." Marjie repeated.

"Why today can you suddenly see her?" Lord Angle turned them away from the others in the room.

"Then you believe me?"

He shrugged. "I think I have to, based on what I've felt and seen."

He looked at where Ane had been standing but was now empty. "What changed from today? Why today could you suddenly see her?"

Marjie cleared her throat. "Them. There are at least six others in the room."

His eyes widened. "It was your accident. That bump on your head has enabled you to see ghosts."

CHAPTER THIRTEEN

Arawn paced back and forth in front of the fireplace in his chambers. He truly did not know what to think about Miss Fitzroy and her claims that she could see Ane and all the other 'ghosts' roaming about the castle. But nor could he see a reason why she would make such a thing up. He glanced over his shoulder, wondering who might be lurking about that he could not see. Lud, had they always been there? Did they watch Arawn's every move?

He shook his head. Why should they not? But why had they not made themselves known before now? The papers on his writing desk fluttered and his gaze bore down on them. Could it be the castle was not as drafty as he had assumed? Had all the 'ghosts' been making themselves known for decades? Perhaps even centuries?

Besides, there were things she had said about Ane—things that were true, that only Ane would know.

It was all too fantastical and unbelievable, yet he could not help but believe it. Indeed, if he had heard this story from anyone, he would have laughed at it as a joke or the talk of a mad person.

He stopped and looked at himself in the mirror. Was he mad? He pulled down on his lower lids, looking deep into his eyes. Was there any indication he was near bedlam? He could not say as he knew what bedlam would look like if he saw it there.

He stood up straight. But then he was not the one saying he could see ghosts. Perhaps it was Miss Fitzroy's eyes he should be checking. His earlobes tingled with warmth at the thought. She did have very lovely eyes.

But there would be no checking Marjie's eyes. He knew she was not mad. While he may not have seen nor heard Ane, he had felt her. And what other proof did he need? He shivered as he recalled the moment Marjie said Ane had walked through him. He had felt it before, always attributing it to a draft. But if he was looking at it from an intellectual point of view, drafts usually did not chill him all the way to the center of his bones the way Ane had.

He wanted to believe it was all true. He wanted to think it was possible for him to speak with his sister again.

He sighed and ran a hand through his hair. But that was his problem, was it not? Was he allowing his desires...his wants to cloud his judgment and make him believe the impossible was possible?

Arawn turned back toward the room and shook his head. "Thunder and turf, Ane. Only you would stay around to haunt Mother and me. And of course, you had to make yourself known when we have guests in the house." He sat down on his dressing chair and yanked at his Hessian. He was in no mood to call his valet for help. He managed to pull the first boot free, and he sunk back into the chair, the boot dropping to the floor. "But if you are here, I'm so very glad for it." He ran a hand down his face. "Even if it means I must face once again what I did to you. Can you ever forgive me for making you jump when you were not ready? I'm so very sorry, Ane."

He did not know why he was speaking to his sister as if she were standing in front of him. Even as a ghost, it seemed unlikely she would venture into his bedchambers.

A knock sounded at his door and Arawn jerked his gaze to the door guiltily. "Arawn, are you dressed? Who was that you were speaking to? I just saw Roberts on his way to the kitchen." What should he tell his mother? Indeed, would she even believe it if he told her? But if it was all true, did she not have the right to speak with Ane too?

He stalked over to the door and pulled it open. "Good evening, Mother. I should have thought you asleep long ago."

She was dressed in her nightdress with a shawl pulled tight around her shoulders. She shrugged. "Sleep eludes me." She stepped inside his chambers when he opened the door wider.

"Yes, I feel the same. Roberts is fetching some tea. Would you care to join me?" he motioned to the couch in front of the fire.

She nodded. "What were you and Miss Fitzroy speaking of this evening? It looked to be a rather heated conversation." She glanced up at him from beneath her lashes. "What were you arguing about?"

He shook his head. "We were not arguing. She simply said something that I found most unbelievable."

His mother tilted her head to the side. "And what was that? I had thought you two were becoming friends."

He laughed. "We are, Mother." He took a deep breath. How would she take his announcement? "It seems possible that since her accident, she has developed the ability to see..." He paused.

"Yes? What can she see?" his mother asked.

He squinted at her. It was best just to say, was it not? Although, she would surely think him daft for believing such a claim. "Ghosts. Miss Fitzroy can see ghosts. Including Ane's."

His mother stared at him, blinking. She did not believe him. How could she? He would not if he had not been there to feel it. If he had not heard her repeat those things only Ane knew.

"Ghosts? She can see ghosts? There is more than one?"

Arawn snapped his mouth shut. That was her first question? About the number of them? Not any "how-can-you-believe-it" kinds of questions? He nodded. "Yes. She said there were five or six in the drawing room last night. She did not mention any others."

His mother narrowed her eyes at him as if she were trying to detect any trickery. "And your sister is one of the ghosts."

Arawn nodded. "Yes. She told Miss Fitzroy things that only she knew. And she called me Ari, Mother."

His mother flinched.

"I should not believe it either if I had not been there."

"Who are these other ghosts? Was your father there?" There was a hopefulness in her eyes that Arawn felt sorry to squelch. He shook his head. "No, Ane said he was not."

"Why not?"

Arawn shrugged. "I don't know. I'm not sure if Ane knows. Perhaps when next you see Miss Fitzroy, you may ask her."

His mother sat silently staring at her hands.

"You do not believe me." Arawn's throat tightened. She must be wondering at the future of the marquessate.

She laughed lightly. "No, surprisingly, I do believe you. I have long felt it was more than just a draft—wondered if there was something supernatural."

"Why did you never say anything?" Arawn gawked at her.

She scoffed. "And have everyone believing I've gone mad? I

think not. Which is why I think this shall remain between the two of us."

"Three of us." He leaned forward. "Do not forget Miss Fitzroy. She is who started this whole thing."

His mother nodded. "Oh, I have not forgotten her. Indeed, I believe Miss Fitzroy and I need to become better acquainted."

Arawn stood in the aisle at the end of their family's bench in the parish church. He motioned for Lady Mariane to go first. She moved into the pew and her daughter made to follow. Arawn reached out and stopped her. "Mother, why do you not sit next to Lady Mariane? While I know you should not speak much during the sermon, I am certain you will both have plenty of opinions on what is being said."

He shooed his mother into the bench. She tipped her head to the side and stared at him, but then scooted in next to Lady Mariane.

Marjie moved in next to his mother and sat down.

Arawn followed her in, taking his favorite spot on the end of the pew. "Where is Ane? Did she come with us to church?" He hissed in her ear.

Marjie shook her head. "Why should she? I should think she has long past the need for anything the vicar might have to say."

Arawn frowned. "What do you mean?"

"It is not as if she can change her ways now, can she?" Marjie lifted a shoulder. "I have not seen her yet today. But she mentioned yesterday that she cannot leave the castle grounds."

"She can't leave? Why?"

The vicar stood up and the voices around them hushed.

"Why can't she leave?" He whispered again.

She lifted her shoulder. "How am I to know? I am not an expert on specters and their travel habits."

"Oh, I thought perhaps she told you." He could hear the disappointment in his voice. While he still had his moments of doubt, he had decided he wanted to believe, and thus, he was risking his heart and perhaps his very sanity.

"She has not. Although, I did not get the idea that she knew the answer any more than we do."

"You mean she is just stuck here, and she doesn't know why?"

Marjie shrugged. "That is my assumption. Otherwise, would she not have remedied the situation?"

"Perhaps she does not want to leave. Hywel is her home." He shifted his weight, leaning away from her.

Marjie shook her head. "I must disagree," she whispered. "I have to think she would be happier if she left."

His mouth dropped open before he clamped it shut. Why did she think Ane would rather leave? Did Marjie not like it at Hywel? She had seemed captivated by it when she first arrived. But maybe her accident had changed her opinion.

His mother leaned forward and shot him a withering look. He sank back into his seat, feeling like a little boy being reprimanded. But just as when he was a little boy, the scolding did not sit with him for long. "Why do you think she would be happier to leave Hywel?" he hissed.

She pulled her lip between her teeth. "I should think it would be very difficult watching her family live their lives knowing she is no longer apart of them."

His shoulders released, and his face softened. Why had he not considered how this situation affected Ane? He had only thought about himself.

She reached out a hand and put it on his arm. "I'm sorry, I

was not implying that she wished to be away from you because she does not love you or Hywel. I can only imagine how lonely her existence is. All she can do is walk about the castle and the grounds. No one can see her or speak to her except others like her. I should not like that, and I doubt she does either."

He leaned forward and rested his elbows on his knees, his clasped hands dangling between his legs. He had never considered what Ane's life—could he even call it that—was like. Marjie had a point. How enjoyable could it be if she was all alone?

While he had spent the last few months avoiding his mother's company, he would not wish it away completely. And in that time, he had been able to speak with Havard, Mathias, and any number of stable hands and servants around the house. But Ane had no one. He glanced over at Marjie from the corner of his eye. Until Marjie.

"I had not really thought about it from her perspective," he whispered.

Both their mothers leaned forward and shot them looks of wide-eyed irritation.

"My apologies," he mouthed.

Arawn looked at Marjie and lifted a shoulder as his lips twitched slightly. It was just as it had been with Ane and him when they were younger.

Marjie smiled at him. "You were not talking to yourself. I believe I shall share in the blame too."

Arawn slouched down on the bench, stretching his legs out in front of him. He had scarcely slept at all last evening, and his body was exhausted and stiff. He dropped his chin to his chest and closed his eyes. It would only be for a minute—just until the burning behind his eyes went away. Although, it did not help that the vicar's voice was so melodious.

An elbow nudged him in the side and his eyes flew open.

He turned and looked at Marjie and then at the displeased face of his mother. "What?" He lifted his hands up to his side as he straightened up on the bench. But before either could answer him, he glimpsed the empty pews around them. The sermon was over? But he had only just closed his eyes.

"You slept through nearly the whole of it," his mother hissed through clenched teeth.

He straightened and grinned down at her. "I must tell Mr. Cartwright this was the best sermon I've heard him give."

His mother's scowl deepened. "You will do no such thing. Do not think for a moment that he did not notice you sleeping."

Arawn rolled his shoulders and neck. "I'm sorry, Mother. I slept very poorly last evening. I shall apologize to the Vicar."

"No, you will not." She nearly screeched. "What if he did not notice that you were sleeping? You will only offend him if you apologize."

"But did you not say he already saw me asleep?"

"How am I to know what he saw? I was just assuming the worst."

Arawn's head was drowning in her logic. "Then what do you wish for me to say to him?"

"You may thank him and nothing else."

Arawn shook his head. Sometimes he did not understand what his mother wanted from him.

They moved out of the bench and down the center aisle.

"When did the owners of Hywel start coming to the parish church rather than using the chapel in the castle?" Marjie hurried up beside him.

"Once the castle moved from royal hands to our family. We have attended the parish church ever since. Unlike the royals, we do not mind attending with the townspeople." He dipped his head toward the vicar and then some of the people standing outside the building. "There is no reason to pay a second clergyman just so he can preach to us." He winked at his mother. "And it would be far more obvious if I fell asleep were we the only people in attendance."

"Please, keep your voice down until we are away from the churchyard." His mother smiled and dipped her head to everyone they saw.

Arawn caught a glimpse of Mr. Radcliffe. Lud, the man looked as though he wished to talk, which Arawn had no desire to do. He was a decent enough gentleman. But he did drone on, and the headache already forming behind Arwan's eyes forced him to ignore the man. If he were going to spend time with anyone, he wished to spend it with Marjie and Ane. Not Mr. Radcliffe.

He put his hand on the small of his mother's back and herded her and the Fitzroy ladies through the arch and into the carriage.

As he placed his foot on the step to swing up, Mr. Radcliffe cleared his throat. "My lord, I hoped I might have a word with you."

Arawn grimaced and closed his scratchy eyes, before turning to greet the man with a large, albeit insincere, smile. "I'm sorry, but it will have to wait. My mother and our house guests are already inside the carriage, and I do not wish to delay. Perhaps you can make an appointment to speak with my steward."

"No offense to Mr. Martin, but I wish to speak with you, my lord."

"I am very busy with the fall harvest and such. Perhaps I can make some room in my schedule in a few weeks." He pulled his body up onto the step of the carriage. "I'll have my secretary reach out."

"I did not know you had a secretary, my lord." The man looked perplexed.

"Would I have him contact you if I did not have a secretary?" Arawn gave him an incredulous look before ducking inside the carriage. "Good day, Mr. Radcliffe." He closed the door behind him and rapped on the side, hoping his driver would see them away before Mr. Radcliffe invited himself into their carriage.

"I did not know you had a secretary." Marjie looked at him with what he could only assume was respect. Although why having a secretary should earn someone's respect, he did not know. He believed it only meant that a man was not organized enough to maintain his own schedule.

"He doesn't," his mother scowled at him. It seemed that was the only face she had for him at present.

He folded his arms across his chest. "Yes, but it will take Mr. Radcliffe some time to figure that out."

"But why would you claim that you have one if you do not?" Marjie asked.

Arawn sighed. "It seemed the easiest way to end the conversation with Mr. Radcliffe. Perhaps by the time he figures it out, I will have discovered an excuse to avoid him all together."

"But why do you wish to avoid him? Is he scandalous or untrustworthy?"

Arawn shook his head. "No. It is not as serious as all that. He is simply tedious. And I cannot abide the thought of listening to him today."

"Or any day, it seems," she added, looking almost as disappointed in him as his mother.

He turned away and looked out the window, unsure why that bothered him so much.

CHAPTER FOURTEEN

A knock sounded at Arawn's study door. "Enter," he called.

The door opened only slightly and Mathias' head poked in. "Good day, my lord."

"Mathias. Please, come in." He motioned the stable master inside.

Mathias came in and stood next to the chair facing Arawn. He motioned. "Please, sit."

Mathias frowned but did as he was commanded. "I wanted to thank you for not taking any action against Arthur yet. Because I found something I think you should be aware of."

Arawn's brow rose. He still was not certain if keeping Gwyn or Arthur was a good idea. Not if there was a chance they could harm someone else. But Mathias had pleaded so convincingly, he had relented for the time being. "Oh?"

"After the accident, I locked the saddle in my office. I didn't want anyone to accidentally use it again."

Arawn frowned. "I do not see how that would make a difference."

"And I've taken Arthur out for a ride every day since and he has not so much as hopped out of place."

"Well, hopping was not really the issue, Mathias." Arawn ran a hand across the back of his neck. "What about when you jump him?"

Mathias shook his head. "I have jumped him over the stream more than a dozen times and nothing. He lands on the other side and continues on as if nothing were the matter. I even jumped him over the hedgerow and ha-has. He was as calm as could be."

Arawn stood up and leaned forward on his desk. "How is that possible? If the problem is not Arthur, then what is it?"

"I think I know," Mathias licked his lips and swallowed.

Arawn made a circular motion with his hand. "Come now, do not keep me in suspense."

"When I found nothing wrong with Arthur, I had a closer look at that saddle."

"It can't be Ane's saddle," Arawn argued. "She used it nearly daily when she was alive." It was odd he did not feel the usual twinge of sadness when he mentioned his sister's death.

"That is just it, my lord. It *was* the saddle. When I looked more closely at it, I found a small nail had been driven into the underside, with just a bit of the head still sticking out. My guess is when the ladies landed back in the saddle after the jump, that nail pushed hard into Arthur's back, causing him to buck."

"A nail?" Arawn's fists clenched. "How did a nail come loose and work its way out that much? I have never seen that happen and I have had my saddle for more than ten years."

The old stable master rubbed at his stubbled chin. "That is the thing, sir. I don't believe it came loose. I believe it was put there intentionally. The location is not one that would have a nail for any purpose other than to cause a problem."

Arawn walked around his desk, stopping directly in front of Mathias. "Someone deliberately killed my sister and very nearly killed Miss Fitzroy?"

How could that be? While he knew no one was trying to kill Miss Fitzroy, the result had nearly been the same. But who would want to kill Ane? Everyone loved her. She, like their mother, was one of the kindest people he had ever met. She treated the servants and staff politely and had never been demanding. "Could the nail have been placed there recently?"

Mathias shook his head. "Not from the looks of it. The iron has stained the wood around the nail. It has been there for some time."

"But why? Why would someone do that?"

"I don't know, my lord. I can't imagine it was anyone in the stable or even any of the gardeners. The saddle was stored on the rack, just like all the others. It would not be difficult for anyone to sneak in and quickly drive the nail in." He sighed in frustration.

"When could it have been placed there?" Arawn tried to control his anger by breathing in through his nose. "Have any stable hands left since Ane died? We can assume Miss Fitzroy was not the target, just unlucky to have used the saddle."

Mathias shook his head. "I was trying to remember that myself. Owain left around that time, but I believe it was before Ane's accident."

"How soon before? Is it possible he placed the nail and left only a few days before?"

Mathias shook his head. "I'm sorry, my lord. But I just don't remember. I will ask around the stables and see if anyone remembers."

"We hosted a musicale only the night before. There were nearly fifty people in attendance. It is possible any one of them did it." Arawn scrubbed a hand over his face. "For now, I would appreciate it if we kept this between us."

Mathias nodded. "Of course, my lord."

Arawn settled back in his chair. "I am glad to know that Gwyn and Arthur were not the problem. It pained me to think of putting down such fine horses."

"Yes, sir. I agree."

"Is there another lady's saddle in the stable?"

The stable master nodded. "The saddler brought your mother's back just yesterday."

Arawn nodded. "Very good. Please keep Ane's saddle locked in your office until we are able to discover who is responsible." He looked up from his desktop. "And would you please not remove the nail until I've had a chance to inspect it? But keep it safe, lest anyone accidently use it again?"

"Yes, my lord."

Arawn smiled. "Thank you, Mathias. I appreciate your help in this matter. It has weighed heavily on my mind."

"It is my pleasure, sir. Do you wish for me to keep Gwyn apart from the other horses?"

"No. And I see no reason why he should be selectively ridden." Arawn did not think his mother or Marjie would be riding anytime soon. But if they did, he did not see a reason why Gwyn should not be offered as an option. He was rather hoping to convince Marjie to ride before too long. Else she might never ride again from fear.

The stable master stood up. "Very well, my lord." He looked expectantly at Arawn.

"If you come upon any more information, please let me know."

The man nodded. "Yes, indeed, my lord."

Arawn stood and led the man to the door. He wanted to

talk to Marjie and Ane about this new discovery. Perhaps they —or more accurately Ane—would have some insight into it.

The old man turned and disappeared through the gate in the wall that led to the outer bailey.

He waited until the door shut behind Mathias and then turned and went in search of Marjie. What was she doing to occupy her time?

He doubted she was in her mother's chambers. He knew she preferred the parlor.

Not wishing to encounter Mathias again, Arawn pushed into the King's Tower and moved up the steps toward the wall-walk. It would take him longer, but he would also encounter fewer people. And he did not wish to be delayed by unnecessary chit-chat.

Marjie sat on the couch nearest the window with a stitchery in her hands. She rather detested sewing, but after several comments made by Miss Penry and Lady Stimple, Marjie had determined to give it another try. Her thread knotted and she gave it a little tug, tightening the knot even more. "Lud, how can anyone find this enjoyable," she muttered. She supposed if it were not so vexing, it might give her a chance to think, but so far, that had not been the case.

"What are you doing?" Marjie jumped slightly at the sound of Ane's voice. Even though Lord Angle's sister had been speaking to her for two days, she still was not accustomed to it. The whole situation still felt odd and rather unbelievable.

"Good afternoon, Ane." Marjie said.

Marjie held up the fabric as if it should be obvious. "I am sewing a sampler."

"But why?" Two little lines appeared between Ane's eyes. "I find embroidery unbearable."

"I must confess, I share your opinion."

"Then why do it?" The creases had not yet disappeared.

Marjie put the sampler in her lap. "Did you not do it also, simply to fit in with society?"

"Yes," Ane dropped down onto the couch next to Marjie.

Marjie leaned over and looked at the underside of the sofa. "How do you not fall through the couch? You can walk through the walls, can you not?"

Ane nodded.

"Then why do you not fall to the floor? Is it not the same principle?"

Ane shrugged. "I have never thought about it. But in truth, there is much I still don't understand. I was given no instruction when I came to be in this state."

"What is there to know?" Marjie asked.

"Why am I still here. I am not the first person to die in this castle. Indeed, my own father died in his bed chambers, yet he does not haunt the corridors."

"Nor the parlor and drawing room," Marjie added.

Ane smirked. "Yes, how could I forget the parlor and the drawing room?"

Marjie finally untangled the knot and set back to work on the flower she was working on.

"Why did you choose to make that flower black?" Ane reached out to touch the fabric, but her hand fell through it.

"You see? Sitting just does not make sense." Marjie looked at her exasperatedly. What good was it to have a ghost for a friend if you could not learn new information about their unusual situation?

"Will you not stop prattling on about my sitting? I already told you I do not know." She pointed at the fabric, rather than touching it. "I have not seen many black flowers."

Marjie held the thread up in front of her face. "Oh botheration." She reached inside her basket and withdrew a pair of small scissors. Using the sharp tip, she began snipping at the threads. "I thought it was dark blue." Or at least she had hoped it was. It was one of the very reasons she detested embroidery.

The door opened and Lord Angle walked in.

Marjie smiled up at him and her stomach fluttered when he returned her greeting.

"Good morning, my lord."

"*Bore da*, Marjie. Is Ane about?" He glanced around before he paused on her sampler. "What is that?"

Marjie scowled at the sampler in her hand. "It was supposed to be a flower. But in the light, I mistook black for blue." It sounded like a logical mistake, did it not?

Her mother walked into the room and let out a small gasp. "Oh, Poppet, what are you doing?"

Gads, must everyone in the household enter the room and gasp over her mistake? "I know, Mama. I mistook the black for the navy blue. But never fear, I'm remedying the error as we speak."

Her mother smiled awkwardly at Lord Angle. "Oh, yes. An easy mistake. Especially in this lighting. Why are you not sewing over by the window?"

Marjie cast the sampler to the side. "It matters not now. I think I've had enough of it for today anyhow."

"I am going to the village with Lady Angle. Is there anything you wish me to purchase for you?" Her mother smiled down at her.

Marjie sighed. "No. But thank you for asking."

She patted her hand. "Very well. I will send Susanna down to mend in the corner, so you have a chaperone."

"I do not need a chaperone, Mama. Ane is here."

Her mother darted a glance around the room. "Lady Ane is here? What of the other ghosts?"

Her mother's willingness to believe in the apparitions had surprised Marjie when she spoke of them last evening. But there had been little other choice. Now that the ghosts knew Marjie could see them, they spoke to her and wished for an immediate answer, without any care of who might be listening. Rather than have her mother think she was near bedlam, Marjie decided it was best to share the news.

Her mother raised a brow. "I hardly think a ghost is a proper chaperone. Especially when you are the only one able to see and speak to her."

Marjie rolled her eyes and released an exasperated breath. "Very well. Send Susanna down."

Her mother nodded and turned toward the door, just as Lady Angle entered. "I am going to fetch Susanna, then I shall be ready to go." Her mother smiled at Lady Angle.

"We are in no hurry, Mariane." She looked at Marjie. "Is Ane here?"

Marjie nodded. "Yes. She is sitting right next to me. Although, I have no notion how she does not drop right through the sofa. But she claims not to understand it herself."

"Enough with the sitting," Ane nearly yelled.

Marjie looked at Lord and Lady Angle. Surely, they had heard that. But they still looked about the room.

"And what of the others? Are they here too?" Lord Angle asked.

Marjie shrugged. "A few. But Gwen and Gilford are not present."

He nodded as he slowly pulled his gaze from the other side of the room and looked at her. "Miss Fitzroy, I have just learned something that might interest Ane."

Marjie kicked off her slippers and pulled her feet up underneath her. Smoothing her skirt around her, she glanced at Ane and then back to Arawn. "Oh?"

Ane scooted closer to her. "What is it about?"

"Go on," Marjie prodded him.

"Are you not going to tell him that I asked, 'About what?'" Ane looked at Marjie.

"No. He does not need to know every word you say."

"But you did not even mention that I said anything." Ane pouted.

Marjie rolled her eyes. "That is because you did not say anything that needed repeating."

"Did Ane say something?" Lord Angle dropped into a chair and leaned forward, his elbows resting on his knees.

"Yes, what did she say?" Lady Angle peered hopefully down at Marjie.

Marjie threw her arms up. "Ane said, 'About what?'" Marjie looked at them with wide, exaggerated eyes. "I promise, if she says something that bears repeating, I shall say so." But then she released a sigh. She was not being very kind. These people had been without Ane for six long months. And now they had a way to speak to her. It was no wonder they wished to know every word she said. "I'm sorry. That was not kind. Please forgive me."

Lady Angle reached forward and patted Marjie on the hand. "Please forgive us. I'm certain playing the go-between is rather taxing on you."

Marjie waved her words away, vowing to be more patient.

Lord Angle leaned forward as if to draw more out of her. "And? What else did she say?"

"That is all. That is why I did not repeat it."

Arawn nodded. "I see."

Marjie sighed and glanced at Ane but then turned back to Arawn. "You were saying?"

"Oh, yes. Mathias came to see me this morning."

"Mathias is the stable master, is he not?" Marjie asked.

"Yes, yes. Do not interrupt." Ane waved a hand in front of Marjie and a slight breeze fluttered over the hairs on her arms. "It feels as if he is about to say the important part." Ane scooted closer, nearly sitting on Marjie. But would she sit on Marjie, or would she fall through her? Marjie shuddered at the thought.

Arawn told them of Mathias' discovery. The ladies sat silently staring at him for a moment.

"Then it was not an accident," Ane murmured.

"It was not an accident," Marjie repeated, not because it was something she needed to repeat, but because she did not know what else to say.

"It does not appear to be. Someone intended to kill you."

Ane's lips quivered, and Marjie sat staring as her thoughts battled. While she knew that the notion someone had killed Ane was more important, Marjie could not help wondering if Ane would—or if she could—shed tears. As a ghost, it seemed unlikely. But were there ghostly kinds of tears?

Marjie stared intently from the corner of her eyes, but no moisture appeared on Ane's cheeks. No sheen came to her eyes. But was it because Ane normally was not a watering pot, or was it because she couldn't?

"But who would do such thing?" Lady Angle asked.

Lord Angle shrugged. "I was hoping Ane could tell us. Mathias and I could not think of anyone. With where the saddle was normally kept, nearly anyone could have snuck into the stable and put the nail in without being discovered."

Marjie nodded. "We need more information. But it happened so long ago, is there any information left to find?" A thought struck her, and she turned to Ane. "Perhaps that is why you are still here."

"What do you mean?" Ane's voice sounded as if she might be crying, but without tears, it was difficult to tell for certain.

"Perhaps that is why you still stay in the castle. You are stuck here until your murderer is discovered."

Ane sucked in a deep breath. "Do you think so?"

"I doth know my killer, yet I still reside within." Margie looked back to see that Gwen had joined them.

Lord Angle leaned forward. "I had not considered that. But you may be right."

"It is a possibility." Marjie did not know why they all looked at her as if she were some sort of ghost expert. She had little knowledge of the subject. If anyone should have the answers, she would think it would be one of the ghosts.

"Regardless, I intend to discover the culprit. They will not get away with this," Lord Angle said at the exact same time that Ane said, "Then you must figure it out."

Marjie nodded. "Yes, that seems our best option." And perhaps the only way to keep her from going completely mad. Being the go-between between Ane and her family was losing its appeal quickly. Didn't Marjie have enough quirks and oddities for one person? Had the fates decided she needed even more?

She regretted her insensitive thought when she looked at Lord and Lady Angle's faces and saw hope and gratitude staring back at her.

CHAPTER FIFTEEN

Marjie stepped out of the tower into the bright noonday sunlight of the bailey. The nights had grown steadily colder, but the daylight hours were still more sunny than not.

"Miss Fitzroy, I was hoping to find you. I am about to go for a ride, and I thought perhaps you could join me."

Marjie's stomach clenched. "Thank you for the offer, my lord. But I believe I shall decline. I am far too busy today."

He tilted his head and gave her a knowing look. "I know you are frightened. After what happened, I cannot say I blame you." He put his large hands on her shoulders. "But the longer you wait, the harder it will be. Your fear will only continue to grow until you are not even able to look upon a horse." He shook his head. "I cannot allow that to happen."

She opened her mouth, and he could see the protest in her eyes.

"I am certain your mother will agree with me."

"What if I don't want to get back on the horse?" she whispered.

He stared down at her intently and she thought for a moment he might pull her into him and embrace her. And just as frightening as getting on a horse was how much she wished he would hold her. Perhaps then she could find the courage.

"I understand that you do not want to. But you must." He released her shoulders and took a step back.

Marjie felt decidedly displeased. But she was not certain if she was angrier at him for backing away or at herself for wanting him closer when she knew it was not to be.

"I will help you and be with you the whole time. You need not worry after your safety." He continued to look intently at her.

"Why do you care so much?" She threw her fist down to her side and stomped her foot, her frustration with him matched only by the frustration she felt for herself.

"Because I know how much you enjoyed riding. I cannot be responsible for taking that away from you."

"But it is not your fault. Did we not discover someone tampered with the saddle? None of it was your fault." She wanted to unfist her hands, but it was one of the only things keeping her from crying. And she did not like to cry publicly. But she especially did not want to cry in front of him.

"But it happened on my estate. Therefore, I hold some responsibility." He reached out and placed a finger beneath her chin, gently lifting it until she was looking at him. "What if I ride with you this first time? Would that help you feel more secure?"

She swallowed hard. Why must he make it so difficult to keep him at a distance? Did he not know that while helping her in one way, he was setting her up for a greater hurt later?

"You will not let this go until I have agreed, will you?"

He lifted a shoulder. "If you will not do it for yourself, will you do it for me?"

He knew how to get to her. But how had he realized that she would do almost anything for him? Indeed, she had not realized it until just this moment. "Then you are to use our friendship to convince me to do what you wish?" She sighed. "Do you manipulate everyone like this?"

He ran his hand along the back of his neck. "I am not trying to manipulate you, Marjie. I tried to show you it was best for you, but you still refuse. If I must use our friendship, then so be it. It will be worth it if you overcome your fear and are able do what you loved so much. Although, I hope it will not be at the detriment of our friendship." He flicked up one side of his mouth. "And I prefer the term 'persuasive,' my dear Miss Fitzroy. Manipulation is not done among friends."

She sighed deeply.

"Have I persuaded you?" He asked.

She had not missed his use of her Christian name. But did he really desire informality, or had he done it as a means of further manipulation? She stared at him, studying him. For all she knew of him, she did not believe him to be so cunning. Perhaps he was sincere, and he only wished for her to overcome this growing fear inside her.

But she could not allow him to think he had won so easily. She put her hands on her hips and scowled at him. She was not mad. Scared? Most certainly. And not just about the horses. The way her pulse ticked up and that little flutter returned to her stomach when he looked in her direction scared her more than the thought of mounting Arthur again.

"You promise you will be there with me the whole time?"

He nodded and took a step closer. "I promise," he whispered.

She swallowed a shaky breath. "You will not let up on this, will you? If I do not do it today, you will simply keep asking me until I either leave or do as you ask."

"That was my plan." He did not even look the slightest bit guilty for being discovered.

Marjie nodded and sighed. "Very well. I will meet you here in thirty minutes."

"*Dyna ferch dda.*" He winked and her heart skipped a beat. She did not even know what he said, but it felt personal and almost intimate. But perhaps that was because of his wink? Even now he smiled at her as if she had just done the most praiseworthy thing in the world. And it made her want to live up to that look.

On the basis of her health, she thought it might be best if he did not look at her in such a way. But then, what were a few palpitations when such a smile was bestowed?

She threw her hands to her side again and grunted. Gracious, she hoped she survived the afternoon. And not just because of the ride.

⟡

Marjie looked out her bedroom window into the courtyard below. She was fully dressed in her riding habit, but she was still debating if she should just cry off. Lord Angle was already pacing about below her, even though she still had seven minutes before she was to meet him.

Was he as nervous about this outing as she was? Likely not, but he looked to be feeling some sort of trepidation. His lips moved as if he were talking himself through something.

She bit her cheek at how appealing he looked.

He had promised he would not let anything happen to her. But could she trust him? He had saved her from being trampled by the horse once already. Why should she not trust him now? A cold shiver traveled down her body as the memories of those moments before she fell to the ground flashed through her mind.

Now that she knew it was not the horse's fault, she should not fear. She knew that in her head. But her shaking hands did not seem ready to understand. Surely, if they did not use the affected saddle, all would be fine, would it not?

She closed her eyes and put a hand to her stomach, her breath sucking in haltingly.

Arawn's very pleasing face, with his altogether too hand-some smile, floated to the forefront of her mind. Her breathing slowed and her body relaxed. He would not let anything happen to her. Of that she was certain. Besides, if he was riding Arthur with her—oh, lud. Her pulse ticked back up and her palms became instantly damp. So much for peace.

She glanced at the clock and let out a yip. Her seven minutes had dwindled down to one. If she did not hurry, she would be late. And the thought of Arawn waiting for her was completely unacceptable.

She grabbed her gloves and bonnet as she hurried from the room. Practically running down the circular steps, she pushed back the lingering doubts. Both about the horse and Arawn. Throwing open the door to the bailey, she pulled up just before ploughing into Lord Angle.

"My lord." She dipped into a curtsy, panting slightly.

"If we are to trust each other so completely, I believe Christian names are acceptable."

"You do?" She smiled shakily. She wanted to think harder on his words—analyze them at their very core. But at that moment, he could have called her a purple potato and she did not think she would care. Her mind was too focused on the ride ahead of them.

"Is Ane following us?" he asked.

She shook her head.

They walked toward the stables, and, with every step, Marjie's feet slowed a bit more, until finally Lord Angle grasped her gently by the elbow and moved her along. "Come along, I'm here with you."

Her heart hammered in her chest. His touch did not have the effect he likely thought it did.

He led her over to the horse he rode on their first outing.

"Dafydd, would you please ready Taran for me?"

"Right away, my lord." Dafydd scurried over and set to work saddling the horse.

Marjie looked up at him. "Taran? I thought we were to ride Arthur."

He shook his head. "I might be persuasive, but I'm not a tyrant. I cannot think you are ready to ride Arthur just yet. I think it better to start slow and on Taran."

She had the urge to throw her arms around him, but she restrained herself, instead muttering, "Thank you, Arawn."

He nodded. "You're welcome, Marjie." Pulling out several carrots from of his pocket, he handed one to her. "Although, I thought while we wait, perhaps you might try feeding Arthur? Maybe it will help to renew your bond with him."

She nodded but could not seem to make her legs move her forward. Why was she so scared just to feed the horse a carrot?

She did not like feeling this way. There was little in the world that frightened her or made her nervous. Not like many other ladies of her acquaintance. They always tittered and whispered about how they were nervous to attend this party or that. Or that they worried that they would not be asked to dance or to partner with anyone at a card party.

Marjie could honestly say she had never felt such feelings. She did not care if certain men asked her to dance. Indeed, she expected men to ask her to dance or partner for cards only once. Once they had a conversation, even a short one, they seemed to realize she was not for them. And Marjie accepted that. She knew she was not like other people.

"I don't know what the matter is. I'm never one to be frightened by things."

He touched her arm. "I think you have cause to be frightened."

"Perhaps." Marjie swallowed. "But it is not in my nature. Even when my father died, there was little fear about what would become of us because I knew my mother would see us through. Or that we would see each other through. But this is different. I do not know how to rely on a horse."

"You need not rely on Arthur. You can rely on me." Arawn moved in closer, and Marjie forgot her fears for a moment. The smell of his soap drew her face toward him so she might breathe it in all the more.

On an intake of breath, she felt movement in her hand and looked over just as Arthur lipped the carrot from her palm.

She let out a squeak and jumped.

Arwan stepped forward, his chest pressing against her back. Taking her hand in his, he held it toward Arthur. Her hand rested in his as he placed a carrot in her palm and stretched their hands a little closer to the horse. "This is a vital part of your recovery."

"My recovery?" Her voice came out tight and pinched. But it was not due to Arthur. It surprised her how much the warmth of Arawn's hand calmed her fears—for the horse. Others, however, seemed to surface. "I feel as though you are being rather dramatic."

"Not dramatic, just practical. Trust me. You will thank me when this is over, and you are riding without a care."

"You ask me to trust you often," she glanced up at him. "Do you feel you have earned such unwavering trust?"

Arthur nipped the carrot from her hand and Arawn closed

their hands, his covering hers nearly completely. "I hope I have."

They took a step back. "You see? That was not so scary, was it?" His whispered voice warmed her ear.

"It was terrifying."

A quiet chuckle brushed over the small hairs at the nape of her neck as his body moved still closer to her. "Shall we try it again? Perhaps this time you can do it without my help."

Marjie was not certain she liked that idea. His help was the only enjoyable part of this whole endeavor. If he took that away, what was the point? "I think I might need more help." Had she sounded convincing? "At least one more time." It was not a complete lie. Her hand still shook when he placed a small, wrinkled apple in it.

"Did I not promise I would be with you the whole time?" He lifted their hands up to the horse again. This time Marjie's heart did not feel like it would pound out of her chest. But that did not mean she was not affected. Quite the opposite. She could not shake the feeling of rightness. And that perhaps frightened her more than Arthur because she knew it was certainly not to be.

"Are you ready to ride? Taran looks to be saddled."

She bit her lip. What would he say if she said no? Would he press her? Perhaps tomorrow he would not be so willing to ride with her. Perhaps tomorrow he would think her capable of riding Arthur while he rode Taran.

"I suppose it is not going away, is it?"

He turned her to face him. "I am not trying to punish you, Marjie. I would not press you if I did not think it was best." He shook his head. "I should have been so kind with my mother."

She looked down at her hands, her head nodding. "I want to ride, I really do. But look at them. Will not Taran feel my nerves and react adversely?" She looked up at him. "Perhaps tomorrow would be better."

He took her shaking hand in his. "They will not shake less tomorrow. I am certain. Indeed, I should think it will only increase, the longer you wait."

She closed her eyes and sucked in a deep breath. "Very well."

They moved outside where Dafydd held Taran and Mathias held the small gray pony.

Arawn looked at her. "Do you wish to ride the pony?"

Her lip quivered. Had he not said he would ride with her? While that notion was fraught with many pitfalls, it was the only plan in which Marjie could see herself atop a horse.

He smiled down at her. "We will not be needing the pony, Mathias."

The stable master frowned. "I thought Miss Fitzroy was to ride with you, sir."

"She is," Arawn winked at her again. Twice in one day? What was she to make of it?

He put his hands around her waist, and Marjie drew in a breath as he set her atop Taran. She closed her eyes until she felt him settle on the horse behind her, his arms nearly wrapped around her waist as he took up the reins. Oh, gracious. Riding together may not have been such a prudent idea.

Mathias cleared his throat, a rather disapproving look on his face. "I will send Dafydd along on the pony as a chaperone, my lord."

Arawn tilted his head to the side, but then shrugged. "Very well." He flicked the reigns and Taran took his first step.

A whimper pushed out of Marjie's lips, and she turned and buried her face in Arawn's chest.

He must have transferred the reins into one hand, because

in the next moment, his hand settled around her waist, holding her firmly against him. "*Dyna ferch dda.*"

She peeked up at him. "What does that mean?"

"It means, there's a good girl." He tightened his arm around her waist briefly. "It means I'm proud of you. You are very brave."

She held up her shaking hand in front of his face. "Does this look brave to you?"

He nodded. "Indeed, it does."

She pulled her bottom lip between her teeth. "Thank you, Arawn."

He dipped his head. "You are more than welcome, Marjie."

CHAPTER SIXTEEN

Marjie peeked into the breakfast room, hoping Arawn was there. She wanted to see him. She had not seen him since they retired to their rooms the previous evening after dinner and visiting nearly—she glanced at the long clock in the corridor —, ten hours ago.

She frowned. She had never been one to count hours since seeing a person. What had happened to her?

Lord Angle is what had happened. Against her better judgement, she had allowed herself to want him. Although, it was not entirely her fault. He must take some of the blame as well. After all, was it not his smile that she missed? Or the feel of his arms around her waist that left her longing for more? But it was more than that. It was the sense that he knew her—the true her—and still he sought her out and wished for her company. Never had that happened to her before. Add to that the feeling of security and peace she often felt when he was with her, and it was no wonder she was very nearly in love with the man.

She pulled up short, stopping just shy of the doorway.

17

Nearly in love? Where had that come from? And why had she ever thought such a thing? She rubbed her hand along her arm where gooseflesh pricked at her skin. Oh botheration. She was much worse off than she originally believed.

Arawn, her mother, Ane, Lady Angle, and Gilford were all in the room. She put her hands to her cheeks. Could they tell what she had just discovered? Would they know that she was in love with Arawn?

She thought about butterflies and honeysuckle and pink daphne. Anything to take the hot sting from her cheeks. But those things did nothing to cool her. Perhaps if she thought of less pleasant things, it would prove more effective. She turned her thoughts to worms and beetles and other creepy crawly things. To her satisfaction, such thoughts caused shudders and she scrunched up her nose in distaste, removing all previous indications of affection.

"Good morning, Mama." Marjie stepped into the room and leaned over to kiss her mother's cheek. Straightening, she looked at Lady Angle but purposefully avoided Arawn's gaze. "*Bore da*, Lord and Lady Angle." Thankfully, Ane was sitting on the other side of the table. "*Bore da*, Ane."

"Ic eom gesund, Þancas þe for frægnesse," said the ghost in hose and a long tunic whose name Marjie did not know. She looked to Ane. "What did he say?"

Ane shrugged. "I understand very little of what he says. But I believe he said he is well. And thanked you for asking."

"And I supposeth I'm to beest ign'red?" Gilford raised an indignant chin.

"I beg your pardon, Gilford," Marjie smiled. "Good morning to you, also."

He sniffed, seemingly unsatisfied with her apology.

Lady Angle put her silverware down on her plate. "I do not see why we cannot suspend with formality while we are in the castle." She looked over at her son. "Do you not agree, Arawn?"

He flicked his gaze to Marjie, a grin on his face, then flicked it back to his mother. "Whatever you wish, Mother."

"Suspend with formalities?" Ane sat up straighter. "Arawn, what is wrong with Mama?" She stood up and moved around the table, leaning in close to examining her mother. "She looks to be well enough. If only I could feel if she has a fever."

Marjie smiled. "Ane is wondering if you are feeling well, your ladyship. She seems to think you are acting out of sorts today."

Arawn chuckled.

Lady Angle pierced Marjie with a look, but she was not certain if it was due to the formal address or Ane's remarks. "You may tell Ane that I feel better than I have in months."

"You don't need to tell me anything, I can hear perfectly well what she says." Ane stalked back to the chair next to her brother.

Marjie bit her lip to keep from laughing.

"What is it?" Arawn asked. "What did Ane say?"

Marjie glanced down the table at Lady Angle. Would she appreciate her daughter's flippant words? Whether Lady Angle liked the words or not, Marjie supposed it was not her right to change them. "She says she hears quite well, and I do not need to restate what you say."

"It seems she is the same Angharad as before." Lady Angle muttered, but Marjie did not miss the smile hovering on her lips. The lady was happy to speak to her daughter, no matter how unorthodox the conversation.

"Do you have plans today?" Marjie's mother asked. Her gaze darted around the room. Her mother did not seem to accept the ghost's presence as willingly as Arawn and Lady Angle. Perhaps it was because she had not been raised with such superstitions. Or perhaps it was because her daughter was not one of the ghosts.

"No, Mama. I do not. Are you in need of me?"

Her mother shook her head.

"Marjorie," Arawn glanced at his mother and tipped his head to the side, as if seeking her approval.

She smiled and nodded.

He continued. "Did you not tell me at one time that you enjoy painting?"

Marjie nodded. "Indeed, I do. Although, I am not very proficient."

She cast a glance at her mother, who raised her brows in concern.

"Splendid," Arawn clasped his hands together. "Mother thought it might be fun to invite several of the ladies from the area to the castle to have a painting party."

"A painting party? With the ladies from the area?" Her voice hitched up. Arawn seemed so excited by the prospect. How could she refuse him? But how would she manage a painting without every lady in the village discovering her deficiency? She would simply have to fetch her own paints.

"I have arranged for easels, canvases, and paints to be set up on the west barbican. It is not the same view you admired on our tour, but I think it is equally as lovely. And you will still be within the protection of the castle."

"Are you anticipating an attack?" Marjie set her plate down on the table and grinned at him.

"No. After learning about the saddle, he's not comfortable with you being outside the castle walls without him." Ane shook her head. "I think he should not care where *I* go. Although, I cannot leave the castle grounds either, so I suppose it makes no difference. We are both to be prisoners here."

Arawn raised an eyebrow at her. "No, I do not expect an

attack. But after your accident, I would simply feel more comfortable knowing you are within the castle's protection."

Marjie nodded. "That is what Ane supposed." It was easy to forget that there might be a murderer still about. And while she could not imagine they would do anything to her, she had to admit it might not be beyond the realm of possibility. "I do not wish you to feel any unease on my account." She smiled at him but hoped he could see in her eyes that she understood. "I will stay on the castle side of the drawbridge."

His shoulders relaxed. "The party is scheduled to begin at two. It is when the sun is at the best advantage."

Ane leaned forward and put her elbow on the table. It sank slightly into the wood. "Do you really like to paint, or is he simply imposing that on you? I find the activity very distasteful, yet he and my mother insisted upon it."

"The talent of painting is to beest admire in all who is't possesseth it." Gilford held a hand up in the air.

Ane rolled her eyes. "I do not believe anyone sought your opinion, Gilford."

"Thou art a v'ry ill temp'r'd young maiden." Gilford scowled at her.

Marjie grinned at the two.

"What is it?" Arawn leaned closer to her.

"Ane and Gilford are having a disagreement."

"We art not for thy amusement," Gilford lifted his chin and floated out of the room.

Arawn frowned. "While I know it likely vexes you, I find myself rather jealous of your abilities."

"My abilities? You act as though I did something difficult to cultivate them. I simply hit my head."

"Regardless, you can see Ane. And Gilford. He is a relation also, is he not?"

"If I could, I should pass the burden onto you." She sighed, but then her eyes widened. "I'm sorry. I should not have implied that seeing and speaking to your sister is a burden." She looked covertly around the room and leaned forward even more. "It is more the others that are burdensome. They swoop in quite without invitation and wish for me to speak with them whenever it fancies them."

He shook his head. "I understand. I'm certain after all this time, all the ghosts are anxious to speak with someone among the living."

Marjie nodded. "Sometimes I long for quiet."

He leaned back. "Then perhaps I should leave you to yourself until the painting party."

That is not what she had hoped for at all.

Lady Angle pushed out her chair. "I am off to the milliner's. Have you set a meeting with Mr. Radcliffe about the ap Tudur celebration? Ever since Mr. Radcliffe spoke with you on Sunday, he has become quite determined to begin the planning."

"No. The celebration is not until April, Mother. I believe we still have time to plan." He wrinkled his nose. "You would think Rhys and Gwilym were his relations, not just national heroes."

"I can understand his loyalty," Marjie said. "I find myself quite drawn to the men also."

"But in *your* case, they are relatives." Annoyance laced Arawn words.

Lady Angle stepped back into the room. "Excuse me? You are a relation of the ap Tudurs?" She looked to Marjie's mother. "Mariane, how did I never know this?"

Marjie's mother smiled. "It is through my husband's family." She cast a look at Marjie. "And it is not substantiated."

Lady Angle clapped her hands. "While I wish to hear all

about it, I am afraid I will be terribly late if I do not leave now. But you are joining me for tea, are you not?"

"That was my plan." Mariane replied.

Lady Angle nodded. "I enjoy our tea together. I shall be disappointed when you return to Yorkshire."

She turned from the room and hurried away, her calls for Halvard echoing through the corridor.

"What are you to do this morning, Marjie?" Arawn asked.

Marjie stood and a footman hurried over to pull out her seat. "I have not yet decided. I thought about going to the stables."

"You're leaving? Are you to make me float along behind you so I can hear? That is not very polite," Ane groaned.

"Is she following us?" Arawn glanced behind him as they stepped into the corridor.

"Yes. She is unhappy we left. Apparently, she does not enjoy floating behind and listening."

He frowned. "I don't think *I* like her floating behind and listening." He shook his head. "You do not plan to ride by yourself, do you?"

Marjie shook her head with wide eyes. "Good heavens, no. I'm not yet ready for that. But I think I might try feeding the horses." She looked up at him coyly. "Although, I shall miss your strong hand beneath mine." What was that? Was she flirting? Where had it come from? She did not even know she knew how to flirt. But she was not completely opposed to practicing it more.

⁂

Arawn fetched her just before two, as promised. He led her out through the gatehouse and onto the cobblestone of the barbican. "I had thought about setting this up on the East Barbican, before mother invited the whole of the village. But it would take far too much preparation on short notice. Boats would have to be arranged. Unless, of course, I allowed everyone to traipse through the family quarters. And I'm not inclined to make those concessions."

She smiled, suddenly nervous. He would surely wish to see what she had painted. Especially after all her talk about forcing Ane to do it. What had she been thinking?

This was not her usual painting where she and possibly her mother would be the only people to see it.

Over the years, she had memorized the paint color names. Her mother had taught her when she was young that the sky was blue, the grass was green, and so on. She could usually manage well enough. Perhaps not to make the painting look identical to the real view, but close.

Besides, it was not the colors that brought joy to her. It was creating texture within the painting. If a tree made a person wish to reach out and touch it, that was what Marjie relished.

But she had never had an audience before.

Easels and wooden stools sat positioned facing the village and fields. Several of the chairs were already occupied as Lady Angle flitted about from person to person making small talk.

Arawn led her over to one of the unoccupied stools. She could not help but notice the gazes that followed their path.

"You sit down, and I will get you your paints."

"No," Marjie nearly shouted. She reached out and grabbed hold of his coat sleeve. "I can fetch them myself. I'm sure you need to go and mingle with your guests." She moved out from behind the easel.

He rolled his eyes. "My mother is taking care of that adequately."

As if summoned, Lady Angle appeared at their side, with a maid in tow. "Here is your color palette."

The maid thrust forward a board with at least ten different colors evenly distributed.

Oh, lud. She looked down at the paints. This was sure to be a disaster. By the time her painting was done, the whole village would know.

He would know. And then what would he think of her?

She frowned down at the brush she was wiping on a towel tied to the palette. Never had she cared so much what people thought of her. She glanced over her shoulder. Or perhaps, she only cared what he thought.

CHAPTER SEVENTEEN

Arawn was curious about Marjie's abilities. She had said she enjoyed painting, but had mentioned she was not proficient.

While Ane had been proficient, he had always felt her paintings lacked something. But after his initial conversation with Marjie, Arawn had wondered if perhaps Ane's paintings lacked a soul. Or however it was that one conveyed enjoyment and passion on a canvas.

He may not know Marjie's talent, but he did not doubt her passion. The question was, would the passion supersede the natural genius?

He could hardly wait to find out.

He looked down at her palette. "Is this enough paint, do you think?"

Marjie stared at the board. "Lawkes, there are so many different colors." She frowned. Did she not have what she needed?

"I believe you received some of every color so you are able to blend the colors to make any other you might need."

Marjie nodded, but her brow was knitted tightly together. "Yes, blending. That is very important."

He stood there for a moment, waiting to watch her make her first brush stroke across the canvas. But sensing her discomfort, he stepped to the side. She likely did not wish to have an audience while she painted. Whatever his mother called this activity, it was not the same as a musicale. He need not spectate.

"Why do I not leave you alone to paint? I need to check with Mathias to see if he has learned anything new."

She smiled up at him. "Oh, yes. You need not stay here. Go and see what you can discover. I am certain Ane is anxious for some answers."

Arawn turned slowly away, watching her as she tilted her head one way and then the other. She looked at her paints, then looked out at the scene in front of her. She glanced at a few of the canvases around her. Was she feeling as though this was a competition rather than a friendly activity?

Perhaps she was simply a true artist, who needed to consider everything before she started her painting.

Or she simply could not start as long as she felt him hovering behind her.

With one last look at her from over his shoulder, he walked purposefully toward the stables. He had to admit he was anxious to know if Mathias had learned anything.

He stepped through the large archway that led into the stable yard. Several stable hands walked about, arms full of feed or leading a horse around their paces. He dipped his head as he passed each one.

The main stable, where Mathias kept an office, was his destination, even if Taran did knicker and dance for Arawn to come visit.

As he entered, he allowed his eyes to adjust to the

decreased light, then moved down the aisle to the door at the back. He knocked twice before dropping his hand to his side.

"James, I told you to put the fee—" Mathias opened the door and took a surprised step back. "Oh, my lord. I did not realize it was you."

Arawn nodded, a hint of a smile on his lips. "Yes, I figured as much." He motioned the man back into his office and shut the door behind him. "Have you learned anything new?"

Mathias shook his head. "I have not. Although, I have not done much questioning of the grooms. You said you wished to keep it between us, and I did not know how to broach the questions without raising suspicions or giving more information than you wished."

Arawn nodded but felt out of sorts. How were they to learn anything if they asked no questions? But the wrong questions could spook the guilty party into disappearing for good. And then what would they do? Besides, was it even possible that the man responsible for Ane's death continued working at the stable?

He rubbed at his temple. When it was thought to be an accident, why should the man have left? Would it not cast a guilty light on him? No, he shook his head. It seemed reasonable to think that the person might still be on the grounds. Unless they had never been employed at the estate at all.

He ran a frustrated hand over his face. He had thought all this through at least a hundred times since discovering the truth, yet he still could not make any sense of it. "I would like to see the saddle."

Mathias licked his lips. "It is out on the wall, with the other saddles, my lord."

Arawn dropped his hand. "What? Why? Did we not agree that you would keep it locked in your office."

"We did. But Dafydd saw the saddle in my office. He had

happened upon me just after I discovered the nail. I did not tell him about it, but my boy is an intelligent one, my lord. He found the nail and removed it so the saddle would be available if Miss Fitzroy should wish to ride on her own again."

"Did he keep it? I have not yet had a chance to look at it." Arawn ran a hand through his hair.

Mathias shook his head. "I know, my lord and I am sorry. The boy was only trying to be helpful."

Arawn released a growl. "I know he meant no harm. I just would have preferred—" He let the sentence trail off. Why belabor the point? The nail was gone and there was nothing he could do about it. "I would still like to see the saddle."

Mathias nodded. "If you will wait a moment, my lord. I shall fetch it directly." He opened the door and scurried out into the stable, returning quickly with the saddle Arawn continued to have nightmares about. Mathias set it on the neatly organized workbench that stood along one wall.

Arawn picked it up and turned it over, laying it on the bench. A reddish-brown stain encircled the rectangular hole in the wood. It was obvious where the nail had been. Just as it was obvious that it had not simply worked its way loose. There was nothing on the saddle of importance within a hands width of where the nail had been. Indeed, it appeared as if the nail had been placed where it would inflict the most pain on the animal.

It was no wonder Gwyn had thrown Ane and Arthur had thrown Marjie. They were surely trying to rid themselves of the thorn, or nail, in their side.

He shifted onto his heels. "Where do we go from here? Do you believe there is any chance we might discover who did this?" He ran his fingers gently over the hole.

Mathias shrugged. "I don't know, my lord. It has been a long time."

Arawn pounded a fist on the bench top. "We must do something. This person, whoever is responsible, cannot get away with it. If we do not catch them, they will believe they are above the law. Imagine what else they might do."

A scratching sound made them both look toward the door. Dafydd stood, his cap in his hands. "Good day, my lord." He turned to his father. "I have finished walking the colt. He is growing stronger every day."

Mathias smiled. "Good, good." He glanced at Arawn. "I was in the middle of speaking with his lordship, Dafydd. Please go check on James and make certain he has stored the feed in the right place this time."

Dafydd grinned. "Yes, sir." But his smile faltered when he glanced at the saddle and then at Arawn. "My lord." He bowed, then turned away.

"I may have been wrong to tell you to keep it between us." Arawn glanced down at the hole in the saddle. "Please make discreet inquiries among your hands. Perhaps one of them saw something but they do not realize what they saw."

Mathias nodded. "I will begin immediately, my lord."

Arawn clasped his hands behind him to keep himself from touching the nail hole again. It held a strangely hypnotic hold on him. "Please inform me if you should learn anything."

"Yes, my lord."

Arawn walked slowly out of the stable. While he had known he likely would not discover anything new, he was still disappointed. They were no closer to discovering who had placed the nail in Ane's saddle than the day it was discovered.

He clasped his hands behind his back again and studied the ground where he walked. The grass was turning dry and brown. It would not be long, and the cold would be upon them.

It had only been a few days since they had learned the truth of Ane's accident. He need not allow himself to wallow in the unknown. Nothing productive would come from that. But he was at least grateful to know that it had not been his fault. At least not entirely.

If he had not pushed Ane to jump the river at the spot she had, would she yet be alive? Until a few days ago, he would have said yes. But now he was not so certain. Ane loved to give Gwyn her head on the beachside path. Would Gwyn have thrown her there instead? If that had happened—Arawn shivered at the thought of the mangled mess Ane would have been had she been thrown down the sharp, craggy cliffs.

He shook off that thought. She would not have been any less dead. But it was possible she could have suffered more.

He walked away from the stable yard and looked over to the barbican. Even with a dozen easels scattered across it, Marjie was easy to pick out. Her deep red hair glistened in the sunlight. But even apart from that, there was just something about her that drew Arawn's gaze to her. A magnetism of some sort.

He stopped and watched for a moment. She was looking at the village to his left, and even from this distance, he could see her head tilt to one side and then straighten.

She looked to be intent on her painting.

Arawn's anticipation grew. And not just at seeing the painting. He continued his walk across the fields. It seemed unlikely she would be done with the painting, but he could still peek, could he not?

He moved as quietly as possible, afraid she might try to hide the painting from him until it was finished. He walked up slowly behind her.

"You need not sneak up on me. Your shadow reached me well before you will."

"I was not sneaking, per se," Arawn let out an exaggerated sigh. "I was afraid you might try to hide the painting from me."

"Why would I do that?" She bit her lip. "Although, I fear I may have led you to believe I had more talent than I do."

Arawn looked over at her painting with a grin. She was surely exagger—

Saints above, what had she painted? The scene was not yet finished. But the parts that were all there—Arawn did not know what to say. He leaned in for a closer look. Her technique was much better than Ane's. And as he looked longer at it, he sensed rather than saw something more.

While the colors were completely wrong—the sky was yellow, and the grasses were a vibrant shade of purple. The only thing remotely painted in the correct colors were the walls surrounding the castle and the village. But even with the odd choice of colors, there was a feeling in the painting that he had never quite encountered before. Indeed, if a painting could have a soul, this painting most assuredly did. It was the only way he could think to describe it.

"Your choice of colors is interesting." He dropped down to his haunches, so he was looking at the painting from a similar angle to Marjie. "Why did you choose yellow for the sky?"

Marjie leaned forward and stared at the painting and then out at the view before her. "Yellow. Yes, I know it is not what one might normally think a sky should be, but..." She just stared out at the countryside before her. "You don't like it." It was not so much a question as a statement.

Miss Penry walked behind them at that moment. "Gracious. What is that?" She shrieked as she pointed to the painting.

Arawn straightened, putting himself between the young lady and Marjie. "What do you mean? It is a painting. And a very fine one at that."

"You can't be in earnest, my lord." She pointed and Arawn noticed many of the other ladies had ceased their painting and craned their necks to see. "The colors are completely wrong."

Arawn flicked his gaze over to Marjie. Her cheeks boasted a deep crimson. And while he found the effect rather pleasing, he knew it was a sign that she was distressed. "I do not believe she was trying to paint the countryside as it appears but rather took a more abstract view of it. By changing the colors, she has evoked a completely different feeling with the painting." He lifted his chin, inviting Miss Penry to disagree with him. If she dared.

Miss Penry took the cue as he knew she would. Her mouth pinched shut, though her gaze bounced back and forth between him and the painting. Finally, she smiled. It was more of a sneer, but Arawn was willing to give her the benefit of the doubt. "I see," was all she said.

He lifted his brows. "Is your painting done? I believe my mother wishes to have a showing in the village once everyone's painting is complete."

Miss Penry shook her head. "No, I have not yet finished."

Arawn smiled, though he felt no felicity toward the woman. "Please, do not let us keep you any longer."

She lifted one brow and curtsied. "Thank you, my lord."

"My pleasure." He turned back to Marjie's painting. "Pay no heed, Marjie," he whispered in her ear and was quite satisfied to see gooseflesh raise on her neck.

"But she is not wrong, Arawn. Most will see it as she does."

He signed. "Anyone who truly looks at this painting will feel the truth of it. It is a masterpiece."

Marjoe swallowed. "You are just being kind."

"I am not. I can assure you." He glanced out at the sea of other ladies perched on their stools painting. "Do you care what others think? I had not thought you would."

Marjie bit her lip and shrugged. "I wish I did not. But I find that I do. Very much." She gazed up at him and a sudden desire to protect her welled up inside of him. He had no notion where it came from.

He grinned down at her. "Well, Miss Penry's good opinion is not worth the effort it takes to receive it." He pointed to the painting. "It's a marvel that you can see the scenery like this. I have never even imagined a yellow sky."

She frowned and squinted at the painting. "Nor have I," she mumbled.

He glanced over at her and a thought struck him. "Marjie, do you see colors?"

She twisted at the corner of her apron, sitting quietly for several beats of his heart. But then her head shook slowly. "No, I don't."

She ducked her head as if she could not bear to look at him.

He looked at the painting with new eyes. It was even more amazing than he had originally believed. He had never encountered someone who could not see color. It explained so much. The mismatched clothing and the black flower on her stitchery.

He put his finger beneath her chin and drew her gaze up to his. "Why did you not tell me?"

She lifted a shoulder. "Mama says we should not announce our deficiencies. Especially among the *ton*."

He stared at her. What must the world look like through her eyes? He had never even imagined such a thing.

He had read about people who could not see this color or that. But he had never actually met someone who had...what did she call it? A deficiency? The word felt so unkind and even more inaccurate. While he might call it a gift, he could see how Marjie might find that word disingenuous or a mockery.

Regardless, it was completely Marjie. Unique and utterly remarkable.

"I do not see it as a deficiency. You simply see the world in a different way. Perhaps we could all do with a bit of color blindness from time to time."

She scowled at him. "I see the world this way constantly, not only from time to time."

He shook his head. "My apologies. I was not trying to make light of your uniqueness."

Her brows rose and he hurried on before he made more of a muddle than he already had. "I am not saying anything right. I'm sorry."

She pursed her lips together. "You need not apologize. Mama says that sometimes I look for a reason to be displeased with the world. Perhaps that is what I am doing now."

"What colors do you see?"

"I am not certain because I have never seen what they should look like, so it is hard to describe them. But Mama is quite certain I only see shades of black, white, and gray."

He nodded. "That is why you did not notice you had embroidered your flower black?"

She sighed. "Ane was the one who first noticed the mistake." She finally glanced up at him. "For as long as I can remember, my mother has sewn flowers into the collars of my clothes. I need only match the flowers to know what coordinates with what. It was very important that I look as if my mother was an accomplished seamstress. And now it is important that I look as though I belong with the *ton*." She lifted a brow and a wicked gleam appeared. "But sometimes I just want to ignore those flowers and wear whatever I choose."

He nodded. So much was explained in this short conversation. He held up a finger. "Are you finished painting, or do you wish to do more?"

"I was enjoying myself, no matter how dreadful it looks."

"I wish you would not call it dreadful." He narrowed his

eyes at the painting as he straightened and snapped his fingers. "Wait one moment." He turned and jogged over to the table holding the paint supplies.

A few moments passed before he hurried back out with a new canvas in his hand and another palette. Careful not to disturb the paint on the partially finished landscape, he moved it down to the cobblestones and leaned it against the back leg of the easel. Then he placed a new canvas in front of her.

She looked up at him in confusion. "You wish me to start over?"

He shook his head. "Not for the reasons you think." He took the old palette out of her hands and stepped back. "Would you please paint the scenery the way you see it?" A new palette, one with only two large dollops of paint—one black and one white—he placed on her lap.

"I'm not certain this will look any better." She tilted her head to the side.

"I doubt that. But regardless, it will help me to see a little bit of the world as you do."

She dipped her brush into the black and pulled a little bit of white to it, moving the brush around, a dark charcoal gray formed. She glanced up at him. "Are you certain this is what you want? It will surely be very dull."

"We shall see." He shook his head. "But I believe quite the opposite will be true."

She tilted her head to the side and drew a streak across the canvas. "Are you to stand there the whole time?"

That is precisely what he wished to do. But he could see how that might draw unwanted attention. He grunted. "I suppose not." He wandered around looking at the paintings of the other women. There were several very accomplished painters in the group. And he supposed he could count Miss

Penry among them, but no one else's work stirred his emotions as Marjie's did.

After looking at each painting and making a kind comment to the artist, Arawn returned to where Marjie sat, her face scrunched up in concentration. She did not even acknowledge him this time.

Looking around, he decided he did not care what attention he drew. Had he not just lectured Majie about not caring what the others thought of her? He wished to stay here and that was what he intended to do. He dropped down to the ground and stretched his legs out in front of him. Putting his hands behind him, he leaned back and allowed the sun to warm his face.

"Are you to stay the whole time?" she asked.

"Will it bother you if I do?" He did not want to admit how much he hoped she would say he could stay.

She lifted a delicate shoulder. "Now that you know what to expect, I suppose I don't mind." She glanced over at him. "If it turns out to be complete rubbish, it is not my fault. You have been warned."

Arawn closed his eyes, "Ah, but it will not be."

She pulled her brush from the canvas and leaned back in her chair. "How can you be certain?"

He looked up at her through one eye, barely able to see much more than her silhouette as the sun shone behind her. "I know because even with the sky painted yellow, your painting evoked something inside me that I have never felt before. In an odd way, you almost made a yellow sky seem right."

She shook her head at him, but he could see her fighting a smile. "I think you might be mad. Besides, what sane gentleman sits on the hard cobblestones if he does not have to?"

He winked at her. "Who are you calling mad? I am not the one seeing ghosts."

CHAPTER EIGHTEEN

"I thought perhaps you might try riding alone today." Arawn cleared his throat. "At least on your own horse. I shall still accompany you."

Marjie crossed her arms. "Do you think I'm ready?" She did not feel ready. Although, she was not certain how much of that was fear and how much was that she just wanted to feel Arawn's arms around her again.

"I do." He moved over closer to her. "Are you still frightened?"

She nodded.

He reached out and took her hand, squeezing it lightly. "Did I not tell you I would let no harm come to you?" He released her hand, and she missed it immediately. What would it take for him to hold it longer? For him to hold her? "And did you not promise you would trust me?"

"Yes, but that was when we were riding together." She sucked in a deep breath. "I have a different perspective today."

He chuckled melodiously and it made her skin tingle.

"I do not think your perspective is different only today."

Her spine stiffened slightly. "What do you mean by that?"

"I have never encountered someone who sees things or speaks as you do."

She guffawed. "That does not seem so incredible. From my point of view, people rarely see things in the same way." Her shoulders sagged. "But you are right, few see things as I do. And even fewer actually say what they are thinking. It is rather unheard of."

As if sensing her defeat, he continued. "I did not mean it as a slight. Indeed, I find you rather refreshing."

"Pray, why?"

Arawn was like no other gentleman she'd ever met. Granted, no other gentleman had paid her much heed beyond the first few minutes of conversation. But as she was wont to do, she almost always said something to offend, and then they would find an excuse and cry off. Indeed, it was not even a defect she could lay at the feet of the *ton*. It seemed her unlikability extended even into the serving classes.

Yet, Arawn did not dismiss her. Indeed, at times it felt as if he sought her out. But why? Why was he different from all the others? What made him stay? Apart from the notion that they were at his home.

At their first introduction, he had seemed like all the others. It was not until the tour that things shifted, if only slightly. Perhaps the key was time. In the future she need only to sequester men until they could find something to like about her.

She grinned, but only momentarily. It was humorous, but only until she realized how disheartening it was.

"It is rare to know what one is thinking within the *ton*. Even when they express their thoughts, one cannot be certain it is not a ruse." He shrugged. "But with you, there is no hidden motive, no question as to your meaning. You say what you think. And while it might sound harsh or unfeeling, one need only come to know you better to understand there is nothing unkind about you."

Marjie discreetly looked at him side-eyed. Could he really mean it? It seemed almost as fantastical as seeing ghosts. And yet, she *did* see ghosts.

The stable master and one of the stable hands already had saddles on Arawn's horse and the pretty horse she had wished to ride the first time. They stood holding the horse's reins, waiting for Marjie and Arawn.

"Ah, Mathias. Thank you for having the horses ready." He stopped and ran a hand down his horse's nose. He looked at Marjie who stood staring at the other horse.

"What is this horse's name?"

"Gwyn," Ane said, and Marjie jerked at her voice.

Marjie put a hand to her chest. "Ane, I did not see you there."

The stable master and the hand gave each other raised brow looks.

Arawn cleared his throat. "Yes, that's right. He was Ane's horse."

"Gwyn. You were Ane's horse, were you? I'm not surprised. You are quite the handsomest horse in the stables." She ran her hand down the horse's neck and Gwyn nuzzled her.

"There now, you need not make Taran feel inferior."

Marjie grinned and turned toward Taran. "Taran knows I will always love him. He helped me both times I needed it the most." She looked over at him from beneath her lashes. "He did have some help, of course."

Arawn stepped close to her. "Are you ready for this?" She could hear the concern in his voice but also confidence. Was it in her?

Her heart raced and her gloves were very nearly soaked

through. But Marjie nodded her head. "No, but I shall do it anyway."

"*Dyna ferch dda,*" he smiled at her.

Her stomach flip-flopped. Lawkes, she loved it when he said that to her. It made her feel special. Like it was his pet name for her.

Arawn lifted her up into the saddle, but far too quickly he removed his hands. His touch made her feel so much calmer, she wished he could keep them there longer. He patted her booted foot and moved over to his own horse.

Gwyn danced lightly as Marjie settled in the saddle. *The* saddle. She could only assume that the nail had been removed, but still, her heart hammered harder in her chest. If she had an apoplexy right then, she would swear off riding for good.

Glancing at Ane, Marjie smiled. This could not be easy on Ane—watching another woman ride her horse and use her saddle.

Marjie held Ane's gaze. "Thank you for allowing me to ride your beautiful horse, Ane."

"You're welcome, Marjie." Ane said as she turned and glided out of the stable.

Marjie's heart ached for the girl whose life had been ended too soon.

The stable master seemed to avoid Marjie's gaze, but she didn't care. Ane had watched everything at the castle in invisible silence for the last six months. It was time she was *seen* again.

The stable hand mounted a horse Marjie had not noticed before. It seemed he was to be their chaperone for the ride.

They headed out across the fields. Gwyn walked as if he could not feel Marjie's shaking body atop him. He was a good horse, and it seemed to Marjie a nail was the only way to get the horse to buck. They reached the stream, and it dawned on

Marjie that if this was Ane's horse, he was the one that had thrown her. She tightened her grip..

Arawn stopped. "Hand me your reins."

Marjie did not question why. She did not know if she could push the words out of her throat. Handing them over, Arawn slowly guided the horses through the water, rather than jumping over it. Apparently, she was not the only one apprehensive about this part of their ride.

Once they were on the other side of the stream, Arawn turned his horse onto a small worn path that went in the opposite direction of the village.

"Where are we going?" Marjie asked.

"I thought to make it a surprise. But from the look on your face, you may not be up for one today." He came up beside her and leaned slightly forward in his saddle. "This trail follows the coastline. There are several places where paths branch off and lead to the water." He looked hopeful. "Are you up for it?"

She was terrified. She could admit it to herself, but she was not about to admit it to him. And if she said yes, would he use his pet phrase again? It was worth the risk, was it not?

She nodded. "If we go slow, I should like to see it."

He winked at her. "*Dyna ferch dda.*"

She beamed at him. When he looked at her like that and said those words to her, she thought she might be able to do most anything he asked.

They fell silent as Angle Bay came into view.

"It's lovely," Marjie gushed on a breath.

He reined Taran to a stop. "Yes, it is." He glanced over at her. "How do you think it compares to the North Sea?"

"We do not live on the coast, but rather inland. I have only seen the North Sea once. It was lovely, but I believe this view surpasses it."

He grinned and she knew she had said the right thing for once.

Again, silence surrounded them, but it was not of an uncomfortable nature.

She shifted in the saddle, only then remembering where she was. The view had quite captured her attention enough that she and forgotten where—or rather on what—she was. Was it possible she could go back to enjoying riding again? Would there come a time when the fear disappeared completely?

"Have you learned anything new about Ane's accident?" She knew it had not been an accident. But she could not bring herself to say the word 'murder.' It just felt so dark and dreadful. And how could one use such a word when looking at such a lovely view?

Arawn shook his head, his frustration vibrating off him. "No. And I'm not certain we will. There has been so much time since it happened. Evidence could have been removed. Indeed, I know it already has." He ran a hand through his hair. "As you likely concluded, the nail was removed from the saddle."

She frowned. "By whom? Was it not locked in the stable master's office?"

He nodded. "It was, but his son found it and removed the nail. He wished to have it available when you decided to ride again." He nodded in her direction. "A wise decision, I suppose."

"It seems not." Arawn frowned. "But what could we learn from a simple nail? It is not as if it was different than another nail."

Marjie shrugged. "I do not know. But nor will we know unless we look at it. Perhaps there is something there we have not considered."

Arawn stared out at the water. "You might be right. I will ask Mathias about it when we return."

"And I think we should speak with Ane. She was there. Perhaps she can tell us if there was anything odd that happened. Or perhaps she will remember if someone was treating her strangely." Marjie shifted again so she could look him more in the eye. "It might also be prudent to write down a timetable of events leading up to and following the event. Maybe there is something there that you don't remember."

Arawn nodded slowly. "It seems as good a place to start as any. Ane might be helpful with the timetable. Mathias is going to question the stable hands. And I will have Roger, the gardener, speak with the undergardeners."

He grinned at her. "Perhaps you should apply to Bow Street."

She laughed, even as warmth crept up her limbs and settled in her belly.

The breeze blowing in off the sea lifted her side curl and blew it into her face.

Arawn leaned over and tucked the curl behind her ear. "While I may not have desired it at first, I am very glad you came to visit Hywel, Miss Fitzroy. I hope it shall not be your only visit."

Marjie swallowed down a nervous giggle. "I should be delighted to visit any time you request it, my lord." She was already dreading the time they would have to leave. In the short time she'd been there, she had developed quite a love for Wales. And for Angle in particular.

He looked out at the water again. "Perhaps you would consider visiting for the holidays? You could arrive in early December and stay on through Twelfth Night."

Marjie noticed a slight uptick in his voice. More than one

would expect from just a question. Could he be nervous? What could a marquess have to be nervous about?

"That is only a few months away. I'm not sure my mother will be up to such a long journey so soon after our return."

He sucked in a breath but did not release it. "Then perhaps you should just stay on and not return home in between."

Marjie blinked at him. Was he asking them to stay at Hywel for another two months? She coughed. "Should you not first speak to your mother?"

He grunted, sounding irritated by her question. "I do not need my mother's permission to invite guests to Hywel." He tilted his head to the side. "Did she not invite your mother and you without my permission?"

Marjie nodded. "Yes, it seems she did."

His shoulders relaxed, and he released his breath. "My mother was quite lonely before your arrival. I'm afraid I was not the son I should have been after Ane's death. But since you came, I have seen new life in her. She is quite the happiest I have seen her in months." He shook his head. "No, I should not think she'll have any objections."

"I shall discuss it with my mother and let you know?"

He nodded. "Take your time. There is no rush."

They reached a place where the path widened enough that Arawn guided Taran around, and they made their way slowly back to the castle. "Do you think you can manage a trot?"

Marjie looked over the cliffside at the sand far below. "Perhaps we could wait until after we cross over the stream for trotting."

He watched her intently. "That is a compromise I will happily accept."

Their horses walked back the way they had come. It was almost painfully slow. But Marjie did not mind. She was with

Arawn, and she did not seem to care what they were doing, as long as they did it together.

"What kind of a name is Taran?" Marjie asked.

"Taran means thunder. Taranis was the Gaulish God of Thunder, but in the old Welsh tales from the *Mabinogion,* he is known simply as Taran."

"What is the Mabin—?" She trailed off, having no idea how to say the actual name.

Arawn grinned at her attempt. "The *Mabinogion* is a compilation of myths, similar to those of the Greeks or the Romans, only the gods are Welsh. In one of the myths, Taran defeats Arawn."

Marjie pushed her lips out and tapped her finger to them. "I had wondered about your name."

"And you did not ask? I believe that may be the only question you have not asked me." He gave her a lopsided grin.

She shook her head. "Oh, no. There are many I have not asked. Mama said I needed to limit my questions. She said we are only here for a short time, and I should not tax you with all my questions from the very beginning."

"That was you being reserved?" His eyes widened and his lips twitched. "I cannot imagine how you held it all in."

She shook her head. "You have no idea how difficult it has been."

"I'm certain it was." He dropped his head back and laughed. A deep, rumbling, belly laugh.

Her breath caught in her throat. She had done it. She had earned a genuine laugh from him.

Lawkes, she loved that sound. Indeed, it was quite possible she loved everything about this man.

CHAPTER NINETEEN

Arawn paced restlessly in front of the fireplace in his study. When his mother had asked, he told her he was distracted by some new information he had learned about Ane's *accident*. No one seemed to be able to say the actual word. But they all knew what was meant.

But Ane had merely been an excuse because he was quite certain he could lay his restlessness at the feet of Miss Marjorie Fitzroy.

It had been nearly a week since he realized she had become a friend to him. Indeed, he would have admitted she was one of his closest friends. However, since riding together the last few days, he could no longer think of her as just a friend.

Those rides had changed things. The feel of her in his arms, even if it had not been an embrace, felt right. Too right, if he was being honest. It was one of the reasons he had wished for her to be on her own horse, yesterday. He could not think straight when she was pressed up against him—breathing in the smell of her—with his arms around her. It made him want more. And that was a feeling he had never encountered.

He had always assumed he would marry someone for political or financial reasons. Duty and honor seemed a more likely path for a marquess. But now, he was not sure if he could do it. For the first time in his life, he thought about marrying for love. It was a novel idea. But one he thought worth investigating.

It was that feeling he had fallen asleep thinking about and that feeling he had awakened to this morning.

He wanted to do something special for Marjie. She had shown so much bravery on the horses, it made him puff up with pride. She had done what even his mother could not.

She had been scared, even if she tried to hide most of it. But still, she mounted and rode. And that alone made him adore her even more.

But what to do? What would show her just how he was feeling? He did not have the luxury of time. Marjie and her mother had been at the castle for nearly a fortnight. If they did not accept his offer to stay on longer, his time with her was ending. And that thought made his stomach clench.

A knock sounded at his door and his mother poked her head inside. "May I come in? I will not be long."

"Of course, Mother. How may I help you?"

She stepped inside with a vase of flowers in her hands. "I thought these might brighten up your study. The blooms in the garden will not last much longer as the nights are becoming cooler."

"They are lovely, Mother. Thank you." He motioned to the table on the other side of the room.

"Mother, I wish to do something for Marjorie, to thank her for speaking to Ane on our behalf. I'm sure it is a taxing chore. Do you have any ideas?"

His mother grinned so wide, he thought she might split her skin.

She nodded to the flowers. "Why do you not take her into the garden? It is simply beautiful with all the different colors."

Arawn grimaced. "I do not think it will have the same effect on her as it would on you or me."

His mother frowned. "I do not see why. She may be a little odd, but I'm certain she can appreciate lovely flowers."

Marjie was not odd. But it would not serve his purpose to argue the point. His mother did not know of her color blindness. Was it his place to tell her? He wasn't certain, but she could not help him if she didn't know. "It is not something they wish to have known, but Marjorie cannot see color." He bit his cheek, wondering how his mother would respond. He knew she would not spurn or mock Marjorie, but would his mother see it as a deficiency also?

A light dawned in her eyes. "Ah, that explains much."

He nodded. "Yes, I thought so too. But you see my point about the garden?"

His mother shook her head. "I do not. I still believe it is a fine idea."

"But how? The flowers will look like shades of black, white, and gray. It almost feels like a mockery."

"You are assuming that the colors are the only desirable part of the garden. For Marjorie, you will simply need to take a different approach. Take her on a smelling tour, rather than a color tour."

Arawn snapped his fingers. "Mother, I think you might be a genius."

She grinned. "It's about time you realized it."

Arawn stepped over to her and placed a kiss on her cheek. "Thank you."

"I should not wait too long. Nearly everything is in bloom, but as I said, they will be gone soon."

Arawn smiled. "I do not need them for much longer than a

day or two. Then I shall not lament them, should they wither away."

She gave his arm a light smack. "Speak for yourself, my dear. I should love to see them for as long as possible."

"Then for your sake, I will hope they last longer."

His mother stayed where she was, staring at him as if she were trying to decide how to broach the subject of the real reason she had come to see him. "Arawn, what have you learned about your sister's accident?"

"Not much. I'm afraid we have lost too much time. I'm not certain if there is anything left to find." He sighed. "Although, on our ride yesterday, Marjie did suggest that we speak with Ane and create a timeline of events before and after the accident."

His mother took a step forward. "Have you spoken with Ane?"

He shook his head. "The ride took a toll on Marjie. She needed to rest afterward. But we plan to speak to Ane this afternoon."

"I cannot believe you are pressuring her to ride again. Especially so soon after what happened." His mother shook her head.

Arawn crossed his arms. "You're proof of why I am. It was not even you that was thrown, and yet you have not ridden since Ane's accident. The longer you wait, Mother, the more afraid you become."

She lifted her chin. "I am not frightened. I simply do not see a reason to ride, that is all."

He stared at her. She was lying. That was evident in her gaze. But he would not mention it. She did not need his disappointment. "I hope you discover a reason soon. I have missed our rides together."

She closed the distance between them and placed a kiss on

his cheek. "While I have not missed the riding, I have missed you. It has been nice to have you back these last few weeks." She turned to leave. She turned just before reaching the doorway. "Do not forget we are having a card party tonight."

Arawn sighed. "As much as I've tried, I'm unable to forget, Mother."

She rolled her eyes before quitting the room.

Arawn stared at the fire burning low in the grate. When should he take Marjie on her scent tour? He snapped his fingers. Why not that very evening? The other guests would keep his mother busy, leaving him free to take Marjie to the garden. Perhaps he need not forget about the card party after all.

He glanced at the long clock. It did not leave him much time to make the proper arrangements, but he could manage it with his valet's help. And he should surely know the names of at least some of the flowers in the garden—if it was to be a proper tour.

He hurried out of his study, hoping his mother was still nearby. She was just pushing into the family parlor, another bouquet of flowers in her arms. Lud, had she left any blooms in the garden?

"Mother, I am glad I found you."

She looked up at him with questioning eyes. "Yes? Did we not finish our discussion?"

He nodded. "We did. But I had a thought after you left." He glanced away, wondering where Marjie was and if he should just hand her the card or if he should have it delivered in some way. "Do you think you could meet me in the garden in—" he pulled out his pocket watch and checked the time, "—in thirty minutes? I have some questions I wish to ask you."

She nodded. "Of course, dear."

"Thank you, Mother." He nodded to the bouquet on the shelf in the alcove. "Your arrangements are lovely."

She did not say anything, but her smile told him enough.

He left her standing in the corridor while he went in search of Marjie. It would be better for him to give her the card himself. If a servant should read what he wrote, it would surely start the rumors flying belowstairs.

He moved toward the parlor. It seemed to be her favorite place, even if she wasn't sewing.

Sure enough, when he stepped inside, his eyes immediately went to the deep red hair showing just above the high-backed chair near the center of the room. Her shoulders were not moving, which led him to believe she was not working on the stitchery she so obviously hated.

Perhaps she was reading. She had asked him several days ago if he minded if she borrowed a book or two. He had been rather embarrassed that he had not thought to give her permission while they were on their tour. But that could not be helped now.

He stood in the doorway watching the back of her head. It was not that there was anything particularly captivating, as much as he was struck with the feeling of rightness. Why did it feel as if everything around him was complete in that moment?

"No, Gwen, I am not reading the *Lives of Saints.*" Marjie glowered at the seat next to her. "Yes, I realize I am surely going to Hell because I'm not of the true faith. I thank you for your concern."

She sighed. "No, Gilford. *You* tell Sybilla to trade seats with you. She does not listen to me any more than she listens to you."

She flopped her book onto the side table. "There is nothing I can do about it. It is not as if I can move her. Lud, how have you carried on for the last seven hundred years? I should think you would have worked out your differences by now." She threw her hands up in the air. "Yes, Gilford. I'm aware you have not even been dead for two hundred years. But that is still ample time to have come to an agreement."

Arawn laughed. It was no wonder she was exhausted every evening. She was busy playing peacekeeper all day.

Marjie turned to look over her shoulder. She smiled. "Oh, good. It's you."

She looked genuinely happy to see him. But he did not know if it was him she was pleased to see or just the notion that she could speak to someone living.

He moved over and stood next to the sofa. "Is Ane here too?" He hated that he could not see his sister. There were times when he just wanted to speak to Marjie privately. But he never knew if his sister was about. It was one of the reasons he wished to start her riding again. Ane could not leave the castle grounds, which meant that was the only time he felt certain he could speak to Marjie alone. Not that he had anything untoward or private to say. But he did not like thinking that Ane was privy to everything between them.

A shadow passed over Marjie's face. "Yes. But I believe she might be sad today."

Arawn sat in the chair next to her. "Why do you think that?"

"She is sitting at the pianoforte away from everyone else."

"And that leads you to believe she is sad? Why should she be sad?"

Marjie shook her head. "I'm not certain. But I imagine it's difficult watching those you love continue on without you."

Arawn picked at the carving in the wooden arm of his chair. "It's not as if we want it this way."

Marjie nodded; her gaze sympathetic. "I know that. And

I'm certain Ane knows it. But knowing something does not always make it easier."

"Ane," Arawn called toward the pianoforte. "Would you come over, please? I should like to speak with you."

Marjie turned, her eyes following a path from the piano until it stopped in front of her. She smiled as if someone stood before her. "Please do scoot over, Gwen. His lordship wishes to speak to his sister, and I will not speak around you." Marjie looked at the seat next to her and raised a brow. "No, Gwen. It is not your turn to sit next to me. Lawkes, sometimes you all act like children." She sighed. "Yes, Gwen, even you."

She turned to Arawn. "I should prefer to have Ane sitting next to me. She does not constantly lecture me and tell me I'm going to Hell." She spoke to Arawn, but the way her voice rose at the end, he assumed she was really speaking to Gwen.

She turned to Arawn. "What did you wish to speak to her about?"

"I thought perhaps we could speak to her about what we talked of yesterday."

Marjie nodded, excitement in her eyes. "Ah, yes."

Arawn looked at Marjie. "Would you explain it to her?" Even though he had come to terms with Marjie speaking to his sister's ghost, it did not mean he was completely comfortable speaking to her himself. Especially not in front of other people. Even if the other person was Marjie. And while this had not been the reason for his visit, it was just as well they discuss the plan sooner rather than later.

"Ane, we thought it would be a good idea if you put together a timetable for the days before the accident. Then Arawn and your mother will add to the timetable the days after. We are hoping we might spot an irregularity that might help us discover who did this to you."

Arawn's esteem for Marjie only grew the more he watched

her interact with Ane, and especially the other ghosts. His head swam just listening to her one-sided conversation. But a part of him hoped that even if they discovered Ane's murderer, she wouldn't leave the castle. Both because he wished her to stay and because he hoped it might convince Marjie to stay too.

Marjie smiled. "She says she cannot write anything down, obviously, but she will think about it and tell me what she remembers."

Arawn nodded. "*Da iawn.*" He smiled. "It means well—"

"Done." She chuckled. "Yes, Ane told me."

Arawn sighed, feeling more hope than he had in months. Maybe this would work. Maybe it would lead them to the person responsible.

He stood up. "I did not intend to interrupt your reading."

She smirked. "*You* did not interrupt my reading." She glared at the other end of the couch.

CHAPTER TWENTY

Arawn smiled stiffly as he and his mother flitted about the room, greeting their neighbors. It was not that he did not like these people. Most of them were a pleasant and friendly sort. But his mind was on other things. Every time he passed one of his mother's floral arrangements, he tested himself by naming the various flowers within. And every time he saw Marjie, he patted the card in his pocket, just to make certain it was still there. It would not do to lose it and have someone else pick it up. Not only would it ruin the whole evening he had planned, but it would also start rumors that he was certain neither he nor Marjie wished to endure. At least not yet.

He approached Seren. "Good evening, Seren. I'm glad you could join us this evening."

Seren grinned. "Miss a party hosted by the reclusive Lord Angle? I would not hear of it."

"Reclusive?" Arawn looked at his friend in question. "Your exaggerations are going to get you into trouble one of these days."

"Perhaps. But not this time, as it is not an exaggeration. It has been nearly a month since I heard you called such, but before then, it had become a frequent topic in the village."

Arawn grunted and shook his head in irritation. "We were in mourning. What did they expect?"

Seren shrugged. He glanced over Arawn's shoulder and let out a quiet whistle. "How is it you seem to attract quite the most handsome guests to your parties?"

Arawn turned around, a smile immediately forming on his lips when his gaze connected with Marjie's. "A recluse must not share all of his secrets." He patted Seren on the back. "But it does bring me to mind. I have a favor to ask of you."

Seren stared at Marjie for longer than Arawn thought proper, before pulling his gaze back to his host. He grinned, not bothered in the least by the scowl he encountered. "Yes? What is this favor?"

Arawn looked around him, not wishing for anyone else to overhear. "I have arranged with Havard to fetch me in an hour's time. He is going to inform me that there is a matter of urgent business which needs my attention in my study."

Seren raised his brows. "Where is the favor?"

"I have not told you." Arawn sighed impatiently. "After about twenty minutes, I need you to tell Miss Fitzroy, rather loudly, that she looks unwell. If she does as I hope, she'll claim a headache. You must then insist that she return to her chambers." Arawn looked at him with wide eyes. "Will you do it for me?"

"Indeed, I shall. But why? To what end?"

Arawn glanced around them again. "I have a surprise for her in the garden."

Seren's head nodded slowly. "Miss Fitzroy. In the garden."

"Yes," Arawn ran a hand along the back of his neck. "But I

need it to not look suspicious. I have no doubt Mr. Pugh will try to monopolize her this evening."

A light dawned in Seren's eyes. "Oh," was all he said.

Arawn frowned, but let it pass. "You will do it?"

"If you are caught, she will be ruined. You must realize that."

Arawn shook his head. "No, there is nothing untoward. Morgan and Susanna, Marjie's maid, will both be there as chaperones. I simply do not wish to give the gossips their fodder."

Seren smiled. "Marjie? You're using Christian names." There was an all too sure tone to Seren's voice that Arawn did not care for.

"Will you do it?"

Seren nodded. "Of course, I will."

Arawn sighed. "Thank you, Seren. I owe you a debt."

"And do not think I will not collect on it." Seren laughed.

"I have no doubt you will." Arawn clapped Seren on the back and moved over to speak with Marjie.

He took her hand in his, the card from his pocket in his palm, and bowed deeply. "Miss Fitzroy. You look very well this evening."

She smiled, even as her brow furrowed when she saw the card in her hand. "Thank you, my lord." She tucked it discreetly into her reticule and glanced over his shoulder. "I should go to my mother, but perhaps we may be paired for a game this evening?"

"I'd have it no other way."

"Ah, Miss Fitzroy," Mr. Pugh's tight, whiney voice sounded behind Arawn, and he clenched his fists at his side. Why his mother continued to invite that man, Arawn would never understand.

Marjie's tight smile was Arawn's only consolation. She did

not seem to like him any more than Arawn did.

"Good evening, my lord." Miss Penry curtsied. "May I claim you as a partner for a hand of whist? I'm very proficient. You'll not regret it."

Arawn smiled. Not because of anything Miss Penry said, but rather because of the slight narrowing of Marjie's eyes.

"Come along," Mrs. Beddoe motioned to their little group. "Here is an available whist table."

Arawn nodded to the others, and they all moved forward. One might think it was Mrs. Beddoe's card party rather than Arawn's mother's.

Mr. Pugh helped Marjie into her seat. And while Arawn would have liked to have been her partner, he was content to sit next to her instead. More than content.

She smiled around the table at everyone, but once all the eyes were directed elsewhere, she slipped the card from her reticule under the table and read his note. She glanced over at him, giving him an almost imperceptible nod.

His plan was a go. His stomach danced and his foot tapped against the leg of his chair.

The first hour was beyond tedious. Arawn partnered the first two rounds with Miss Penry but was then saved by Miss Griffiths for the next round.

Just when it looked as though he must partner with Miss Penry again, Havard approached. Arawn had never been so happy to see the man. The butler leaned forward. "I'm coming to speak with you as you requested, my lord," he whispered.

Arawn furrowed his brow and nodded. "Are you certain it can't wait until tomorrow?"

Havard shook his head. While he did not know what this was about, he did know his part and played it well. "I'm afraid it cannot. I'm sorry to interrupt your evening, my lord."

Arawn heaved a heavy sigh. He flicked a glance at Marjie

but looked away quickly. Watching her would surely foil their ruse. "No need to apologize. It cannot be helped."

Arawn pushed back from the table. "My apologies, Miss Penry. I have an urgent matter I must attend to. I'm afraid you'll need to find another partner."

She scowled at the table.

Arawn made his excuses and headed toward the door. He was nearly free when his mother reached out and grabbed his arm. "Arawn, what is the matter? Why must you leave now?"

He did not like what he was about to do, but it was the only 'matter' he could think of that would cause his mother to excuse him from this party. "Mathias has learned something. He does not believe it can wait."

His mother's face slackened and the guilt in Arawn's stomach burned hotly. "Then you must go."

He tried to smile, but it felt hollow. He was a terrible person. Using his sister's murder to escape a party. That he would be meeting Marjie only made him feel marginally better. If only Ane would remember something.

He kissed his mother on the cheek and left the room, heading straight for the wall-walk where he was to meet Marjie.

Arawn paced the allure between the Chapel Tower and the Stockhouse Tower trying to expel his nervous energy. He had gone through and unlatched all the tower doors between the South Tower where Marjie's room was and the gardens.

He looked down into the inner ward below him. It was dark and quiet. Just as he liked it.

The outer ward had seen dozens, if not hundreds, of parties and guests throughout the centuries. Even for the card party that evening, they greeted everyone in the outer bailey as they entered the castle. But the inner ward was a different story. It was reserved for family and only the most special of guests. It was their private wing, the family quarters, and they did not open it up to just anyone.

But Marjie was not just anyone. No, she was different. She *was* the most special of guests. And Arawn wanted her to love it all, just as much as his mother did. Just as much as he did.

The garden in question was located on either side of the east barbican. Visitors either had to pass through the inner bailey or come by boat. But the wind and waves made a boat approach out of the question. Arawn knew this because he had seriously considered it.

The private gardens were his mother's project. She had picked every plant there, even if they had been planted decades, or in a few rare cases, centuries before. If his mother did not like them, the plants did not stay in her garden, no matter their age.

Only this afternoon, he had gone through the garden with her, and she had told him the name of each plant.

The door in the old Stockhouse Tower let out a low, slow groan. It did not matter how many times the hinges were oiled, it would not be silenced. It was as if it wanted to remind everyone of just how old it really was.

Marjie poked her head out the door. She smiled when she saw him. "Am I early? Shall I wait here?"

He nodded nonchalantly. "Yes, I'm sorry, but the rules say you may not enter until ten o'clock straight up."

She grimaced as she nodded. "Very well. I will wait here until it's time."

She made to duck her head back out, but Arawn hurried over and pulled the door open. "I was jesting with you. Please come in."

She released a nervous laugh. "My apologies. You must think me daft. But as I do not know what you have planned, I was uncertain. I thought perhaps it was a castle rule I had not learned." She raised her brows at him. "Perhaps my castle tour did not teach me everything I need to know."

"Your castle tour was very thorough. Of that, I am certain." He offered his arm to her, patting her hand when she placed it on his. He sucked in a deep breath, suddenly nervous. This scent tour had seemed a splendid idea that afternoon, but now he questioned the decision. What if she thought he was mocking? Or what if she did not like the smell of flowers? Could they make her sneeze? He had seen that happen with others.

He cleared his throat to stop the tide of doubts. "Is Ane with you?" He looked around as if he could see her himself.

Marjie shook her head, frowning. "No. I have not seen her since the parlor this morning."

He sighed, grateful to have the time with just Marjie. Even though he could not see Ane, the thought that she might be lurking—could a ghost lurk?—listening to what they spoke about, made him uncomfortable. Although, he could not say why. It was not as if he would be completely alone with Marjie. His valet, Morgan, would be acting as chaperone. But Morgan did not feel compelled to insert himself into the conversation, as Ane so often did. Indeed, all the ghosts seemed to speak and add their two pennies worth. Arawn was simply not in the mood to share his conversation that evening. "I thought we could tour the family gardens. It was something that you did not see, at least not up close, on the tour."

Marjie smiled, but he could tell she was not as excited as he was, which served only to fuel his doubts. However, he hoped that changed once they entered the garden and he explained his idea.

"Come this way. I have something I wanted to show you."

He led her into the Chapel Tower and motioned her down the stairs. At the bottom, he motioned to the door leading out onto the east barbican. They stepped out onto the cobblestone terrace.

Hanging lanterns lit the garden path, adding a sparkle to the already lovely garden. The colors of the flowers were not immediately discernible, but it did not take away from the glittering beauty.

"It's lovely," Marjie said, but her voice did not hold the awe that true beauty evoked. She must simply say what she had heard everyone else say about such things. It must be her way of blending into a society that likely would not embrace her differences.

"It is lovely, but that is not what we are here for."

She looked up at him and her brow creased. "Then why are we here?"

He leaned forward. "I thought we might take a scent tour of the garden. Their fragrance is just as lovely as their color."

She tilted her head to the side, a slow smile spreading across her face "You planned this just for me."

"Do you see anyone else here with me?"

She swallowed hard, her face glowing and her eyes twinkling in the lamplight. "No one has ever done something like this for me." The awe that had been absent now filled her voice. "Thank you, Arawn."

Never had he seen such a true picture of happiness, and it brought a piercing to his chest. It made him want to see it every day.

"Then it is about time someone did." He held his hand out. "Our first flower is the purple lavender." Marjie leaned over to smell the bloom. When she stood up, Arawn took her place. He was overwhelmed by the floral, woodsy smell that filled his nose. Suddenly he was grateful he'd not taken his mother's advice and smelled the flowers when he'd been there with her. It was so much better discovering it with Marjie.

They moved to the next flower. "Ugh," she wrinkled her nose. "That smells terrible."

Arawn laughed as he joined her with an up-turned nose. "Those are daisies. While they are rather pretty, their appearance does not make them smell any better." He tilted his head to the side. "I suppose you see them similarly to how they actually look."

She reached out her hand and felt the petal.

"This is my favorite," he said as they approached a large bush. "My mother brought a vase of them into my office this morning and I could not help but smell them."

"Yes, I like roses too." She leaned over and sucked in a deep breath. "And their petals are so soft."

"Do you have a favorite flower?"

She pulled her bottom lip between her teeth. "I do. But they're not grown much here. The climate is too cold. But I smelled it in the orangery at Dindale, my uncle's estate. It is called a gardenia."

Arawn put his finger to his lips. "I have never smelled that flower. At least not that I remember."

She looked down at the floor. "You may have, but just did not realize it. After we returned home from Dindale, my mother found a soap with the scent. I have used it ever since."

Arawn was tempted to lean in and smell her, even though it would be completely inappropriate. But he did not, because he did not need to smell her then to know what gardenia smelled like. The smell was forever imprinted in his nose since he'd ridden with her on Taran.

Instead, he led her to the honeysuckle.

"I think perhaps gardenia is my favorite flower also."

CHAPTER TWENTY-ONE

"Is Ane here?" Arawn asked as he entered the parlor.

Marjie's smile faltered. "No. I have not seen her yet today." Why must he ask after Ane every time they were together? While she understood that Arawn and his mother were happy that they still had communication with Ane, no matter the limitations, there were times when Marjie wondered if perhaps the reason he sought her out was in case his sister was nearby and he might have an opportunity to speak with her. Sometimes Marjie felt like she was just his go-between and nothing more.

Although, last evening in the garden did not feel like a go-between situation. Which is why she often felt confused and frustrated.

"The weather is nice today, but I worry it may change before too long. I wondered if we might go for a turn?"

Did he wish to walk around the castle in the hopes they might discover Ane?

Marjie smiled, but she knew it surely did not look sincere. "Of course." She placed the ribbon in her book and stood up.

"Let me put on my half boots and spencer. I will meet you in the outer bailey in ten minutes?"

"You speak as if you have lived in a castle all your life." He winked and her stomach fluttered. How could he make it do that even when she was feeling out of sorts with him? It was quite vexing.

"I believe you are exaggerating, my lord. But to what end?" She raised a brow at him. "I hardly sound as if I've lived in a castle. Rather like I've visited one for nearly a fortnight."

He chuckled. "If you were to accept my offer, I wager no one would know that you haven't always been here."

Marjie hugged her book to her chest. "I spoke with Mama. She said she was not opposed to the idea, but she wished to discuss it with your mother."

Arawn nodded. "I expected nothing less."

She set her book on the side table and moved toward the door. "Give me a moment and I will be ready."

Marjie trudged up the stairs. While she wanted to spend time with Arawn, she did not like feeling as though she were just the means to find who he really wished to spend his time with.

She stepped into her room and closed the door behind her, leaning back against the wood. Why was she allowing herself to worry over such things? It was as if she thought that without Ane, he might find her interesting and wish to spend time just with her. Which was a ridiculous notion. They were from different societies. For him, society revolved around him and those like him. While she stood barely on the outskirts. Even the outskirts were new to her. How could she ever even dream that someone like Arawn would take an interest in her? No, she needed a ghost or some such thing to draw the attention of a gentleman like Arawn.

She moved over to her window and looked down into the courtyard.

Arawn paced back and forth, muttering to himself.

Marjie sighed. She should not keep him waiting. She would just need to remember what she was to him. She was the odd girl who could see and speak to his sister. That was all.

Grabbing her half boots, she hurriedly put them on and shoved her arms into her spencer as she made her way down the stairs.

He stood staring at the door as she stepped out. His gaze traveled from her bonnet to her hem. "Did you match flowers today or is this your own picking?" He stepped next to her.

She looked down at her clothing. "Perhaps a little bit of both."

He motioned her toward the door leading to the west barbican and they set out.

"Where are we going?" she asked.

"It's a surprise."

She grinned. "You are full of those lately."

They crossed the drawbridge and skirted around the walls, walking through a small arched gate in the village wall attached to the castle.

"What is the point of a wall around the village if there are several gates built into it? Does that not defeat the purpose?"

He stopped her on the other side and pointed to a recessed rectangle. "At one time, there was a drawbridge there." He pointed at the ground. "Where we are standing here, there was a small moat. It enabled people to leave the village, but enemies could not get in. But now that it is not needed for defense, there is no need for moats and drawbridges. But it does make it easier to get to the shore without having to go around the village."

"The shore? Is that where we are going?" Marjie clapped

her hands together. The shore was beyond where Ane could go. Or at least Marjie thought it was. Could that mean he wanted to be with her and not Ane? She did not allow herself to continue that thought. It would surely only end up in disappointment.

"I thought we could search for seashells."

"Seashells?" While it did not appeal to her, she was content just to be with Arawn. And if it was a pastime he enjoyed, she did not mind going along.

"I thought we could see how many shells we could find. Then we can sort them into shape and texture—see how they differ."

"Not by color?" She watched him from the corner of her eyes.

"Now what would be the fun in that?"

Her chest squeezed and it was painful to breathe past the lump in her throat. "Thank you, Arawn." She was saying that a lot of late.

"For what?" He acted as if he did not know.

"For creating activities that embrace my deficiency, rather than pretending it does not exist."

He ran a hand through his hair. "You keep calling it a deficiency. But it is not."

"There are few who would agree with you." She tipped her head to the side. "Most see my color blindness as an embarrassment or want to hide it away."

He shook his head. "I disagree. It should be neither hidden nor an embarrassment. It is merely a single piece that makes you who you are. Indeed, I would say it has helped to form your personality and character." He stopped and stared at her. "Perhaps it is why you care so little for society and their opinions."

She averted her eyes. Perhaps that was true at one time,

but she no longer had the luxury not to care. Too much of her future depended on the opinions of those within society.

She cleared her throat, hoping to release the tightness. "Regardless, I appreciate you trying. It is more than anyone else has done for me." She grinned and chuckled lightly. "I never knew that a scent tour was an event. And no one has ever taken me to find seashells." She sighed. "Except, perhaps, for my father. I have a vague memory of searching for them with him." She eyed him. "You remind me a bit of him."

Arawn straightened. "I do? How so?"

Marjie put her finger to her lips and tapped. "He did not see my blindness as a deficiency, either. He said it made me special."

"I believe I would have liked your father, Marjie."

A warmth spread through her, even as the wind whipped her skirt and loose hair around her. "I believe he would have liked you too."

They stepped off the stone stairs and onto the sandy beach. The tide rolled in and out, coming up a little farther each time.

"On the few occasions I've been to the beach, I've never found many different varieties. I hope you are not disappointed if this adventure is not successful."

"Poor form, Marjie," he laughed. "You have already doomed me to failure, and we have yet to look for a single shell."

She shrugged. "I simply do not want you to be disappointed."

He winked at her again. "Why do you not let me worry about that? For now, let's see what we can find."

He handed her a small satin satchel. "Here you are. You may collect your shells in this."

She took it with a smile and looked down at the ground. "Goodness, there are a great many shells on your beach." She was shocked to see shells scattered as far as she could see. And not just the small shells she remembered seeing with her father. There were shells of differing sizes and shapes.

He nodded and gave her a knowing smile. "This is the best place in all of England and Wales to find shells."

The way he looked at her, she thought he might be hiding something. But she had no notion what it could be.

She walked hunched over, picking up shells as fast as she could walk. About twenty rods down, she stood up and called out to him. "It is very odd. The shells seem to end here. I have never seen anything like it."

"Yes, that is very odd, indeed." He called back. "Perhaps it is because that is where Hywel ends, and the next estate begins. After all, it would not do if there were two beaches that had the best shells in all of England and Wales."

Marjie picked up a shell and studied it. How could it be that the shells were only on this stretch of sand? It did not make sense.

Her hands dropped to her side as her mouth gaped open. He didn't…. She looked down the shore at Arawn. He would not have purchased this many shells just for this outing, would he? It would have been very costly. But Marjie could not imagine how else the shells could have come to be on this stretch of beach.

"Arawn," she walked toward him, holding a larger shell up in front of her.

"Yes?" he asked.

"Did you—" She looked back at the section of beach they were on and shook her head. "No, it is not possible."

"What is not possible, Miss Fitzroy?"

She looked at him and then at the shells in her hands. "It is almost as if these shells were deliberately discarded here. And it is odd that there are so many different kinds. Almost as if they were—" She looked up at him. "You didn't, did you?"

"I didn't do what?" he asked.

"These shells look like something one might buy at a sundry shop. They are used to make art."

His lips twitched and his shoulders bounced as if he were trying unsuccessfully to hold back a laugh. "And how would that be a problem?"

She looked around them. "There are so many shells. Several of them were hand-picked. How could you spend so much money on something so frivolous?"

He scoffed. "Are you enjoying yourself?"

"Very much, but that is not the point."

He reached out and took her hands—and shells—in his. "If it brought you joy, it was not frivolous. It was worth every shilling."

She shook her head, but her eyes kept drifting down to their hands. "That is ridiculous. You cannot put a cost on joy."

He shrugged. "Oh, but I can, and I did." He held her hands a little tighter, then pointed out a shell partially covered with sand as the tide washed over it. "Look at that one. You have not collected one like it yet, have you?"

She gave him one more hard look before pulling her hands from his.

He scowled.

She bent forward and dug the shell out of the sand. It was just smaller than the size of her hand and in the shape of an open fan.

Marjie ran her fingers over the ridges on one side of the shell, then she turned it over and did the same thing on the smooth shiny side. How had she never realized how amazing shells were? Thankfully, Arawn had corrected her earlier folly by showing her what she had been missing. This shell was different from all the others. But then, most of them were different from each other.

Arawn grinned.

She looked up at him, the shell sitting in her open palm. "Why did you do this?" He had said her joy was worth the cost. But why did he want her to have joy? What benefit was it to him if she were happy or sad or angry or frustrated? Why did he care?

"Why did I do what?"

"Why did you buy all these shells? We could have looked for shells without you buying them and placing them here." It was not precisely what she wished to ask him. But how could she ask what was truly in her heart? Did he care for her? Was there a chance they could be more than dear friends? Even Marjie, with her penchant to speak without thought, knew she could not simply blurt out those questions.

"That would not have been special. This shore does not have many shells naturally. Those that are here are all the same and usually crushed or broken. How much fun would that have been to pick up the same shell one after another?"

"I appreciate what you did for me." She looked down at the shell in her hand. "But you realize it would have been special because I was hunting for shells with you. It is not the shells that make it enjoyable as much as discovering them together." It was the closest she could come to telling him outright that she loved him.

He heaved a dramatic sigh. "Then we will have plenty of special time together. The beach is full of shells."

She shook her head. "This must have taken you a great deal of time."

He shook his head. "Not as much as you would think. I simply tossed them out onto the sand and water. The waves did most of the work."

"Do you think we will find all of them?" There had to be a hundred shells, maybe more, still littering the beach.

He smiled down at her. "Perhaps over the next five years or so, we will finally collect them all."

She looked at her bulging bag of shells. "I like that idea very much, my lord." He thought they would still see each other in five years? But would that be merely as one friend visiting another or something more? Could she stand to see him every year, knowing how she felt and knowing he did not feel the same?

Opening her satchel, she grabbed a handful of shells and threw them out into the water.

"What are you doing?" He gaped at her.

"I should like to find them for longer than five years, my lord."

"Does this mean you will be here next year to look for them with me?"

"I will always come when you ask it of me." She looked at him, realizing that if friendship was all he could offer, she would take it, simply for the chance to be with him. "If that is what you wish."

He pushed her side curl away from her face. "I can think of nothing I wish for more."

CHAPTER TWENTY-TWO

"Marjie. Marjie, wake up. I have remembered something that might be important."

Marjie squinted into the darkness, wondering who was babbling in her ear when the sun was not yet up.

Ane sat on her bed and leaned close, her hand out as if she wished to shake Marjie awake but without any way to do so.

"Ane? What are you doing? And why are you doing it so early? It is still night."

"I was thinking about the timetable, as you suggested, and I remembered something. But I do not know if it means anything."

Marjie sat up and rubbed her eyes with the palms of her hands. "You remembered something?"

"Perhaps."

Marjie yawned and nodded. "Let me light a candle so I might see you better. We shall write down the timeline and see if what you remembered is of import."

She threw her legs over the side of the bed, reaching for the candle holder she'd left on the side table before retiring. Padding over to the fireplace, she stirred the coals until a small flame appeared. Thrusting the candle into the flame, she added a small amount of light to the room.

As she secured it into the holder, she could not help but notice the time. Two twenty-four. Lawkes, Ane had better have remembered something important.

She released a sigh and sat down at the writing desk. "Now, tell me what you remember." She pulled a sheet of paper from the desk drawer and picked up the quill.

Ane moved from the bed to a chair nearby. "I am not certain it has anything to do with my accident—"

"But it might?"

Ane shrugged. "I do not like thinking that someone set out to deliberately kill me. It has been difficult to think of it in that context."

"But that is what happened," Marjie's voice softened. She could not imagine what it must feel like to know that someone killed her intentionally.

"Yes, I know." Ane pulled her bottom lip between her teeth. "Several days before the accident—"

"How many days? Two? Three?" Marjie drew a line across the paper, making a tick mark in the center and writing *accident* beneath it.

"I do not remember the exact day. Perhaps two?"

Marjie made a mark at the beginning of the line and looked up. "What happened?"

"Dafydd drove me into the village so I might buy some supplies. We were to have a musicale that week."

Marjie wrote *village with Dafydd*. "When was the musicale?"

"The night before my accident."

Marjie's brows rose. "Interesting. I had not realized there were guests in the castle the evening before."

"Do you think one of the guests did it?" Ane asked.

Marjie shrugged. "I have no idea. But it does increase the number of suspects."

"What happened in the village? Anything suspicious?"

Ane shook her head. "No. We saw Mr. Griffiths and Lord Stimple. Oh, and I think we saw Mr. Pugh and Miss Penry." She frowned. "Or maybe that was at a different time." She bit at her fingernail and nodded. "No, I'm quite certain it was the same trip because Miss Penry mentioned the musicale. Which was odd, because neither of them had been invited. It was an awkward conversation."

"Miss Penry was with Mr. Pugh, not her father, Lord Stimple?" That seemed odd, but Marjie did not think it was strange enough to contact the constable.

"Yes, they were." She frowned. "I had not thought about it until you just mentioned it. But that is odd, is it not?"

"Perhaps." Marjie raised her shoulder. "Why were they not invited to the musicale? Since I've been here, they have both been invited to every event."

"It was Arawn's doing. He insisted if we must have a musicale, he did not wish for them to be present. Miss Penry is a thorn in his side and has been for years. She is constantly trying to gain his attention by any means necessary. It's rather vexing."

Marjie nodded. She could not agree more. Miss Penry was one of the biggest flirts Marjie had ever encountered.

"I do not know why, but Arawn has never liked Mr. Pugh. It stems from their childhood. But I don't remember the particulars."

"Did they seem angry about the slight?" Marjie asked as she made a note on the paper.

"No. Indeed, Mr. Pugh mentioned he already had accepted another invitation for that evening. And Lord and Lady Stimple had an event of their own planned. It worked out for the best."

Marjie covered another yawn. "What happened next?"

"I visited the sundry shop and made my purchases. Then Dafydd returned me to the castle."

Marjie rested her elbow on the tabletop and her chin in her hand. Why had Ane thought any of this information needed to be discussed at two o'clock in the morning? Nothing seemed so urgent as to warrant the early interruption.

"On the way back to the castle, Dafydd put his hand over mine. At first I thought it was an accident, but when he didn't remove it, I realized it was intentional."

Marjie sat up straighter. "What did you do?"

Ane bit her lip. "I pulled my hand away and laughed, like I thought it was an accident."

"What did Dafydd do?"

"He apologized and then became very quiet. When we arrived at the castle, he disappeared, and I did not see him again. At least not while I was alive."

Had Dafydd intended to pursue Ane or was it an isolated event? He had to have known it would not be reciprocated. Even if Ane loved him, it did not seem likely that Arawn or Lady Angle would give their approval. Unless Ane went against her family's wishes and married him anyway.

Marjie frowned. Such circumstances were not unheard of. Her own mother had chosen that path. But Ane had given Marjie no reason to believe she would take such actions.

"Had you flirted with him? What would have given him the belief that you would accept him?" Marjie could not picture Ane flirting as she could Miss Penry. But then she had not known the living Ane. Perhaps her character had changed in death.

Ane looked away. "Dafydd and I have always been close. We are nearly the same age and often played together as children. But he knew what was expected of me—of him. He could not have believed anything would come of it."

Ane had not denied it. So perhaps there been some flirting involved.

"Did he threaten you?" Marjie asked.

Ane shook her head. "No, never. Dafydd has never been anything but kind to me. That is why I keep thinking it could have nothing to do with my accident."

"Did you see Dafydd the morning of your ride?"

Ane shook her head. "No. One of the other hands saddled Gwyn for me."

That may or may not be suspicious. He could have avoided Ane because he was embarrassed that he had tried to hold her hand. Or he could have avoided her because he knew about the nail. "And you did not think to mention any of this before?"

"It did not seem important. It was a single event that was never discussed." She sighed. "And I simply cannot believe he could do something like that. We were friends. His family has been in our stables since we bought the castle. How could I suspect him of such a terrible thing?"

Marjie pushed the paper back on the desk and stood up. "I think we need to discuss this with Arawn." She was not to have a full night's sleep. Why should not Arawn have one?

Marjie moved to the bell pull in the corner.

"What are you doing?" Ane asked.

Marjie yawned again. "I am ringing for tea."

"But I thought you wanted to speak to Arawn about it."

"I do. But he is surely asleep, and I see no reason to wake him. Nothing will change in the next few hours." Just as it would not have changed if Ane had waited until morning to wake Marjie. But there was nothing to do about that now.

"But what if Dafydd leaves?" Ane glided to the end of the bed.

"Why would he leave tonight? He has continued to live at the estate the entire time. What makes you think in the next four hours that he will suddenly decide that this morning is the time he needs to leave?" Marjie shook her head. "It is a ridiculous notion."

Ane frowned. "Must you be so mean?"

Marjie's body sagged. "I'm sorry. I did not intend to be mean, Ane."

Ane folded her arms across her chest. "You said I was ridiculous."

"No," Marjie mimicked Ane's stance. "I said the notion that Dafydd would flee, after staying all this time, was ridiculous. You were never mentioned."

"It is the same thing." Marjie did not miss the whine Ane had added to her voice. She had surely been a persuasive one when she was alive. Although now that she thought on it, it seemed to be a family trait.

"Why do we not finish filling out the rest of the timetable. Perhaps it will reveal even more that we might discuss with Arawn, once he is awake."

"I suppose you would think differently if it was you that had been murdered."

Marjie rolled her eyes. Now she used the word 'murdered.'

A very tired looking Susanna entered the room. "You rang, miss?"

"I'm sorry to wake you, Susanna, but I simply cannot sleep." She cast a glance at Ane. "Would you please bring me up some tea. Perhaps that will help."

Susanna nodded and turned from the room.

"Now, come over and let's see what else you can remember."

Marjie pushed out from the desk and stretched her muscles. It was nearly five and she had a nearly completed timetable. Or at least Ane was fairly certain it was complete. Marjie had her doubts.

"It is late enough I think we may go see my brother now." Ane said, her arms folded across her chest. "I'm certain he will be up and readying for his ride."

Marjie was not so confident. Would he be about the castle already or must she seek him out in his bedchambers? "Let me change into a morning gown before we leave. This is already improper enough. I need not show up at his door in my night clothes."

"Make haste then," Ane said impatiently.

Marjie went to the wardrobe and pulled out a morning gown. Hastily, she slipped it on and reached for a wrap. She turned around to Ane's frowning face.

"Are you to wear that wrap with that gown?"

Marjie narrowed her eyes at the girl. "Do you wish to critique my clothing or speak to your brother?"

Ane gave a hasty smile. "You are right. Let's go speak with Arawn."

They moved down the tower steps and through the corridor next to the Great Hall. The castle was eerily quiet. Normally there would at least be sounds from the kitchen, but in the castle, the kitchen was on the other side of the outer bailey, surrounded by thick stone walls. "Do you think he is at breakfast, or must we inquire at his bedchambers?"

Ane shook her head. "He does not eat breakfast until after his morning ride."

Marjie grunted. "I do not think I should go into the inner bailey without his permission."

Ane gave her a bland look. "I am still part of this family and I give you permission. Go, tell Arawn what I remembered."

"I'm not certain the rest of the family will see it that way," Marjie muttered through gritted teeth. But she pushed open the gate into the inner bailey. "I do not even know where Arawn's chambers are."

Ane pointed straight ahead. "It is up those stairs."

Marjie sucked in a deep breath, barely believing she was about to do this. A lady did not knock on a gentleman's door at this time of the morning. But Ane would not be put off any longer.

When they reached the door, Marjie stood on the landing with her hand poised to knock. But she couldn't do it. What would he think of her? She had proven to him time and again that she was completely improper. She spoke whatever came to her mind with nary a thought about it first. But this was beyond the pale. She was invading his private spaces and before the darkness had even left. He would surely throw her out at first light.

"Go on, knock," Ane said impatiently.

Marjie closed her eyes as she rapped three times. "Arawn?" she called out.

The door flew open, and he stood before her, his hair rumbled, and his shirt tucked haphazardly into his breeches. "Marjie? What is wrong?" His eyes looked widely around as if he thought the castle might be under attack.

Marjie opened her mouth to speak but her tongue refused to work when she noticed the hair on his chest peeking out of his shirt at the base of his throat. A breath pushed out of her gaping mouth.

Lawkes, he was even handsome when he was rousted out of bed.

He stepped forward and gently put his hands on her upper arms. Worry clouded his eyes. "Marjie, what is wrong?"

She licked her lips, and his gaze dropped, but he hurriedly refocused on her braid hanging over her shoulder. She released a shaky laugh. In her haste, and amid Ane's nagging, she had forgotten to twist it up into a knot. Her fingers instinctively lifted and trailed down it. "Ane insisted I hurry. I must have forgotten my hair."

He seemed to realize the danger was not imminent, because he relaxed and leaned against the doorway. "You should not scare me like that. Although," he lifted a hand to touch her braid but dropped it before he completed the task, "I find I do not mind the state of your hair."

She laughed awkwardly.

Ane nudged her, but instead of a solid poke of an elbow, all Marjie felt was an intense coldness that pricked all the way to her bones. It was a feeling Marjie could not say she had enjoyed, nor become accustomed to. "Tell him what I remembered."

"Ane came to me this morning—"

He sighed. "I should have known it was Ane. Tell her we are doing the best we can, but we have too little information."

Ane stomped her foot, but no noise sounded, making her cry out in frustration. "I would figure it out myself if I could. But I cannot."

Marjie put out a hand to the side to calm the agitated ghost. "She remembered something that may be helpful."

"Then why do you not meet me in my study." He gave her one more appraising glance, smiling when he reached the wrap secured tightly around her shoulders. "It is the room just below."

"Thank you, Arawn. And I'm sorry for waking you. Ane

thought it important to catch you before you left on your morning ride."

He glanced out the door. "Yes. She must have neglected to tell you that would not happen for several hours yet."

As soon as Arawn's door was securely closed, Marjie rounded on Ane. "Why did you make me wake him? I told you he would not be awake," Marjie muttered out of the side of her mouth. She hurried down the stairs. "He is surely unhappy with me."

Ane gave her a pert look. "Arawn looked anything but angry. Indeed, I half thought he might try to kiss you."

"What?" Marjie's fingers flew to her lips. How did she know it was Marjie's greatest wish?

The door to Arawn's study opened from inside and he motioned them in. His hair was not quite as disheveled, but neither was it combed. It was more like he had run his fingers through it to tamp down the worst of it.

Marjie paused, the thought of running fingers through Arawn's hair rooting her in place. Would she ever grow accustomed to seeing him in these different situations? Not that she would be at Hywel long enough to grow accustomed to it.

"Marjie, he is waiting for you to speak." Ane's insistent voice sounded next to her.

Marjie jerked. "I beg your pardon?" She asked as she slid into the chair opposite his desk.

Arawn grinned at her as if he knew exactly what she was thinking. Her face burned with embarrassment. "What did Ane tell you?" He leaned forward, resting his elbows on the desk.

Marjie leaned forward also, although she did not know why. "She remembered something from the day before the *accident.*" She looked over at Ane and her eye caught on a painting hanging on the wall just inside the door. And not just any painting. *Her* painting. The dreadfully miscolored landscape she had done on the barbican when he had discovered her defic—she stopped, knowing he did not like that term—discovered what made her unique. But why had he hung it in his study? Perhaps so no one would see and wonder at it? But why hang it up at all? Marjie would likely have tossed it into the fire.

"You mean her murder?" Arawn's raised voice pulled her gaze back to him.

Marjie threw her hands up in the air. "Yes, exactly." She turned to his sister. "You see Ane? You are the only one who does not think of it in that way."

Arawn grinned, but then became serious. "What did she remember?"

Marjie told Arawn everything Ane had told her about Dafydd, with Ane jumping in and adding anything that she remembered or that she thought Marjie had not covered adequately.

Arawn sat back in his chair and sighed. "Dafydd? I have a hard time seeing him as a plotting killer."

Ane sat back in the chair next to Marjie. "I don't like the thought either. But it is the only thing that seems out of place."

Marjie repeated Ane's words. She leaned in even farther. "This does not mean he did it, Arawn. You must talk to him—let him explain himself." Her voice was barely above a whisper. She had met Dafydd and agreed with Arawn and Ane. He did not seem like one who would exact revenge. He had been nothing but kind to her.

"But if it is true, it will kill Mathias to have Dafydd imprisoned." Arawn looked weary.

"Wait, imprison Dafydd?" Ane nearly shrieked.

Marjie glanced over at her and then turned back to Arawn. "Ane seems to think imprisoning him is too harsh."

"He killed her," Arawn said empathically.

"*Possibly* killed her. We hardly have irrefutable proof." Marjie nodded. "Perhaps it would be best if you asked him if he saw anything suspicious. Or questioned him about his intentions toward Ane, rather than accusing him outright."

Arawn's brow creased. "It would explain some things. Dafydd has been acting oddly of late. He did not want you to use that saddle the first time we went riding. At the time, I thought he felt as I did. That it was simply because it was Ane's saddle. But perhaps it was because he already knew the nail was there."

"But if it was him, why had he not removed the nail already?" Marjie wondered. It seemed the most logical thing. "Dafydd is in the stables every day. It would be simple enough for him to remove it without anyone noticing. Why leave it in the saddle to be discovered?"

"Perhaps he forgot. Or maybe the chance never presented itself. The stables are busy, and he would not wish to draw attention to himself. In the aftermath of the accident, there was so much going on. And when it was seen as an accident, he had no reason to worry. He likely meant to do it, but then forgot as time went on. You were the first to use either of the side saddles since Ane." Arawn rubbed at the stubble along his jawline and Marjie was momentarily transfixed. Was it possible he looked even more handsome unshaven? "It is also odd that he is the one who withdrew that nail after it was discovered."

"None of this proves he did it," Marjie interjected.

"No, but it does mean we need to speak with him. If he did not do it, perhaps he knows who did."

He leaned back in his chair.

"But if he knows, would he not have said something sooner?"

Arawn nodded. "Which does not speak in his favor that he has not."

"Or it says he does not know anything more than you or I do." She slouched in the chair. "What will you do if your suspicions are correct?"

"I don't know." He shrugged. "I will see what he has to say for himself first." He looked at the empty seat next to her.

Marjie nodded.

He sighed. "I'll speak with Dafydd after breakfast. One way or another, I hope to have our murderer identified by the end of the day."

CHAPTER TWENTY-THREE

"I still cannot imagine it is Dafydd," his mother said as they walked toward the stables. "And how are you going to tell him you learned this information? You can't very well tell him that Ane's ghost told you. The Welsh people are superstitious by nature, but I don't think they will believe you. At least not until closer to All Hallows Eve."

Arawn looked over at his mother. "I had not considered it. But we can hardly wait until *Nos Galan Gaeaf* to speak to Dafydd. It's still months away. What shall I tell him?"

His mother slowed. "Would waiting ensure Ane was here longer?" She twisted at her fingertips. "I confess I would be willing to ignore what Dafydd did if it meant Ane stayed, even if she is just a ghost."

"You cannot mean that, Mother. We cannot allow the person who killed her to go free just so Ane stays. We do not even know that she will. She could disappear tomorrow, regardless of what we do. We simply do not know." He swallowed as another realization struck him. "And once Miss

Fitzroy leaves, we will have no way to speak with Ane even if she is still haunting us."

"I would hardly call what she does haunting, Arawn." She tilted her head to the side. "But does it not make sense that she is only here to discover what happened to her?"

Arawn shrugged. "I do not believe so. After all, Gwen and Gilford know the detail of their deaths. It is not a great secret. Yet, they remain."

"You are right." His mother sighed. "I just feel as if we are losing her all over again."

Arawn placed a hand on his mother's shoulder, giving it a squeeze. "I know, Mama. But at least we had another fortnight with her."

His mother nodded. "You have not called me Mama since you left for Oxford." Her voice was full of nostalgia. She squared her shoulders. "If Dafydd is responsible, do you really feel comfortable having him around the estate? What if he should kill someone else?"

"I highly doubt he is dangerous to others. I believe he did what he did during a fit of jealousy or revenge." He perked up. "We will say we found Ane's diary."

"That may work," her steps slowed as they arrived at the stables "I don't know if I can do this," his mother whispered. "What about poor Mathias?"

"We don't have a choice, Mother." He sucked in a deep breath and walked through the archway.

Mathias was in the center of the yard, talking to Owain, his youngest son. He lifted his eyes to them and smiled. But his smile dropped when he saw their faces. He hurried over. "My lord, have you discovered something?"

"I am not certain, yet. I had hoped we might talk to Dafydd."

"Dafydd?" Mathias licked his lips. "I already spoke with him, and he said he did not see anything."

"Mathias, I wish to speak with Dafydd. Unless you know more than you are telling me?" Arawn did not like intimidating people, but he would if he must.

Mathias' eyes widened. "No, my lord. I do not know anything I have not already told you. I will have Dafydd fetched immediately." He looked at Owain and snapped his fingers. As if understanding the signal, Owain hurried into the stable on the right.

Moments later, Dafydd's head poked out into the lowering sunlight. He stepped out and his shoulders hunched more than usual. He walked slowly over to them. "Good day, my lord."

Arawn's eyes narrowed. Could he really have killed Ane? He thought back over the months since the accident happened and realized it was around the same time that Dafydd's appearance had begun to change. Was it due to the guilt he felt? Arawn's mouth set into a hard line. If it had been his fault, he deserved to feel guilty.

"It has come to my attention that you attempted to hold Ane's hand when you took her to town in the days before her murder."

Dafydd flinched at the word and Arawn was happy to see he had hit his mark.

"Where did you learn of that...my lord?" He hastily added.

"I am not required to explain myself to you," Arawn bore his gaze into the man. "But as I have a very serious charge to lay at your feet, I shall tell you. My sister kept a diary. She wrote of the incident and how you refused to speak to her afterward. She was surprised by your behavior, and I must admit that I am as well."

Dafydd's already pale complexion whitened even more.

"Yes, I did as she claimed." He licked his lips. "But when she so kindly allowed us to pretend it was an accident, I realized my folly. I know an alliance between us would never have been accepted," he dipped his head to Arawn and his mother, "by society." He swallowed. "I was embarrassed by my actions. That is why I did not speak to her. Not because I held any ill-will."

Arawn took a deep breath. "Then you did not put the nail on the underside of the saddle?"

Dafydd's mouth dropped open in what appeared to be genuine shock. "I beg your pardon?" He glanced over at his father and his body seemed to curl in on itself. "Of course not, my lord. I could never harm Ane. We were dearest friends. I could never—." His face paled even more, and he looked as though he might be sick. A mark in his favor but not proof he was innocent.

"Do you know who did put the nail in the saddle?"

Dafydd shook his head. "No, my lord. I have tried to remember the events leading up to that day. But nothing stands out as odd."

Arawn's jaw worked. The man seemed sincere. But perhaps he was simply acting the part of the innocent.

His mother put a hand on his arm. "I believe him, Arawn."

The problem was, so did Arawn.

Mathias twisted his cap nervously. And rightly so. His son's fate was in Arawn's hands. And even if he could not prove his responsibility in Ane's death, Dafydd could be turned out from the estate for even attempting to hold Ane's hand.

"Devil take it!" Arawn slammed his hand into the palm of his other hand. They were back to the beginning. Where were they to go from there?

Marjie had decided that after church would be the perfect time to work on her painting. Apart from the bit she painted that first day, Arawn had not seen this picture. She did not know why she wished to wait to show it to him until it was complete. Perhaps because the first one had been such an utter disaster. She shook her head, still baffled at why it hung in Arawn's study.

She wanted him to like her new painting. Even though she knew it would never be as skillfully painted as someone who could see color, she wanted him to admire it for what it was. Her view of the world. In a sense, a rejection of the painting would be a rejection of her. And while she expected it from others, Arawn had been different thus far. But how much longer could that last?

She squinted at it critically. Looking out over the landscape, she could say the painting looked remarkably similar. Lovely, in fact. It was one of her most proficient works. And yet, she knew it was inferior to those with the proper colors. But how was she to ever compete with those pieces when she knew nothing other than what was on the canvas in front of her.

She was nearly finished. All that remained was to add a little more depth to the clouds in the sky and a few waves to the water, visible only at the far side of the painting. Then she would take it to her room to allow it to dry.

Arawn need not even know it was finished. She need not show it to him if she did not wish to.

"That is very pretty." Ane's voice sounded over Marjie's right shoulder. "I confess, when Arawn mentioned that he had only given you the colors black and white, I did not leave much hope that the picture would amount to much. But I find I am very much surprised."

Marjie was not surprised. Not with how the picture looked

nearly finished or by Ane's assumption of what it would look like. Many people could not imagine that something only in black, white, and grays could be beautiful. But Marjie knew differently. While she knew not what color looked like, she thought the world around her was lovely.

She was tempted to add some flowers—maybe some roses and gardenias—even though they were nowhere to be seen in her current view. It would serve as a reminder for her when she and her mother left Hywel and returned home. A reminder that there were good people, even in the *ton*. Her painting would always remind her of Arawn. And even Lady Angle. She had been nothing but kind to Marjie and her mother.

"I knew it would be pretty. But then I already had the finished painting in my mind." Marjie turned and looked at Ane.

Ane came and stood at her elbow. "I would not have thought you could achieve the amount of depth and texture with so limited colors." She looked out at the view in front of them. "But you have done so masterfully. You are much more proficient at painting than I ever was."

"I am certain you are proficient. But if you did not enjoy doing it, I should think it would reflect your lack of passion."

"Is that what makes yours so inviting? Passion?" She squinted at the painting, turning her head at different angles.

"I believe you can feel if a person enjoyed themselves while they created it."

"Hmmm," Ane clasped her hands in front of her. "Perhaps you are right." She looked back at Marjie. "Has Arawn learned anything new about my *accident?*" She said the last word lower and slower.

Marjie nearly rolled her eyes but paused. The situation must be very hard on Ane. "He spoke to Dafydd."

Ane's eyes widened. "And what did he say?"

"He said he would never harm you."

"I did not think he would." And smiled sadly. "I feel bad for even bringing it up."

"He did say he avoided you because he was embarrassed by what he'd done."

"Do you want to know a secret?" Ane leaned in closer. "Knowing what I do now, I would not care about society and the rules. I would marry him if he asked." She cast her gaze downward. "But that realization came much too late."

Marjie reached out to put her hand atop Ane's but it dropped through, giving her a cold shudder instead. "I'm sorry, Ane."

Ane shrugged. "Then we are back at the beginning? We have no other clues?"

Marjie grimaced. "That is my understanding."

Ane's whole countenance fell.

"Marjie," light footsteps sounded behind her, and her breath caught in her throat.

Arawn.

If he found her now, he would surely see the painting. But what could she do? She could not deny him the chance to see it if he asked, could she?

She stood up and placed herself between the canvas and Arawn.

He smiled as he approached. "Is Ane here?" he asked as he nearly always did when he approached her within the castle grounds.

Marjie's eyes narrowed slightly, but just as quickly she pushed it away. What did she care if he only wished to be with her so he might speak to his sister?

"She is."

His brow furrowed. "*Diwrnod da,* Ane."

"*Diwrnod da*, Arawn."

He looked at Marjie. "Good day, Marjie. I hope you had a pleasant time at church. You were rather quiet in the carriage on the way back."

Marjie shrugged. "I was just excited to come and paint."

He grinned. "Ah, the painting. I have been anticipating its completion." He twisted his head slightly and raised a brow. "Is it finished?"

Marjie shook her head. "No, not yet."

Ane peered around her back. "It looks finished to me."

Marjie ignored Ane's comment. Sometimes it was beneficial that she was the only one who could hear Ane. "I don't want you to see it until it is finished."

He frowned. "But the anticipation is going to be my undoing." He produced a rather pitiful-looking pout. "Please?"

Ane sighed and rolled her eyes. "When did he begin doing that? It does not suit him."

Marjie chuckled. "Your sister says pouting does not suit you."

The smile fell from his face and the tips of his ears reddened. "I very nearly forgot Ane was here."

"Oh, Marjie. I think you embarrassed him." Ane looked only slightly repentant.

"Me? I should think it was you who embarrassed him. I was only repeating what you said." Marjie tried to hold back her grin. It was surely rude to laugh at his discomfort.

His brow knit for a moment and then he lifted his eyes to Marjie. "Would you like to go for a ride? There is something I think you would enjoy seeing."

"And we must use a horse to get there?"

He shrugged, "I suppose we could walk, but it would take the whole of the day."

While she was not as frightened as she had been immediately following the accident, she still did not love riding as she had before. Yet, Arawn seemed hellbent on her overcoming her fear and being comfortable on a horse again. She supposed she should be grateful to him for that. It would be a shame if she never rode again, especially when she had enjoyed it so much previously.

"Very well. When do you wish to leave?"

"I believe the perfect time to see the place will be at two."

She nodded. "Perfect. That will give me time to finish my painting."

He stood looking expectantly at her. "Finish it alone?" He turned a wicked grin on her. "Perhaps I could go off into the distance and you could paint me into your picture."

"I hardly think that proper, Arawn."

"Very well," he grumbled but then winked at her. Her stomach did a sort of flip-flop.

"Then I can see the painting before we leave?"

She shook her head. "I am certain it will take several days for the paint to dry completely." And perhaps by then, he will have forgotten about it.

He took a step closer to her. "Why do I get the feeling you are trying to prevent me from seeing it?" He lifted his head as if trying to see over her shoulder.

She shrugged. "I suppose I worry you will be disappointed. You have very high hopes for this painting. I am not certain even Da Vinci could live up to them."

His lips pushed out, his head moving back and forth. "I expect nothing but a little insight into how you see the world. That is my only expectation."

"I do not know why you will not show him," Ane said. "I am certain he will like it."

But she did not want him to simply like it, she wanted him to love it. She needed him to, what? Understand it? Or rather understand her. Because perhaps if he could understand and love a black and white painting—he might be able to love her.

She pulled her bottom lip between her teeth. "Then I suppose you may see it now. It is finished." She did not like how invested she was in his opinion. It seemed to her that no matter his response, it would only end in heartache for her. If he hated it, what did that say about his opinion of her? But if he loved it? She shook her head. There was nothing to be done if he loved it. They were of two different societies. And even if he thought, only for a moment, that it did not matter, she did not believe she could ruin his reputation. No matter what he believed.

He put his hand to his heart. "You were lying to me? Miss Fitzroy, how could you?"

She rolled her eyes as she stepped to the side, and he moved closer, leaning over so he was seeing it at eye level.

A soft whistle sounded, but she did not know if it was a good whistle or a bad one. She leaned toward the latter as whistling in general tended to be frowned upon. "It is magnificent." He breathed out. He lifted a hand, almost as if he wanted to touch it, but she swatted it away. "The paint is still wet in some places."

He glanced over at her. "I'm sorry. I was not thinking." He smiled as he stood up straight and took a step back. "I should like to buy this painting for the Lesser Hall."

"Wh-w-what?" she stuttered. "Why should you wish to do that?" Could she sell him this painting? It was all she would have to remind her of Hywel. After a time, would she remember all the details without the painting to remind her?

"Because it—," he turned to look at her and there was a look in his eyes she had never seen before. "I just do."

She rolled her eyes again. "You need not buy it. I will give it to you." She had not anticipated how much it hurt to offer it to him. "You did buy the canvas and the paints, after all." Perhaps she could make a trip into the village and purchase another canvas so she might quickly paint another piece that she could take with her back to Yorkshire.

Ane stood there silently watching them. Her brow was crinkled, and her lips pushed out slightly. But what she was thinking about, Marjie had no idea.

CHAPTER TWENTY-FOUR

Marjie pushed Gwyn through the thick grasses and underbrush, trying to keep up with Arawn. They had passed through the village and ridden to the opposite side of the peninsula from where they had ridden before. Poor Dafydd rode a fair distance back, surely still feeling the sting of being accused of killing Ane. He did not look angry, simply...defeated. And perhaps sad. Was it possible he missed Ane nearly as much as Arawn and his mother?

"How much farther?" she asked, ready to dismount and walk for a bit.

"It is just up ahead." He looked back over his shoulder, a hint of concern in his deep brown eyes. "Is there a problem?"

"No, I would simply prefer to walk for a bit. That is all."

The bushes opened up, and she saw an old, ruined building. "What is it?" She nodded in front of her.

He grinned. "That is what we came to see. It is an old abbey."

She flicked the reins, quickening Gwyn's trot. "Oh, Arawn. I love it." She looked at him from the side of her eyes. "How did you know to bring me here?"

He shrugged. "There is little you have seen that you have not enjoyed. I thought this would be no different. And the coloring is such that I thought we might both see it similarly."

She slid off the saddle and tied the reins to a nearby fence railing. Where the walkway had once been, weeds and grass grew up between the cracked and broken cobblestones. The roof of the abbey was no longer present and much of the structure had crumbled, leaving only partial walls and the bell tower standing.

Arawn came to stand next to her. "What do you think?"

"It is charming. How long ago was it inhabited? I would guess, as many others were, that this abbey was sold as a private residence?"

He looked to be thinking. "I should think it has been at least fifty years since someone lived here. I do not believe it was inhabited even in my father's lifetime. But I am uncertain about my grandfather's." He motioned her forward, and they walked through what had once been a doorway but now was just a large hole in the wall. Piles of rubble lay on either side of the entrance. The stones of the floor were still intact, although several patches of grass pushed up through the cracks.

"It is both sad and wonderful to see it like this."

"How do you mean?"

She sighed. "It is sad that no one cared for it enough to keep it up. It is like so many of the old castles that are only ruins."

"And what is wonderful?" He asked.

"That these old buildings resist disappearing for good. It is as if they refuse to be forgotten."

"I think this old abbey might be a bit like you, Marjie."

She snickered. "And how is that, my lord? It lacks all color?"

He shook his head. "No, just like the abbey, I do not believe I will ever be able to forget you."

She swallowed and ducked her head, uncertain of what to say. What was even the proper reply? No one had ever said anything like it to her, so she had no idea.

Instead, she chose to ignore it. She turned and looked around at what would have been the interior of the nave. It was open to the sky above. However, the bell tower at the far end shaded it from the sunlight.

"Is the bell still there?"

Arawn nodded. "As far as I know. Mr. Potter, the vicar, comes once a year to check that it is secure. The last thing I would want is for it to fall on someone visiting."

"Does it ever ring?"

Arawn put his finger to his lips and twisted his head slightly. "If you listen closely, you can hear the wind ring it."

Marjie followed his lead and turned her head toward the tower. A slight echoing hum drifted on the breeze. "Has it ever been rung for real? More than just the wind?"

He nodded. "The bell rings every year on Easter and on every day leading up to Twelfth Night."

She sighed. What would it be like to hear it? He had invited her mother and her to stay on until then, perhaps she might come to know if it sounded as rich as she believed.

They walked through the nave and out into the cloister. It seemed to be the most intact part of the abbey. It still had the roof overhead and most of the rock walls separating it from the courtyard garden. But there were several places where the rocks had collapsed, providing many smaller entrances into the garden. Marjie stepped over some stones that filled the walkway and moved out into the courtyard. "Does this have several other names, or is it just a courtyard?"

Arawn looked confused for a moment, but then a smile

split his face. "I don't believe so. But then I have never lived in an abbey, so I cannot be certain." He looked around at the clumps of now wild sage and lavender. "It may have been called the garden or even an herbarium, as this is likely where they would have grown such things."

Marjie lifted her face, looking up at where the upper floors had surely been.

Arawn came to stand next to her, looking up at the same place.

The bell in the tower rang loudly, causing both Marjie and Arawn to jump. But once the initial surprise was over, Marjie grinned at Arawn. "I knew it would sound beautiful."

It rang loudly, covering the sounds all around. But instead of the sound growing quieter, it only grew in strength until hundreds, perhaps even thousands of birds flew out of the bell tower. They flew in all directions, including through the cloister and into the garden, squawking and flapping to find their freedom.

Marjie let out a scream and buried her face in Arawn's chest.

He wrapped his arms around her and held her close, protecting her from the birds swooping around them. "You need not worry. It is only birds, not bats."

"It does not matter. I do not care for either of them." Her muffled words sounded as tense as her body felt beneath his fingers.

The noise was nearly deafening. But after what seemed an eternity, the only sound was her whimpering.

"Marjie, are you well? They are gone now. You are safe." His arms stayed wrapped around her as she slowly lifted her head and looked up at him.

He looked at her, worry lines creased around his eyes and mouth. "Marjie?"

She realized she had not answered his earlier question. She nodded. "I am fine. I-I just don't like birds or bats."

"Yes, I believe I made that discovery on my own." He smiled down at her. "I can understand bats, but what is wrong with birds?"

"When I was little, I was throwing small seeds to the birds while I waited for my father to load his shipment onto a cart. All at once, a million birds swarmed me, pecking at me if they could not get to my seeds. I have hated them ever since." She bit down on her lip to keep from cringing. "I can admire them from afar. But I do not like to see them up close."

He grinned. "A million birds, you say?" His voice was soft, with a hint of laughter in it.

She nodded and smirked. "Yes. *At least* a million."

His gaze turned serious. "That must have been frightening." He reached up and pushed a stray hair away from her eyes.

"It was," her voice came out sounding small and quiet. Not for the first time, Marjie wondered what it would be like to be kissed by Arawn. She could not remember ever desiring it as much as she did then. But then, she had never felt for anyone what she felt for Arawn.

It would surely be a mistake, but perhaps a mistake worth making. He had said that he would never forget her. And while she could surely say the same about him, would it not hold especially true if he kissed her? Surely, she would never forget such a thing.

His head dropped closer to her, and she thought her hopes might come true.

She stretched up on her tiptoes, inviting him to kiss her if he wished. She closed her eyes. Lud, she hoped he wished to.

He closed the distance, his lips brushing against hers before pressing down and taking her lips in his.

Fireworks popped inside her brain, and her knees felt weak. Lawkes, it was so much better than she had imagined. A fire warmed inside her chest and wisped its way to the tips of her toes and fingertips. She leaned closer, grabbing his coat and curling her fingers into his lapels, needing it both for support and to be nearer to him.

He deepened the kiss, and Marjie thought she might burst from sheer joy, until the cackle of laughter jerked them apart.

Four young boys stood gawking through the large holes in the walls of the abbey.

Marjie's face heated and Arawn took a step back.

Dafydd yelled at the boys and chased them away. Marjie did not miss that he averted his eyes from them.

Arawn cleared his throat. "Perhaps we should return to the castle. I believe you have had enough surprises for one day."

Marjie nodded but then ducked her head as she put her hands to her face to cool it. But it did little good. Her hands were nearly as warm as her face. Saints above, what had she done?

CHAPTER TWENTY-FIVE

Marjie did not know what to think. She pulled the satin bag from her side table and pulled out the large, fan-shaped shell she and Arawn had found on the beach the day before last.

What kind of man spent a small fortune on shells just so he could spread them along the beach for them to find? And then they had not even collected them all, leaving some so they might be found later. A later time together.

She ran her finger over the rough ridges. She might think he was simply being a proper host, if not for the kiss they shared yesterday after church. A kiss that still left her lips tingling.

She lightly brushed her fingers across her mouth.

What would she do when she and her mother finally returned home? They had accepted the offer to stay on until after Twelfth Night, but then what?

While neither had expressed their feelings aloud, after the kiss Marjie thought Arawn's feelings might be similar to hers. But no matter how much she thought about it or what scenarios she came up with, she could not see a connection between them working out. They came from two different worlds. And her world did not fit inside his. At some point in time, even if he loved her, he would come to resent her. Society did not look favorably on those who tried to elevate their stations. And they did not appreciate those who aided in it.

A tightness formed in her chest, and she rubbed at it.

Perhaps Arawn and his mother would come to Yorkshire to visit. The tightness increased as she thought about how unlikely that would be. Besides, where would they stay? She and her mother did not have a large estate. They could barely afford the small cottage with only three servants.

She should reconcile herself that she would not be looking for more shells on the beach with him in the years to come. Nor was she likely to see him once she left Wales.

Arawn said he would never forget her. But could he promise such things? As much as she hated to admit it, she no longer remembered every detail of her father's face and she had looked on it for more than a decade. How long would it take for Arawn to forget about her? A year? Or perhaps only a month or two?

For the first time in her life, anger toward her grandfather and all they had suffered at his hands welled up inside her. But she quickly tamped it down. Would she be the same person if she had been raised within the *ton* rather than outside it? If her mother had not been a seamstress, would Marjie have the same views or opinions? It was possible she might still have met Arawn, but would they have become friends? Would he have kissed her in the abbey? Or would she have turned out more like Miss Penry?

Perhaps she should not place blame on her grandfather after all. For all the questions about their future, Marjie would not change the last fortnight for anything. Nor would she trade the friendship or whatever it was she had with Arawn.

Arawn had made Marjie feel something she had not felt since her father died. He had made her feel special. He had made her feel as though she had something to give that no one else could. And he was interested in that something. He wanted to know what she thought—how she saw the world. And that was better than any gift she could imagine. Even if it was only for a few months while they were in Wales.

She flipped the shell over and pressed the smooth, shimmery side to her cheek, delighting in the cool sensation. What would she do when she returned to being the insignificant daughter of a former modiste that no one cared what she thought or how she saw the world?

A knock sounded at the door and her mother poked her head in. "Poppet?"

Marjie smiled at her mother. "*Bore da*, Mama."

She stepped inside and raised her brows. "You are speaking Welsh now, are you?"

Marjie shrugged. "I only know a handful of words. Most of it still sounds like gibberish to me."

Her mother picked up the fan-shaped shell off the table. "What is this?"

Marjie feigned ignorance. "It is a shell, Mama."

"I am aware of what shells look like, Poppet." Her mother looked at her blandly. "I simply wondered where it came from."

"I found them while taking a turn on the beach with Lord Angle." Marjie motioned to the bag on the table. "They all came from the beach."

Her mother reached for the satin bag and opened it, dropping several more shells into her hand. "The beach? These do not look like shells collected from the beach. At least not any

265

beach near here. They look like something purchased from a shop for shell art."

Marjie nodded. "Yes. I believe that is the case."

"Then how did you find them on the beach?" Her mother took in a frustrated breath.

Marjie smiled softly. "It was Lord Angle's doing. He wanted us to have an activity to do together. And as their beach has very few shells, he felt he needed to supplement it."

Her mother blinked at her, still clearly confused.

"He suggested we go shell hunting because he said that in most shells, it is not the color that makes them unique and pretty but the shape and texture, which are both things that I can see."

Her mother nodded slowly. "He knows you do not see color?"

Marjie guffawed. "It was rather obvious when he saw my first painting."

"But you know where the colors should go. I know it usually does not look exactly like the scene you are painting, but you do well enough."

Marjie gave her mother an exaggerated look. "Lady Angle was very helpful and had a maid collect the colors for me."

Her mother grimaced. "Good gracious, I am certain it was hard to hide it after that." She looked down at the shells. "He purchased all these only to spread them out on the beach so you could find them?"

Marjie nodded. "Yes. We did not even collect them all. He said maybe next year we may see what else we can find."

"He has asked you to come back?" her mother asked. She looked as though she were trying to hold back a smile.

"He did not ask for a specific date, but he did infer that he would like us to come back." She shook her head. "But I am not certain it is wise."

"Why, Poppet?"

Did she dare confide in her mother? She had never hidden anything from her before. Why should she start now? "I'm afraid it will hurt too much when it is time to leave again."

"And why is that?"

Marjie closed her eyes, feeling Arawn's warm breath on her cheek and the whisper feel of his lips as they brushed against hers.

She sucked in a deep breath. "Mama, how did you know you were in love with Papa?"

The shell stilled in her mother's hands. "I did not realize it at first. It was nothing I had ever felt before."

Marjie frowned. "That does nothing to help me understand. There are many feelings I have never experienced before. Such as when I ate the *rarebit* and the *bara lawr*."

Her mother smiled. "I see your point." She bit her lip but did not say anything more. Marjie knew she was not ignoring the question, but rather thinking on the best way to answer it.

"I think perhaps there were several things that told me I loved your father."

Marjie scooted forward. "Such as?"

"For one, I could not imagine living without him. Just the thought of leaving him to return home was unacceptable. It was one of the first signs. But it was also how he made me feel." A soft smile formed on her mother's lips. "He made me laugh, but he also made me think. He treated me like I was the Queen herself, doing everything he could to make me happy." She sighed. "I thought leaving everything behind—my father, my dowry— proved to him that I loved him. But then I realized it might really mean I was simply immature. It was when I realized that I would let him go, if that was what was best for him, that I knew I truly loved him."

"But you didn't let him go." Marjie frowned.

"You're right, I didn't. But I would have. My father made many threats against him and his business. I told your father I could not allow him to take such risks for me." She smiled. "But your father said I was worth the risks. And that was when I knew he loved me too. He married me even though I had no dowry, no title, and nothing to bring to the marriage." A little tear formed in the corners of her eyes. "And then he worked to his dying day to see that I was happy. It was not always easy, and I was not happy every single minute of every single day. There were still vexations. But your father always made me feel loved and cherished."

She glanced over at Marjie. "Poppet, do you think yourself in love?"

Majie nodded. "I believe I am. Oh, Mama. I have never felt this way about anyone. The thought of returning to Yorkshire leaves an empty hole in my stomach and heart. But I know nothing can come of it. And I do not know if I can go through it again next year."

"Are you in love with Lord Angle?"

Majie swallowed and nodded.

"Does he love you in return?"

"He has not said it. But there are times when I believe he might. But I know we are too different. It can never be."

Her mother nodded thoughtfully, looking back at the shell. "Yes, this was very thoughtful of him."

Marjie nodded. "Yes, since he discovered my uniqueness—"

"Your uniqueness?" Her mother raised her brows.

"That is what he calls my color blindness. He says I should not look at it as a deficiency. Because it simply makes me unique in the way I see the world."

"Oh, does he?" A soft smile played at her mother's lips.

"Since he discovered my uniqueness, he has planned

several things such as that." She motioned to the shell in her mother's hand.

Her mother's head tipped to the side, and again that earlier look came over her. "Oh, pray, what else has he done?"

"He invited me on a turn about their private gardens. Only, instead of looking at the color of the flowers, we smelled them. He took me to the ruins of an abbey. He said we could likely see it in a similar way because there was not much color in the stones."

Her mother smiled and there was moisture in her eyes. She could feel it too. Arawn was different from other gentlemen— different from other members of the *ton*. "It sounds as if the two of you have grown very close."

Marjie nodded. "Yes. It has been the best fortnight of my life. And I will be disappointed to leave."

Her mother patted her leg. "Then I suppose it is fortunate that we are staying on until Twelfth Night."

Marjie grunted. "Perhaps. Or it will only make the farewell more difficult."

CHAPTER TWENTY-SIX

Arawn sat in his chair behind his desk. Sometimes he wished he had a window in his study so he could look out over the sea and contemplate his troubles. He would surely be able to figure them out better if he had a window. But that is one thing castles had in short supply. And it hardly seemed worth a trip to their Anglesey estate just to look through a pane of glass.

He leaned forward and dropped his head onto his arms resting on his desk. "Ah, Ane. Why should it not have been me who hit my head and allowed me to see and talk to you? There is so much I wish to speak to you about, but I can hardly do it through Miss Fitzroy."

He had kissed Marjie the day before and he had thought of little else since. It had not been a thorough kissing, thank the heavens, but neither had it been brief. Indeed, he could still feel a warmth spread through his limbs and his stomach. It had only confirmed his belief that he loved her. But unfortunately, it left him with more questions than answers.

"I don't know what to do. I need someone to talk to—someone to help me figure out my future. But who can I speak with? I cannot talk about such things with Mother. There is Marjie. I feel like I can talk to her about anything. I know she will tell me what she is thinking, not what she thinks I wish to hear. The problem is—lud, Marjie is the problem. I can hardly talk to her about my feelings for her." Or maybe he could. If he had ever met a person who could give an honest opinion about something like that, it was Marjie.

But still, he did not think he could do it. At least not yet.

Although, in truth, he did not know if he could speak to Ane, if he could not see her. He was still not used to speaking to an empty room and expecting someone to listen. Besides, even if she did hear him. It was not as if she could reply.

"Lud, who does that leave me with?" It seemed he must work this out himself.

He ran his hands through his hair. Perhaps if he simply talked it out to himself, it would accomplish the same thing. But was that so very different from speaking to Ane?

He pushed out from the desk and paced in front of his fireplace. When had he become a pacer? It seemed to be all he did of late.

He clasped his hands behind his back and allowed himself to speak the thoughts that had been swirling around in his mind.

"Ane," it seemed best to pretend he was speaking to her. Otherwise, it felt odd. Speaking to his dead sister was odd enough, but he would dwell on that point another time. "I'm sorry for the part I played in your death. I should not have pressured you to jump. Not until you were ready or comfortable with it. But I didn't wait. I made you do it even though you did not wish to. Can you ever forgive me?" Even if she would, he was not certain he could forgive himself. "I miss you, Ane. And not just because you distracted Mother and made her pay me less mind." He paused. "I miss our weekly rides. And even if you hated it, I miss seeing you paint." While he did not feel wholly better, his shoulders did feel lighter.

"But that's not all that is troubling me, Ane. You see, I kissed Marjie." He shook his head, still unable to believe it had happened. Did she think him a rake? Or did she realize he was in earnest?

Oh, yes. He had been earnest. And that was the part that troubled him most. Wondering what would have happened if those boys had not been there to stop them.

Arawn liked to believe that he would have acted appropriately and pulled back before he thoroughly ruined her. But he had never felt like that about anyone. It made it difficult for him to know at what point he would have stopped.

"Why did I kiss her, Ane? She did not deserve to be treated in such a manner. Not that I regret doing it. Indeed, I should like to do it again, only better next time. I should like to kiss her so thoroughly that she cannot let me go. Ever." He sighed. "But regardless of my feelings, it has complicated things." Botheration! Talking about his problems was of little help, especially with no one there to reply or make any comments. He did not feel any more certain of his next actions than he had before his one-sided conversation.

He ran a hand down his face and sighed.

"Do you think she is angry with me? Lud, Ane, I took advantage of her when she was scared. What kind of man does that?" He shook his head. "Not a good man, that is for certain. She likely thinks me the worst kind of rake." He sighed. "And that disappoints me because I desire her good opinion above anyone else's."

He dropped his head back and stared at the ceiling. The dark timbers combined with the lack of a window kept the ceiling almost completely in shadow. In that moment he was grateful for the lack of windows. It fell in line with his mood. "What vexes me most is that it does not matter how much I like her. It is not as if anything can come of it. She is the daughter of a merchant and a former seamstress. While I don't care about that, I do think Mother will object."

"Which perhaps is for the best, Ane. The *ton* will surely not accept her, even if she were my wife." He sat back. The anxious ball sitting in his stomach eased for the first time and a calm settled over him, relaxing his shoulders and warming his chest.

The notion of being in a marriage with Marjie did not frighten him in the least. Nor did it make him nervous or anxious. It simply felt right.

It was everything outside the castle and their immediate life there that brought about the anxiousness. The thought of taking her to London or other social events made him break out in a cold sweat. Not because he was embarrassed by her. Nothing would make him prouder than to have her on his arm. But he feared for her. He knew society could be cruel.

After all, was that not one of the reasons she disdained society?

"I'd only make her life worse if I married her and society rejected her. I could not stand to see her hurt. But you know as well as anyone, Ane. They *will* hurt her."

He released a heavy sigh. He was all talked out. What more was there to say?

Whoever said that putting voice to your concerns was beneficial was full of fustian nonsense. He felt no better. Indeed, he felt worse than he had before because now he knew he wanted to marry Marjie, but he also knew there was little chance that he could. How had this little exercise been beneficial?

"Lud, Ane. Why are you never around when I need you?" He grumbled and dropped down into his chair.

A knock sounded at the door and his mother peeked her head in. She looked around. "Are you meeting with someone? I thought I heard you talking."

Arawn rolled his eyes. Not at his mother, per se. But at the situation. He had been caught trying to speak to his sister's ghost—which he did not even know if she was in the room. The whole thing was beyond ridiculous. "No, there is no one in here but me."

His mother opened the door wider and stepped inside. She smiled down at him, before glancing around the room. "Were you speaking with Ane? I do it too. I don't always know if she is in the room. But I like to think that we are still conversing as we always did." She shrugged. "And sometimes Ane will reference our private conversations when Marjorie is there to speak for her."

She walked around the sofa and paused in front of a picture propped up on the table behind his desk.

"That is a lovely painting. Where did you get it?"

Just looking at it made him smile. "Marjorie painted it."

His mother looked at him over her shoulder. "Was this her idea or yours?"

"It was mine. I wanted to see the world how she saw it." Arawn stood and moved beside her. "Indeed, I think the absence of color is what I like most about it." It made him feel closer to Marjie. And right then, he wanted—needed to feel closer to her. After all his talking and thinking, he felt as if she were slipping away from him.

"Yes, it does evoke a certain emotion." She looked up at

him. "She gave it to you? That was very kind. I know she wished to have something to take with her back to Yorkshire."

Arawn grimaced. "It was more like I took it from her. I offered to purchase it, but she would not hear of it." He was not certain how he would feel about it once she left. Perhaps then he would need to move it somewhere he would not see it every day. "But I did offer to purchase her a new canvas so she could paint one for herself."

"That was very giving of you, son." Her voice sounded anything but proud. "You take both of her paintings," her gaze flicked to the one already hanging on his wall, "and think yourself magnanimous because you offer to buy her a new canvas?"

He frowned. He did not think himself magnanimous. He had thought she would enjoy painting another picture. Especially since she and her mother would not be leaving for another few months. She had time to paint what she wanted. Indeed, he might just buy her a dozen canvases. What could his mother say then?

He grunted. "Thank you, Mother." He turned away from the painting. It only seemed to remind him that he had made no progress at all on his current troubles. "What was it you needed?"

Lud, she sat down. That could only mean she intended to stay for a little while. "I thought we could talk. We have not done that much of late."

He gave her a dry look. He knew he should be kinder—happier to speak to her, but he had things he needed to think about. Although, it had done him little good so far. What could it hurt to speak to her for a few minutes?

He settled onto the sofa next to her. "What did you wish to speak about?"

She tilted her head to the side. "You seem to be happier the last few weeks."

Arawn arched a brow. She obviously could not sense the turmoil surging through him.

"I am glad for it." She leaned slightly forward and put a hand on his arm. "And you do not look as if you are going without sleep anymore. I must say I am quite relieved. I was worried about you."

Arawn shrugged. He had been sleeping better since learning he had not been wholly responsible for Ane's death. But it did not follow that the nightmares had completely vanished.

He rubbed the back of his neck. And now he was also having dreams about kissing Marjie. While they were more than pleasant, they did leave him feeling rather exhausted and unsettled in the mornings. "I suppose I am sleeping better."

"And what do you attribute it to?" His mother was obviously trying to wheedle information from him.

"I cannot say as I know." He was not in the mood to discuss his sleeping habits. But he flicked a smile at her so she could not accuse him of being grumpy. "Perhaps it is simply that the weather is cooling. I always sleep better when the air is cool."

"Yes, I do too." She twitched her lips to one side. "But I thought perhaps it was something else."

"Oh? And what would that be?" he asked dryly.

"I wondered if it might not be Miss Fitzroy." She raised a brow. "You have been spending a great deal of time with her."

He sighed. If she thought he was going to tell her about his feelings for Marjie just so she could tell him it could not happen, she was sadly mistaken. "Did you not tell me to be polite? That is what I have been doing."

"You are simply being polite? I had thought perhaps you were becoming friends." She looked almost disappointed.

"And would that be so wrong?"

His mother shook her head. "Of course not, my dear. I have

wondered if perhaps Ane's death would not have hit you so hard if you'd had another friend to help you through it." She smiled. "If you have found that in Miss Fitzroy, then I am happy for it."

Arawn narrowed his eyes, waiting for the 'but' that he was certain was to come. "I have friends, Mother. Or have you forgotten about Seren?"

"No. I suppose you are right." His mother stood, looking less happy than when she had entered the room. He looked at her questioningly. She was giving up already? That was not like her. She usually wheedled for much longer. "Is that all you wished to discuss?"

His mother shrugged. "For the most part."

Arawn shifted, sitting on the edge of the sofa. "What else did you wish to speak about?"

She studied him intently, as if she were debating whether she should say more. "Now that we have put off mourning, you need to think about marrying. Your sister's death has put me in mind that you should delay no longer. If something should happen to you..." She trailed off and Arawn knew she was thinking about losing Arawn but also about his idiot cousin, Pwyll, inheriting Hywel and the other Beavin holdings. "I simply think it is time for you to be settled."

Was this his mother's way of saying that Marjie was fine as a friend, but she expected him to look for someone different— someone *better*—for a wife?

His jaw worked as he scrubbed his hand over his face. "Why do we not revisit this later?"

"But you will leave for London in January."

"Then we shall speak about it in January, Mother." He pushed up and looked down at her. He had no intention of thinking about marrying anyone, except for Marjie. Which was not helping his mood.

She looked just over his shoulder at Marjie's painting hanging on the wall. "You have obligations, Arawn."

"And I'm fully aware of them, Mother."

She moved toward the door. "I did not intend to make you angry, son. I just thought it something you should begin to think on."

"Do not worry, Mother. I have thought about it more than you could imagine."

CHAPTER TWENTY-SEVEN

Marjie sat in the chair near the fireplace reading a book as rain pelted against the windows in her mother's chambers.

Her mother sat across from her, a stitchery in her lap.

"I do not know how you can stand to do that now that you do not have to." Marjie glanced over the top of her book.

"But I enjoy doing it. It is one of the reasons I chose to be a seamstress. It feels much less like work if you enjoy what you are doing."

Marjie turned up her nose. "I hope I never have to make such a choice."

"Have you done any other activities with Lord Angle since the beach?" Her mother did not look up from her sampler.

Marjie shook her head. "No. But we only went to the beach a few days ago. You cannot expect him to plan an activity like that every day."

Her mother shrugged. "I did not expect it, dearest. I was just asking if you had seen him."

Marjie stopped reading. "No, Mama. That is not what you asked. You asked if we had gone on any other activities. But then you know we have seen each other since then. Do we not eat dinner with them every evening?"

Her mother sighed. "Yes, you are right, Poppet." She was quiet for a moment. "What do you and Lord Angle find to talk about?"

Marjie looked over at her mother. "I dare say the same things you speak to Lady Angle about."

"I highly doubt that," her mother murmured.

"We speak about his sister and art and history. Those types of things."

They fell into a comfortable silence.

Marjie thought about what her mother had said. What would she do for a profession if she had to take one? Would anyone hire her as a governess? While she'd only had a year of schooling, her mother had taught her very well. She knew Latin and some French. She could also teach art and other types of skills. Perhaps not embroidery, but the pianoforte was not beyond her.

But would it not be better if she need not seek out employment? She looked at her mother. "Mama, did you ever regret marrying Papa?"

Her mother shook her head. "Not once."

Her mother sewed for a moment longer before she spoke again. "Has Lord Angle mentioned marriage?"

Marjie shook her head. "No. I do not even know if he cares for me in that way."

Her mother looked at her incredulously. "How can you not know? The gentleman went to the sundry shop just to purchase shells so you could find them on the beach together. He took you on a smelling walk that was meant solely for you. He has taken you riding every day to stop you fearing horses."

She took Marjie's hands in her own. "He keeps *both* of your paintings in his study. What hasn't he done to say he loves you?"

"He has not said it aloud." Marjie looked at their hands.

Her mother nodded slowly. "Would you accept him if he asked?"

Marjie frowned. "I don't know."

"Why not? It would be a very advantageous match for you."

Marjie nodded. "I know. But it would not be for him. I worry what marriage to me would do to his reputation and standing. I'm certain, in time, he would grow to resent me for it."

Her mother shook her head. "You cannot know the future, Poppet. He may or he may not lose his standing. You may live happily together for a very long time. There is no way of knowing. The only thing you do know is that there is no chance of either of those things happening if you do not take a risk."

Marjie sucked in a deep breath. She did not like these feelings of doubt that swirled around inside her. "But there is also a chance we'll both end up hurt."

Her mother put her sewing to the side and turned to fully face Marjie. "That is what love is. It's a risk. But if you never take the risk, you will never know the happiness. I would not give up the happiness I had with your father for anything. It was worth all the possible heartache."

Perhaps her mother had a point, but it was all for naught, as Arawn had not made an offer, nor had he indicated he would.

Marjie pressed her lips together, wanting to feel the slight tingle that came when she thought back on kissing him.

Should she tell her mother about the kiss? Marjie held back

as her feelings warred within her. It had been such an intimate act. One that Marjie held very close to her heart.

But what would her mother think? Would she think Marjie ruined? Would she demand they marry? That was the last thing Marjie wanted. If Arawn married her, she wanted it to be because he loved her and wanted to be with her. Not because he was forced to.

Marjie set her book to the side. "Mama, I need some air. Do you mind if I excuse myself for a bit?"

Her mother shook her head. "No. I quite understand the feeling. Take your time. And if you happen upon Lord Angle, you have no need to hurry back." Her mother grinned down at her stitches.

Marjie rolled her eyes. "Thank you, Mama." She ducked out of her mother's chambers, relieved to be away from her mother's questions.

"Ah, Marjie. I am glad I found you." Ane floated up next to her.

Marjie turned toward her. She was not in the mood to play the go-between for Ane and her family. Her head ached and her heart was heavy. "I don't know where your brother or your mother are, Ane."

"That is fine. It is you I came in search of."

Marjie looked over at her. "Oh? What could I possibly help you with?"

Ane grinned. "I need help writing a letter or two."

"Pray to whom? I should think they might faint dead away if they received a letter from you now." Marjie smiled to herself at the thought.

"It is to Arawn and my mother, if you must know. And I do not think it should cause him any ill should I write it to him." She wiggled her fingers. "Or rather have you write it for me." She pushed out her lip in a pout. "Please, Marjie?"

Marjie nodded. "Come to my chambers and I will help you."

Ane clasped her hands together.

Marjie stared at her. Ane's hands did not go through each other. That was interesting and rather unexpected.

They moved up the stairs into Marjie's room and shut the door behind them.

Marjie sat at the writing desk beneath the window and set to sharpening her quill. She pulled a paper and the ink well forward and looked over her shoulder at Ane. "What did you wish to say to him?"

Ane walk-floated back and forth. "*Annwyl Arawn, hoffwn ateb eich cwestiynau o'n sgwrs ddoe.*"

Marjie looked back at Ane. "Excuse me?"

Ane sighed with exasperation. "This may take a while." She began to spell out each word. "A-n-n-w-y-l space A-r-a-w-n comma."

Marjie looked down at the paper. "That is how you spell Arawn?" She squinted down at it, sounding it out. She shrugged. "I suppose it's spelling would have it rhyme with lawn."

She looked back and released her breath. "What next?"

"H-o-f-f-w-n space a-t-e-b—"

Gracious, Ane was right. Writing this letter by spelling every word out was going to take forever. Marjie lifted her eyes to the ceiling in a prayer for patience. But then she hurriedly set to writing those letters she had missed.

She tipped her head to the side. It would surely make Arawn happy to see his sister's words written out for him. Which made it worth the effort.

She thought back to what her mother had said. That love was doing what would make the other happy. A warmth filled her chest and spread through her body.

If it meant Arawn would be happy, Marjie would help Ane write all of her letters in Welsh.

Marjie smiled, but then realized she had missed several letters. "Oh, wait. I think I missed some."

Ane stopped and looked over Marjie's shoulder. "You missed nearly the whole paragraph. This will take much longer if you do not pay attention."

Marjie nodded. "Yes, I am aware of that. I will try to stay focused."

"A-t space y-m," Ane resumed her letter recitation.

Marjie kept her head down, intent on listening to the letters so she would not have to spend any more time than necessary on this chore. *It is for Arawn.* She repeated the mantra enough to keep her focused but not so often that she lost track of Ane's droning voice.

Finally, Ane closed the letter. "E-i-c-h space u-n space c-h-i comma, Ane."

Marjie put the quill down on the desk and arched her back, then stretched out her neck and shoulders. "Shall I seal it with anything?"

Ane shook her head. "No. But if you would please see he receives it."

Marjie nodded as she stood. She leaned over the desk and folded the paper, then wrote ARAWN across the front. "I'll give it to him as soon as I see him."

"May I write one for my mother? It will be much quicker as I do not think it needs to be in Welsh."

"Of course," Marjie moved to sit back at the desk.

Ane moved across the room and put her hand on Marjie's arm. Or rather it hovered just above it. "Thank you. It provides me great relief to be able to answer their questions. For months, all I could do was listen but never provide any answers. It's been one of the most vexing parts of my situation."

Marjie moved to cover Ane's hand, but her hand slipped through, resting on her own instead. Iciness shot through both her hand and her arm. But it was not as bothersome as before. "I am glad I can help, Ane." And she meant it.

CHAPTER TWENTY-EIGHT

Arawn walked around the garden, closing his eyes and smelling the flowers as he had when he and Marjie had taken their scent walk. It was like a whole different world had opened up to him that day. Now it seemed he could not pass any plant without bending to smell it.

He opened his eyes to look at the pink daphne and the last of the yellow lilies and frowned. While he knew they had both enjoyed the scent tour, it still saddened him to know that Marjie would never see the beauty of them. He looked out at the blue-green sea and the green and yellow fields beyond the castle. She would never see the beauty of the world. And that made his chest hurt. He wanted her to have everything she desired. But he could not give her that.

"Arawn?"

He turned his head at the sound of her voice. His lips immediately turned up.

"Mrs. Prosser gave me permis—what is the matter? You look sad." She looked around the garden. "Has one of the flowers caused you grief?"

He shook his head and chuckled lightly. "No. I was simply thinking that you have never seen the beauty of these flowers. And while their fragrance is delightful, it saddens me that you are missing one of the best parts about them."

She looked at him blandly. "I am not completely blind, my lord. I can see beauty."

He scoffed. "But how? It is the color that is beautiful."

She shook her head. "Richard Hume said that beauty in things exists merely in the mind which contemplates them."

He raised his brows skeptically.

"He meant that anyone can find beauty in the world."

He tilted his head to the side. While he wanted to believe it, for Marjie's sake, he was not certain that he could. The yellow petal with the deep orange center is what made the lilies beautiful.

She pointed to the yellow lilies he had just smelled. "Look at the lilies. While I do not know what color they are, I can see that they are beautiful when I look at each petal individually. The shape of the petals and the way they curl away from the stamen in the center. It is delicate and lovely."

She bent and smelled the flower. "While I may not know what color they are, I can see the color variation on each petal. It darkens in the center and grows lighter as it moves toward the edge." She turned back towards him. "Please, do not pity me for not seeing beauty in the world. Color is not the only beautiful thing. Indeed, sometimes you must look past the color to see the true beauty."

His heart pounded in his chest. Never had he heard truer words. Nor had he ever been more tempted to pull her to him and kiss her soundly.

He saw her truth every time he looked at her. While she was a beautiful woman—one that surely turned heads until the gentlemen deemed her too common and too improper—it was what he had discovered inside her that drew him to her. She was like no other woman he had ever met. She was not afraid to be herself. Even when she knew it might drive people away. Indeed, how could he not love her?

They stood silently staring at each other. He did not know what she was thinking. He only knew that if he moved, he would surely act upon his desires and kiss her quite thoroughly.

Marjie took a step forward, which nearly made him kiss her anyway. But she lifted her hand and thrust a paper toward him.

"What is this?" He stared down at it.

"It is from Ane. She said you asked her some questions, and these are her answers."

His eyes widened. Ane had been in his study that night? And she had told Marjie about his one-sided conversation with her? How could she be so high-handed? His face and ears blazed. What must Marjie think of him? She must surely know he loves her now. But she must also know that he does not believe anything may come of it. That realization pierced his heart. He had hurt her without even meaning to. At least not yet.

"She had you write it, I assume?"

Marjie nodded, but there was no spark of humor, anger, or sadness in her eyes. Indeed, she didn't look as if she knew anything she should not.

He unfolded the pages and laughed. "It is all in Welsh."

Marjie nodded. "It was the longest letter I have ever written. She had to spell every word for me. And the only thing I understood was *diwrnod da*." She shook her head in exasperation. "Even that she had to spell for me."

Without thinking, he reached forward and pulled her to him, placing a quick, light kiss on her cheek. The thought came to him that he was only inches from her lips, but he pushed it away and took a step back. "Thank you, Marjie. You do not know what this means to me. Ane was my only confidante. We told each other everything. Since she died, I have not had that."

Marjie stared at him. "I'm glad I could help. I know we've talked of many things. But I suppose I am no substitute for your sister."

He licked his lips. He could say with certainty, he did not think of her as a sister.

He looked down at the paper in his hands and Marjie turned away. "I will leave you alone with your letter." She waved a second one in the air. "I have one for your mother, also."

Unwilling to have her leave so soon, Arawn called after her. "Will I see you later?"

She stopped and looked over her shoulder. "The castle is not so big as to become lost. I would assume we will happen upon one another at some point."

He chuckled to himself. "I am certain you are right. I shall look forward to the encounter."

She turned back and headed the way she had come.

Arawn found a bench and sat down with the letter. What did Ane have to say?

Diwrnod da, Arawn.

He sighed, hearing his sister's voice as he read the words.

I wish to answer your questions from our conversation last evening. Let me address your concerns about my death first. Even before we discovered the nail in my saddle, I never held you responsible for my accident. I know you think you pushed me too hard, but the truth is, without your gentle pushing, I would never have done anything difficult. We both know I tended toward the timid and sometimes scared. I needed you to push me. Was it not you that encouraged me when the French or Greek became too difficult? And let us not forget the spurring on that I needed for dancing.

Jumping that stream was not pushing me too hard. Please stop blaming yourself. It was not your fault.

And now about your thoughts on Marjie...

He smiled at the dots showing her thoughts trailed off, just as if she were speaking to him. He could see her with her finger perched on her lips, tapping softly as she thought about what to tell him. Or perhaps it was how to tell him.

You may find my perspective changed since my death. I felt as you do, thinking that mother's approval was the only option. However, I have had time to think these many months, and I have since changed my mind. Had I to do it over, I should not have allowed society to tell me who I could love. I would have accepted Dafydd. I have loved him for as long as I can remember. But I pushed it aside, knowing it would never be approved.

If anyone knows how short life can be, my dear Ari, it is me. My life was over before it had even begun. Don't let that happen to you. If you love Marjie, do not let Mother's or society's opinions chart your course. Make your own way. If Marjie makes you happy, which, from what I have seen, she does, then do not wait another minute. Ask her for her hand and set about living every day as if it were your last because it very well could be. And it is not agreeable to walk these corridors knowing I have regrets. Regret that I did not go to London for a Season. Regret that I did not attend more of the twmpaths. Regret that Dafydd will never know my feelings for him.

I like Marjie a great deal. She is like the sister I never had. But that should not play into your decision, as we do not know how much longer I shall be at Hywel. Do what makes you happy. Follow your heart, Ari.

But be careful with her feelings. While she may not care what others think of her, she cares what you think. Do not cause her hurt, else I shall never leave, and I shall haunt you until your dying breath.

Much love,

Ane

He stared down at the paper, reading it over again. It was easy for Ane to advise him to disregard everyone else's opinion and do what his heart wanted. Ane did not have to live with the consequences. He frowned at the calloused thought. But Arawn did not have the luxury of thinking only about himself. Marjie, his mother—even her mother—would all feel the consequences of his actions. Could he really toss all that aside and do whatever he wanted?

He sighed.

She had regrets. And she could never remedy them. She did not have time to do the things she wished she had.

But what about him? If he did not follow his heart and ask for Marjie's hand, would he have regrets? The pinch in his chest told him he would. But would the regrets outweigh the repercussions of going against everyone in his life who would advise against it?

Perhaps he needed to speak with his mother and determine her thoughts on the subject. If she did not object, could he ignore everyone else?

CHAPTER TWENTY-NINE

Marjie lay in her bed, reading her book by the small flame of the candle on her bedside table. Her mother would surely lecture her, saying she should have at least one more candle lit to provide better light. But Marjie did not care.

The flame flickered. One thing she had discovered about living in a castle was that it was by far more drafty and therefore colder than living in a regular house. She pulled the counterpane up a little higher. There was no way she was stepping out of bed, just to retrieve another candle.

A soft patter on the glass turned Marjie's attention from her book. Was it starting to rain? She listened for a moment, but no other sound came. Perhaps it was just the wind. She returned to the book but had only read a sentence or two when another tink on the glass made her sit up. She replaced the ribbon and set her book to the side, just as another patter sounded. What was it? She had never heard rain sound in such an irregular pattern.

Grunting quietly at having to leave the warmth of her bed,

she padded over to the window. She looked out. No water drops were on the pane. She opened the window and a pebble sailed over her shoulder and into her chambers. "Ahh," Marjie screeched.

"Marjie, did it hit you?" Arawn's frantic whisper sounded from the bailey below.

She looked down. "No. But why are you throwing pebbles at my window?" She hissed.

"I wished to get your attention." He looked like a little boy standing there, looking around him to make certain he was not caught. "Meet me on the allure, I have something to show you."

"But it is late. Can it not wait until morning?"

He shook his head. "No. It will be gone in the morning." He sighed. "Please, Marjie?" He gave her the look that Ane rolled her eyes at.

She looked longingly at the fire burning in the grate. She would surely be chilled to the bone. But Arawn was worth a little cold, was he not? "Oh, very well. I will be down in a moment." She closed the window. How had he known she was not asleep? She glanced at the low-burning candle on her bedside table and raised a brow.

Pulling her night-rail over her head, she dropped it in a pile on her bed. Shivering from the cold, she pulled a gown off her changing screen and pulled it on quickly. She fastened the few buttons she could reach. There were two or three still unbuttoned, but her spencer would cover them. She was not waking Susanna for a few buttons.

Slipping on her half boots, she yanked at the laces and tied them with trembling fingers. What could Arawn have to show her? It must have been something very special if he risked waking her and others in the castle. What was so important that it could not wait until morning?

She closed her door quietly, not wishing to disturb her mother. Pushing on the door to the wall-walk while simultaneously lifting the handle, Marjie swung it open. The carefulness worked as the door let out only a quiet groan rather than its usual moan.

A gust of cold air caused a ripple of gooseflesh on her arms and legs.

She took several steps onto the stone walkway and looked around. Where was Arawn? Surely he'd had time to make it up there in the time it had taken her to change.

Arawn stepped out of the shadows of the kitchen tower and walked over to her. Placing his hand on the small of her back, he motioned her toward the crenel in the center of the battlement. She nearly stumbled on the slightly uneven stones. For a split second, she realized it may not have been her most prudent decision. While she did not doubt Arawn meant no harm, if someone should see them alone and in the dark, it would not prove beneficial to her reputation.

Another man stood a few feet away. In the dim light of the moon, Marjie could just make the face of Morgan, Arawn's valet.

"*Noswaith dda,* Morgan."

She could just make out his smile. "Good evening to you, Miss Fitzroy."

Looking up at Arawn, she put her hands on her hips. "What could not wait until morning?"

A door moaned and Marjie turned to see her mother and Lady Angle emerge onto the allure. "Are we too late? I do not wish to miss it." At least she need not worry about being ruined any longer. But what could be so important?

Arawn shook his head. "No, you are in time."

He put his hand on her hips, and she sucked in a breath, any chill suddenly gone and swiveled her around, so she was looking through the crenel. Then standing close behind her, he lifted a hand and pointed up toward the sky. "Look there," he whispered into her ear.

Lights shot across the sky leaving glowing tails trailing behind.

She leaned back against him, her head resting on his chest. "It is beautiful. How did you know about it?"

"It happens nearly every year at this time. I saw them last night and thought you might enjoy them."

"What are they?"

"Shooting stars." Lady Angle said, and Marjie straightened, nearly forgetting the lady and her mother were there.

But Arawn pulled her back against him, resting his chin on her head.

"It's one of the most beautiful things I've ever seen," she whispered. It was as if the heavens were having a party, and someone had released fireworks. "How are there so many of them?"

"I have no notion how it is done. I simply know it is amazing."

She felt his hand brush against hers and she longed for him to take it. But she kept her eyes on the stars, watching each one, even as her thoughts were on his hand.

"In early times, the Welsh people would have believed that those are the *Cŵn Annwn.*"

"What is that?" Her mother asked before Marjie could pull her thoughts together enough to ask for herself.

"*Cŵn Annwn* are the Hounds of Annwn. It is believed in some myths that Arawn was the king of the otherworld. He was the lord of the wild hunt. And his hounds would chase evildoers across the sky until they were driven into the ground, just as they had done to their victims. It was believed they would only hunt on specific nights, but as St. Martin's Day was a fortnight ago, I am not certain what to make of that super-stition."

She glanced over her and could see a faint smile on his lips. "You are named after the devil? That hardly seems right." Nothing in his character had made her believe he was aptly named.

He looked down at her. "The Welsh did not believe the underworld was a place for punishment as the Christians did. It was more like the Fields of Asphodel in Greek Mythology. It was a place of plenty and eternal youth...a place you hoped to enter. It was very different than the Christian's Hell."

"It sounds much better." Although, at that moment, she thought she would likely enjoy any place if Arawn was there with her.

"It does, doesn't it?" He brushed her hand again, but this time he intertwined his fingers with hers.

Marjie could not help but smile that it was her hand closest to Morgan rather than their mothers.

Silence settled over them. Slowly, Arawn's thumb rubbed back and forth along the side of her hand, sending a thrill through her.

"I am very pleased you are enjoying the stars, but how is that helping me?" Ane's voice sounded behind them, and Marjie turned to look at her. "I'm sorry, Ane. But what is to be done at this time of night?" Marjie slackened her hand, but Arawn held on firmly.

He sighed behind her. "What does Ane want now?"

"She says the stars are lovely, but they are doing nothing to help her."

Arawn released a breath and growled. "I think perhaps she should wear a bell about her neck so as to alert us to her presence."

Marjie smiled up at him. "I do not think a bell would stay

around her neck. I believe it would slip through her just as my hand does when I try to touch her."

"More's the pity." He leaned closer to her. "And it is just my luck, is it not?"

"I do not know what is to be done at this time of night. But it feels as though everyone is having a lovely time, while I am stuck here." Ane folded her arms across her chest, her lips turned down in a deep frown.

Marjie sighed and looked over at Lady Angle. It was difficult to make out much of her expression, but she could guess the lady was concerned over her daughter. "I believe Ane is simply feeling sad that she cannot join us in watching the stars."

"And why can she not?" Lady Angle asked.

Marjie grinned. "Yes, Ane. Why do you not join us? I believe there is a spot next to your mother."

Ane bit her cheek. "I suppose there is nothing to be done tonight. And I do love to watch the stars." She glided over and stood beside her mother. Ane touched her mother's shoulder.

Lady Angle shivered but looked over at the space where her daughter stood. "I am glad you came to join us, Ane."

Arawn stared down at Marjie, his gaze dropping to her lips. If her mother and Lady Angle weren't there, would he kiss her again? From the look in his eyes, she wondered if he would kiss her anyway, regardless of their mother's presence. It made her pulse tick up.

She grinned and pulled her bottom lip between her teeth.

He swallowed hard and pulled her back to him. He leaned down, his lips close to her ear. "You are a wicked young lady, Miss Fitzroy. Testing me when our mothers are not ten feet away."

Marjie chuckled quietly.

Lady Angle pointed. "Look at that one. I've never seen a tail so long."

Marjie nodded. "Nor have I."

He shifted, but his lips stayed next to her ear. How did he manage that without putting a crick in his neck? "Thank you for coming out, Marjie," he whispered. "I know it took a leap of faith that what I wished to show you was important. Thank you for trusting in me."

She turned her head, their lips nearly touching, but her eyes stayed focused on his. "I've never trusted anyone more." She winked at him and was just as surprised by it as Arawn seemed to be. "But maybe next time you can avoid throwing pebbles at me."

He squeezed her hand, and his thumb began to sweep up and down the side of her palm. "I'm just glad you believe there will be a next time."

CHAPTER THIRTY

"Marjie, what are you doing in here?" Arawn asked as he stepped inside Ane's room.

Marjie looked up from her spot on the floor beside the bed. "Ane told me she has a diary and that she keeps it under this side table. But I cannot seem to pull it out. It seems to be stuck on something."

"Is there something in the diary that will help us?" Arawn moved inside, intent on helping Marjie retrieve the book. The sooner they solved her murder, the sooner he could stop feeling guilty for not bringing the culprit to justice. He moved the candlestick holder to the bed along with the few books sitting on top. Then he tilted the table back, allowing Marjie enough room to put her hand underneath. "Can you retrieve it now?"

She grinned and lifted the leather-bound book in the air. "Yes, I believe this is it."

Arawn reached for it and Marjie held it tightly to her chest. "I beg your pardon. Ane did not give you permission to read her diary. She only gave it to me."

305

He rolled his eyes. "What does it matter at this point? It is not as if I will tease her."

Marjie dropped her head to the side. "I will not betray her confidence unless it relates to finding her killer."

"Then she believes there is something in there that will help us?"

Marjie shook her head. "No, but what can it hurt? Perhaps there is something she simply did not realize was important."

Arawn put out his hand to help her up, but he did not let go of it once she was standing. Instead, he tugged her to him.

"Marjie, have you ever thought to live in Wales?"

She pulled her lip between her teeth. "Not until recently. But since our arrival, I've developed a fondness for the country and the—," she held his gaze. "And the people."

The slight smile turned his lips. "Then you would consider moving to Wales? Your family has a history here."

She shrugged. "I suppose it would depend on the opportunity."

"And if it was a marriage proposal?" He knew he was being very bold, but the obstacles of offering for her had plagued his mind and he wished to know if her acceptance was one of them or not.

"I suppose it would depend on the gentleman. I've recently realized that nothing short of love will entice me into matrimony."

"And if the gentleman were Mr. Pugh? Or perhaps Mr. Lloyd? Both men seemed interested."

She grinned. "While I enjoy Mr. Lloyd's company, I do not love him."

Arawn's shoulders relaxed. While he did not believe she did, knowing he had not missed a connection between them was a relief.

"As for Mr. Pugh, he is the only reason I can find not to move to Wales."

He did not say anything, only stared at her and nodded slowly. "I hope Mr. Pugh will not deter you should an offer from the right gentleman come your way."

"If the right Welshman asked, nothing would deter me." She pulled her lip between her teeth, and he tugged her closer to him. He hoped she meant what she said. Because in spite of all the obstacles in their path, he had every intention of asking for her hand. Although, perhaps not in his sister's bed chambers. He could bring his mother around to his way of thinking. He was nearly certain of it. And if he couldn't? She would simply have to be disappointed in him. He had decided he could bear that notion more than not having Marjie.

He looked down at her and she smiled at him. Lud, he loved her smile.

"There was something I wished to do last night," he cocked a brow. "But we never seemed to be alone." He looked around them. "However, now—"

She hit him lightly on the chest with the diary. "However, nothing." She took two steps back from him. "I am going to see if I can find anything of use in here." She held up the diary.

He folded his arms in displeasure. But she had a point. The last thing he wanted was for her to think he married her simply because he had marred her reputation. He must be more careful. "Marjie, is Ane in the room?"

Marjie shook her head. "I have not seen her since last evening."

He leaned against a post on Ane's bed. "When did she tell you about her diary? I did not know she kept one."

"Most young ladies do," Marjie leaned toward him and loudly whispered. "I believe she told me of it a day or two after you confronted Dafydd. I did not think much of it then because she said there was nothing of use in it. But after what she said last night, I thought it would not hurt to at least look."

He took a step closer to her. And only partially because he wanted to see the book. How was it possible that he missed her when she was standing not five feet away from him? "Do you not think it would go quicker if there were two sets of eyes looking?" He lifted his chin, trying for a look of wisdom and knowledge.

Marjie tipped her head to the side, her eyes narrowing. "Ane only gave me permission."

Arawn motioned toward the door. "Then perhaps we should seek out my sister and gain her permission for me to read as well. The longer we wait, the more the trail goes cold."

"Where do we begin our search for her? I confess I have never intentionally sought any of them out. They always manage to find me on their own."

Arawn thought. "The library and the wall-walk were always her favorite. She always loved the view from up on the walls."

"Let us circle the wall-walk on our way to the library." Marjie kept the book held tightly to her chest.

He reached out a hand and placed it on the small of her back, grinning when she sucked in a deep breath. The action made his own breath hitch. He was glad to see he was not the only one affected by the other's touch.

When they passed through the Stockhouse Tower, Marjie grinned. "Ah, there you are, Ane. We have been looking for you."

"We were on our way to the library, but obviously, you are not there." Arawn stood behind Marjie, directing his gaze where he thought she was looking. Since speaking with his sister the other night in his study, he had become less self-conscious about speaking to her. Unless a servant was nearby.

Marjie positioned herself, so she was looking out a crenel, and a sad smile turned her lips. "Is that Dafydd?" She asked in a small voice.

Arawn leaned forward, looking over her shoulder, just making out the groom in the distance.

Marjie released a little shutter, and Arawn wondered if it was the result of whatever Ane had said or his closeness. He hoped it was the latter.

"Is this why you like the allure so much?" Marjie asked, and he assumed it was meant for Ane. "Is it not too cold?" She paused, but she continued to watch Dafydd and Arawn felt a moment of jealousy. It was not something he wore well.

"You do not feel heat or cold? Hmm. I suppose it makes sense. How could you keep warm if a pelisse falls right through you?"

"She does not feel the cold?" Arawn asked. Why had he never considered such a thing? "Is that normal?"

Marjie nodded. "I should think it is not unique to Ane." She glanced over at the next crenel. "Ane, Arawn was wondering if he might help me look through your diary. It will move quicker if there are two of us reading."

She glanced back at him and grinned. "Ane is not certain you can be trusted."

Arawn threw up his hands. "Thunder and turf, Ane. Do you wish us to discover who killed you or not? You cannot be angry that it is taking too long to discover if you are not willing to help when you are able."

Marjie's eyes widened and she lifted a hand but then dropped it back to her side. "I do not believe he is angry with you, Ane. But rather frustrated." She cast him a look over her shoulder and Arawn felt a moment of regret.

But then he pushed it aside. What had he said that was so wrong? While he was grateful that Marjie could see and speak to Ane, it frustrated him that they all did not have that special talent. He raked a hand through his hair. "Please, let me read your diary, Ane. There may be things that Marjie may not know to be a clue. She does not know all the neighbors or grooms. She may not know if she reads about something that is out of their character." He grumbled. "And I promise not to tease you about it. But if there is information that can help—" he sighed and allowed the rest to go unsaid.

Marjie reached behind her and squeezed his hand. "Thank you, Ane. I promise we will both treat the information with utmost respect."

Lud, it was about time she agreed. And it was about time Marjie was the one to take his hand.

She moved to pull it back, but he closed his fingers around hers, holding it securely in place.

Her shoulders rose on a sigh and Arawn chuckled in her ear.

"Ane, do you wish to come with us? I think we shall read in the library." Marjie nodded. "I understand."

Marjie moved back toward the Stockhouse Tower with Arawn following along behind so he would not have to relinquish her hand. But he was forced to anyway when they entered the library, and she sat down at the table.

He took the seat beside her, but she rebelliously placed both her hands on the table. He thought he saw a slight twitch to her lips when she glanced over at him. She was a vexatious woman.

She opened the book but then stared across the table. "I think we need not read the whole thing. Perhaps just the fortnight leading up to the accident? If we do not find anything then we will look further back."

Marjie opened the book to the back, turning the pages forward until she reached the last entry. Then she turned more pages to find her starting point. She read quietly, Arawn reading nearly over her shoulder, he was so close. Lawkes, how was she supposed to concentrate with him breathing her neck, making her skin ripple with gooseflesh?

"I do not see anything unusual on that day, do you?" He whispered.

She shook her head; uncertain she had complete control over her voice. Flipping the page, she read, forcing herself to concentrate on every word.

"Nothing there either." Arawn released a frustrated sigh, as did Marjie. But she wondered if they might be for different reasons.

The next full week of entries was the same, nothing out of the ordinary had been written about. Was it simply that Ane was unobservant and had missed something? Or was there simply nothing to write about?

Marjie shook her head as Ane walked into the room. "Did Dafydd leave?"

Ane nodded. "He went back inside the stables."

"What is it? Why did you shake your head like that?" Arawn straightened next to her, and she felt both relief and disappointment at the space created between them.

"I am simply frustrated. Either Ane did not witness anything relating to her death, or—," she paused. It was not very kind to infer someone was not observant. It felt equal to calling her stupid.

"Or what?" Arawn persisted.

"Or Ane simply was not paying attention." Marjie expected some kind of outrage or at the very least irritation from Ane for the slight. But Ane simply stared at Marjie with elbows sinking partially into the table and her chin resting in her palms. "I'm not certain that was not the case. I did not have to pay attention to much. That is what Arawn and mother were for."

Arawn ran another hand through his hair. "There must be something in there, else what are we to do? How are we to discover the truth?"

Marjie put her hand on his arm. "We might have to resign ourselves to never learning the truth. Sometimes there is not an answer to the question."

He shot out of his seat. "I cannot accept that."

"You may not have a choice," Marjie whispered.

Arawn pushed the book away from him and moved away from the table, pacing back and forth.

Marjie pulled the book to her and continued reading. It was far easier to do it with Arawn halfway across the room. "Who are Lord and Lady Retford?"

Arawn came closer and squinted down at the diary. "I went to school with their son, Mr. James Aldwick." He motioned to the entry with a flick of his chin. "We were invited to attend a fair they were hosting. But had to decline the invitation as our schedules would not permit it."

"It seems Ane was disappointed to miss it." Marjie turned the page.

"Yes, Ane was disappointed by many things I did." He sounded resigned.

"That's not true," Ane said. "I have always been one of Arawn's fondest admirers. I simply wanted him to leave the castle more often."

Marjie smiled at Ane, then looked over her shoulder at Arawn. "Ane says you are mistaken. She was rarely disappointed by you."

Arawn flicked up his brows in obvious doubt, but he did not argue. Instead, he continued to pace.

She read quickly but thoroughly. When she came to an

entry for the day before the accident, she paused. "Wait. I think this might be something."

Arawn paused. "What? Who did it?"

She dropped her head to the side and raised her brow. "Did you really think it would simply tell us the murderer's name?"

He shrugged. "I can hope, can I not?"

"What is it, Marjie?" Ane asked.

"You wrote here that Miss Penry visited on the day before the accident."

Ane's brows creased but then her head nodded. "Yes, I remember that. I did not remember it was only the day before, but I do remember her coming for a visit."

"Miss Penry came to visit?" Arawn stopped his pacing and came to stand behind Marjie. "I do not remember that."

"It was the day the horses got free, and it took all the stable hands and grooms nearly two hours to capture them."

Marjie repeated what Ane said.

Arawn nodded. "I had forgotten about that. Are you sure it was the day before your accident, Ane?"

"Your horses escaped, and you forgot about it?" She looked at Arawn.

He shrugged. "My sister had an accident and died the next day. There are many things from that week I likely have forgotten."

Marjie tried to give him a reassuring smile. "I suppose that is understandable, under the circumstances. But it also is likely what the killer is counting on. You must remember all you can." She looked to Ane.

"Miss Penry was here when the horses escaped. If my diary says that Miss Penry visited the day before my accident, then that is when both events happened."

Marjie looked at Arawn and nodded. "She says it was the day before." Marjie pushed out her lips in thought. She did not know why it bothered her that Miss Penry came to visit that day. Had not Ane said that Miss Penry was not invited to the card party that same evening? "Why did she come to visit?"

"Do you think that odd?" Arawn asked.

"If you consider that she and her family had not been invited to your card party that evening, then yes, I find it odd."

Ane frowned. "I believe that was why she said she came. She wanted to make certain we knew the family held no ill will for the slight." Ane shrugged. "I did not believe it. But lying for politeness' sake is not unusual in society."

Marjie looked to Arawn and repeated what Ane had said. She twitched her lips to the side. "Perhaps Miss Penry's visit itself is not so odd as I originally thought." She tapped her finger to her lips. "But knowing that it occurred at the same time as the horse incident? I do not know what to think."

"Could Miss Penry have set the horses loose for some reason?" Arawn asked.

"Ane says that she was in the Lesser Hall with her when the horses escaped."

"Then she was not involved," Arawn took up his pacing again.

Marjie shook her head. "We're missing something." She bit her cheek. "Could Miss Penry have been working with someone else? I cannot help but feel as though these events are linked to Ane's death."

"Do you believe the horses were used as a diversion?" Arawn leaned on the table, his face very close to hers. He stared intently at her.

The pressure to discover something helpful pressed down on Marjie.

She lifted her shoulder, not entirely certain what to think. "Ane said it took nearly two hours to gather all the horses. Were the stables empty for all that time?"

Arawn stood up. "Not the whole time. As horses were caught, they were brought back to the stables. But there would have been plenty of time to drive a nail into Ane's saddle without being detected."

"Miss Penry did leave as soon as we were told of what happened. She said she wished to check on her horse and make certain he was not one of those running wild." Ane's eyes narrowed.

Marjie raised a brow and repeated the new information to Arawn.

His thumb tapped up and down on the tabletop. "Giving her plenty of time to drive the nail." He straightened. "We need to speak to Mathias and the grooms. One of them must have seen something."

Marjie stood. "May I come with you?"

He nodded and helped her out of her seat, taking her hand before she could find something else to do with it.

CHAPTER THIRTY-ONE

Arawn led Marjie out to the stables, her hand firmly held in his. He knew this may not be a proper place for a lady, but he needed her with him. Both to feel her strength and to know she was safe. The notion that they were closing in on the culprit made him anxious that no one inside the castle was safe.

When they entered the stable yard, Mathias hurried over to greet them, and he released her hand. "Good day, my lord. Are you wishing me to saddle your horse?" He glanced at Marjie, who was obviously not dressed for riding.

"No, Mathias. We came to speak with you. And perhaps your grooms." Arawn said.

Mathias dipped his head, but there was wariness in his gaze. "Have you discovered something?"

Arawn nodded. "While looking over Ane's diary, we found a reference that is curious." He leaned toward the stable master, lowering his voice. Although why he felt the need, he did not know. No one present was a suspect. "Do you remember the day the horses escaped the yard?"

Mathias nodded. "Indeed. I have yet to discover how that came to be." He frowned. "Do you believe it had something to do with Lady Angharad's death?"

Arawn shrugged. "Perhaps it's nothing, but I wish to speak to everyone who was there that day. I have reason to believe that may have been when the nail was placed. Perhaps one of the grooms saw something but they do not remember. Or they thought as you did, that it is not connected." He motioned over to Dafydd who looked on cautiously from down the row of stalls.

Dafydd moved forward. "Yes, my lord?" He'd been rather aloof of late. Arawn guessed that was understandable considering the earlier accusation against him.

Arawn regretted his assumptions. But could he really be blamed for questioning everything that had been out of place? Ane was his sister.

"Dafydd, when you were helping to secure the horses back in the stable on the day they broke free, did you happen to notice anyone come into the stable while it was mostly empty?"

Dafydd shook his head. "Not that I recall, my lord."

Arawn's body sagged. Was this just another fruitless clue? He raked a hand over his face. "Would you please ask among the other hands? I only wish to know if anyone other than those employed in my stables was seen."

Dafydd nodded and ducked away, heading toward a few men farther down the row. As he spoke with them, they each shook their heads.

Mathias grunted. "It may take some time to speak with everyone, my lord."

"We do not have much time left." Miss Penry would be at the castle the day after next for the dinner party his mother had planned for the conclusion of Marjie and her mother's stay. Even though they were to extend their stay, the party had not been cancelled, much to Arawn's chagrin. If Miss Penry had been involved, then Arawn wanted to know before she entered the castle again. Arawn lifted a brow. "This is important. I'll wait."

Mathias' brows lifted as he nodded and turned away. "I will enquire of those outside."

"Thank you, Mathias."

"What shall we do now?" Marjie leaned in closer to him. "Do you intend to stand here until everyone has been asked?"

Arawn nodded. "I do. I cannot go on hoping the next clue will be the one. This must lead to something." He sighed. "It simply must," he whispered.

Marjie nodded, and he half expected her to turn and leave. But instead, she quietly stepped closer to him and wrapped her hand around his. It was not lost on him that she hid their hands in the fold of her skirt. But he did not care. That one small gesture lifted so much pressure from his chest, he could scarcely believe it.

It was simply one more argument in favor of making her his wife. He had thought to ask her at the dinner party, but he did not know if he could wait that long. Indeed, he found the thought of waiting for the banns to be read almost unfathomable.

Dafydd approached, his cap in his hands. "I'm sorry, my lord. But no one seems to have seen anything."

Arawn smiled at him. "Thank you for inquiring, Dafydd." He paused and Dafydd turned away. "Dafydd?" Arawn called him back.

"Yes, my lord?" He looked wary.

"I apologize for thinking you might have had something to do with Ane's death. I now know that Ane loved you, just as you loved her. I should never have thought you capable of harming her."

The sheen covering Dafydd's eyes told Arawn it was the truth. "Then she did love me? I hoped it might be true. But she never declared it."

Arawn nodded. "Yes. Her diary has been very informative." While he had not learned that information from the diary, he did not feel the need to explain where he had discovered it.

A beam of light spread across the stable floor as the door opened and Mathias stepped inside. His face was pensive, but he wore a slight smile. "I believe we may have something, my lord."

Arawn stepped forward. Careful to pull Marjie with him so he did not have to release her hand. "Yes? What is it?"

"Baglan said he saw a young woman in the stable. She said she was checking on her horse and gig. While he did not know her name, from his description, I believe it to be Miss Penry."

Arawn's pulse sped up. That was it. That was what they needed. A stable hand could put her near the saddles. She must have been the one to put in the nail. It would not take much effort. A woman surely could have accomplished it.

"But why?" Marjie asked next to him. "What would have been her motive?" She looked to her side and shrugged. Arawn could only assume she was speaking to Ane.

Arawn sighed. "Perhaps she was angered that her family was not invited to the musicale."

Marjie's brow furrowed. "I cannot imagine someone taking such measures just because they were not invited to a party."

"Sometimes people act rashly. There is no accounting for it."

Marjie lifted her shoulders, but her brow less convinced. "What are you to do? It is not as if you can go to their house and accuse her. What proof do we have?" She looked apologetically at Mathias and Dafydd. "Her father will surely object. And I do not believe the word of a stable hand will stand up against that of a lord or his daughter."

"You are surely correct." Arawn shook his head. "I do not know what to do. Her family has sent their acceptance for dinner tomorrow next. But I do not wish to have them within the castle."

"Perhaps she will do something while she is there that will confirm your suspicions?" Dafydd sounded hopeful.

"Perhaps," Arawn did not feel the same hope. It seemed very unlikely. Especially after such a long time. She surely believed she had escaped any suspicion.

"If the conversation should turn in that direction, she may say something. Or at the very least, give a look that confirms it." Marjie squeezed his hand.

"You wish me to allow her to come?" He swallowed at the thought. How could he do such a thing? After what she had done to Ane? What if she did something to his mother? To Marjie? Sweat broke out on his brow.

"We do not know for certain she did anything. You cannot uninvite the family to the party, Arawn. It simply is not done."

He frowned. "I do not care what is proper and what is not in this case." He turned to face her. "I cannot put you and my mother in danger."

She dropped her head to the side. "We do not know that there will be any danger."

He stared at her. "Do we not?"

"No." Her head shook. "But what if you had a few more men brought inside the castle to keep watch? Do you not have a few extra livery available? We could have several of the grooms dress and help watch at the party for anything suspicious. And those that are not inside could watch over the stables. Would that satisfy you?"

Her green eyes looked on him with such confidence, his shoulders relaxed.

"I know you will not allow any harm to come to me." She smiled. "Nor to either of our mothers."

The tightness gathered in his chest. "I thought that of Ane too."

She reached out and took his other hand in hers, this time not bothering to hide them. "You did not know there was danger then. But now that you do, I feel completely at ease. You will be on your guard."

He wished he felt her certainty—her confidence.

She grinned. "Besides, there are other less *noticeable* eyes that will be watching the castle. Nothing will go amiss."

She was surely speaking of the ghosts. But could he count on them? From what he had seen with Marjie, all they seemed to do was bicker and act like children. But perhaps they were better than nothing.

He nodded. "Then I suppose we should speak to my mother and inform her of what we have discovered."

Arawn caught Mathias' grin as he glanced at their clasped hands. Normally, Arawn would be irritated by the observation, but he did not care. Indeed, it pleased him that other people knew of his affection for Marjie and that the stable master approved. With Arawn's father dead, Mathias was the closest thing he had to a father any longer.

The older man smiled wider when he caught Arawn's eye and gave him a subtle nod of approval. And while Arawn surely did not need it, it pleased him to receive it. "We will see to the stables, and I will speak with Price to have him coordinate the undergardeners."

Arawn nodded. "Thank you, Mathias."

Mathias dipped his head. "We will all keep the ladies safe, my lord. You have nothing to be concerned about."

Arawn sucked in a deep breath, releasing it through his nose. Knowing everyone at the castle would be watching over them did make him feel better.

But that did not make him any happier about having to see Miss Penry again.

CHAPTER THIRTY-TWO

Arawn sat on the family bench in the parish church. His mother had been grateful to know what they had learned. But like Marjie, she was not yet ready to condemn Miss Penry. If Arawn had his way, the lady would already be on a ship bound for New South Wales.

But he supposed they were correct. Caution and prudence needed to be used in this situation.

Mathias and Price had reported that everyone had been spoken to and the castle would not be caught unaware again. There would be no opportunities for anyone to harm someone Arawn loved again.

Unlike the first week Marjie and her mother had attended church with them, Arawn stayed awake for the whole of the sermon. Not because he was listening. He could not repeat a single thing the vicar had said. But he likely would not receive any glowering looks from his mother. He was considering the outing a success.

When the sermon ended, Marjie nudged him in the ribs.

He looked over at her. "What?"

She grinned, but it did not quite reach her eyes. "I was uncertain if you were asleep or not—as church seems to be your favorite place to nap. I thought it best to save time and just nudge you now, rather than waiting until your mother discovered you."

He glanced to the side and his jaw clenched at the sight of Miss Penry and her family. She caught his gaze and smiled widely. He lifted a brow but dipped his head to her. Her smile faltered.

He had the urge to pick up Marjie's hand and feel her confidence. And if Miss Penry happened to notice, all the better.

The sermon ended and Arawn stood up slowly, stretching out his back. With how uncomfortable the benches were, it was a wonder he had ever slept there.

He moved out of the bench and headed toward the door. Once outside, he put his arm out to Marjie.

His mother and Lady Mariane locked arms and chatted amiably as they walked behind them.

Mr. Pugh stepped into their path. "Good day, my lord." He smiled far too familiarly at Marjie for Arawn's liking. He pulled her closer to him. "Miss Fitzroy, you are looking very handsome today."

She smiled politely at him but moved even closer to Arawn. "Thank you, Mr. Pugh. I'm certain it is the fresh air."

"I had thought to ask if you might do me the honor of taking a turn with me tomorrow afternoon."

Marjie flicked a glance up at Arawn, a panicked look on her face.

Arawn opened his mouth to tell the man Marjie was otherwise engaged when his mother stepped around him. "Oh, I'm sorry, Mr. Pugh. But I have engaged Miss Fitzroy's assistance in readying for the party tomorrow evening."

Arawn had to commend his mother. She seemed genuinely disappointed in having to share the news with him.

Mr. Pugh's nostrils flared slightly. "Perhaps another day."

Marjie nodded. "Yes. That would be lovely."

Mr. Pugh bowed to them and turned, disappearing into the crowd of people leaving the church.

"Arawn, could we please hurry to the carriage?"

He looked down at Marjie and his brow creased. Lud, she looked ill. "Marjie, you look very pale. Are you unwell?"

Her eyes flitted shut for a long blink. "I have a headache forming. That is all. I am certain I simply need to rest."

"Are you certain it is just a headache?" His pulse ticked up. What if she was ill?

She nodded. "The sun is very bright today, is it not? And I did not sleep well last night."

He certainly understood that feeling. He had not slept since learning of Miss Penry. While he knew everything was in place to keep the castle and its occupants safe, he still could not seem to rid himself of dark feelings and images.

"Let us see you home quickly."

From the corner of his eye, Arawn saw Mr. Radcliffe heading their way. "Lud, is there not a Sunday when I shall escape him?"

"Escape who?" Marjie looked around.

"Good day, my lord." Mr. Radcliffe stepped in front of them, blocking their path.

"Good day, Mr. Radcliffe." Arawn moved to go around him, but Mr. Radcliffe stepped to the side, blocking their path again. "I stopped at Hywel the day before last to inquire after your secretary. He still had not contacted me to set up an appointment. When I asked after him, your butler informed me that you do not have a secretary." He thumped his walking stick on the ground. "I wish to speak to you, my lord. If I must have the conversation here in the churchyard, then so be it."

Arawn narrowed his eyes at the small, rat-faced man in front of him. "You are not giving me an ultimatum, are you, sir?"

Mr. Radcliffe swallowed. "That was not my intention. But I need to speak with you. It is about the ap Tudur Day celebration. I know it is still months off, but if it is to be a successful event, there is planning that must be done."

"This is not the time nor the place for such a discussion. We are having a dinner party tomorrow eve. Please, join us and we may discuss it then." Arawn was dreading the party more and more. Not only did he have to endure Mr. Pugh but now Mr. Radcliffe also. Saints above, who else must he tolerate for a whole evening? Thankfully, Seren would be there and could help to distract the men from monopolizing Arawn's time. Although, from the look Mr. Pugh had given Marjie, it did not appear it was Arawn's time he wished to occupy. He glanced back over his shoulder, but the man was nowhere to be seen.

He turned back to Mr. Radcliffe. "Please, bring your wife also." Mr. Pugh, Mr. Radcliffe, and now his wife. The evening was only improving, he thought sarcastically. While she was not as bothersome as her husband, she had a rather unfortunate sounding voice. Arawn grimaced at the thought.

"My lord, may we please leave?" Marjie asked.

At least Marjie would be there. Arawn believed he could endure almost anything if she were with him.

"At present, Miss Fitzroy is ill, and I must see her to Hywel immediately."

Mr. Radcliff nodded, too eagerly. "Capital. Very good, my lord. I shall see you tomorrow evening."

"Until tomorrow." Arawn dipped his head as he guided

Marjie toward the carriage. "Shall we stop at the apothecary on the way home and fetch some powders?"

Marjie shook her head. "No. I think rest is all I need."

Arawn settled in the carriage across from her. He had thought to make his intentions for her known tomorrow at the party. The garden seemed a proper place. Besides, it was *their* place. Or that was how he thought of it. Although, he felt that way about the castle ruins and the west barbican also.

But the garden felt right because it was there he had first seen the world through her eyes. Which was something he had never experienced before. But the ruins were where he had first kissed her—the kiss that made him realize just how much she meant to him.

Both held a special place in his heart. But, then, did not the wall-walk, beach, and even the parish church? If he were being honest, nearly every place within view of the castle held a special memory of Marjie. Perhaps it was just further proof that she belonged here. That she belonged with him.

He bounced his leg up and down, impatiently waiting for the carriage to return them to the castle. The many reasons why she might reject his offer repeated in his mind.

He glanced over at her and released a heavy sigh. What would he do if she said no? Could he live without her? He could. But it would certainly be a miserable existence.

"Is something the matter, my lord?" Marjie's quiet voice sounded across from him.

He smiled at her. "No. I'm simply worried about you is all."

"I will be well. You need not worry, Arawn." She leaned her head against the window. Lud, she did not look well.

The carriage finally stopped in front of the gate. Arawn stepped out and handed out his mother and Lady Mariane. The two older ladies moved off to the side as he waited for Marjie to step out. When she did, she shielded her eyes from the sunlight.

"Do you wish for me to carry you to your chambers?" He could not deny he hoped she agreed.

She shook her head. "Do not be ridiculous. I am not sick or injured. I only have a headache."

He did not bother to hide his disappointment. "But it pains me to see you in distress. It is written across your face."

She smiled widely, but he could tell it was forced. "I will be well. I simply need to rest. A nap will set me to rights."

"Very well." He held her hand as she stepped down from the carriage. He held on to it, the thought of letting her go was unacceptable. "When you are feeling better, would you consent to take a turn with me?"

She nodded and a genuine smile turned her lips. It wasn't huge, but he would take it over the larger false one. "I would be honored." She turned and hurried into the south tower, leaving him standing with his mother in the outer bailey.

He turned and headed for his study, paying little heed to his mother.

He pushed open the door and was surprised as his mother breezed past him and sat down in the chair across from his desk. "We need to talk."

Botheration. That could not be good. She had surely noticed his attentions toward Marjie and wished to make her objections known. Arawn was not anticipating the conversation. His mother would be disappointed when he did not bend to her way of thinking.

He sat down and stared across the desk at her. She reminded him of Marjie in a way. Or maybe it was the other way around. They were both strong women who knew what they wanted and would not settle for anything less. "Arawn, you must do something before Mr. Pugh has the chance to take that turn with Marjie. I fear he has set his sights on her, and we both know they are not well suited for each other." She clasped her hands firmly in her lap. "Indeed, I had thought you would have already taken such measures. I cannot imagine what is taking you so long."

Arawn stared at her. What was she rambling about? It was not the lecture he had anticipated. Indeed, if he did not know better, he would almost think she was reprimanding him for not already proposing. But she was surely just worried about Marjie falling into the clutches of a man like Mr. Pugh. On the surface, he seemed a proper enough match. He had an adequate living and his estate, while not grand, was presentable. It was his demeanor and character that were lacking.

But even if he were the perfect gentleman, he would not be right for Marjie. There was only one man who fit that role, and Arawn intended to show her himself just who that Welshman was.

He steepled his fingers in front of him. "You need not worry, Mother. Marjie and Mr. Pugh will not be taking that turn."

Her face softened into a smile. "Oh?"

Arawn lifted his chin, putting on his most authoritative stare. He did not like to use it, especially on his mother. But she needed to see that Marjie was best for him. And if he must intimidate her to make her see that, so be it.

"I will brook no opposition, Mother. But I plan to offer for Marjie tomorrow before the party."

His mother clapped her hands. It was not exactly the resistance he had expected. "Lawkes, Arawn. It is high time you did. I have had to endure watching you moon over her this last fortnight, and I have hardly tired of it. Indeed, I do not know why you are waiting until tomorrow. Are you not to take a turn with her today?"

Arawn blinked at his mother several times. "You approve?"

"Why should I not?" She guffawed. "She makes you happy, which is something I've not seen much this last year. Indeed, you have always tended toward the sullen. I believed it was simply your nature. But Marjorie seems to know the secret in putting that aside."

Arawn nodded, somewhat befuddled by his mother's revelation. "Her family connections will not garner her success among the *ton*."

"To the devil with the *ton*," she said.

Arawn raised his brows. *To the devil,* did she say? "That is easy for us to say, but the reality may not be so pretty." What was he doing? Had he not planned to show his mother why the match was suitable? Why then, was he only pointing out the obstacles? She had completely befuddled him out of his preplanned argument.

His mother waved him away. "You are a marquess, Arawn. Act like one. Demand the respect you deserve and expect nothing less for your wife. People will overlook her connections if you do. But if you continually apologize for them, society will not be kind to her."

Arawn sat back in his seat. His mother had not refrained from lecturing, it was simply on the opposite side of the argument than he had expected. *Act like a marquess.* Her advice may not be as terrible as he thought.

He sighed. "What if she declines my offer because she believes she is saving me from the scorn of society?" He leaned forward on his desk.

"*Hir yw'r dydd,* Arawn. You must help her see that by marrying you, she is helping you to be the best you can be. Show her she can make society conform to her, not the other way around. Show her you believe in her. That is all she needs to know, and I have no doubt, she will grow into a great marchioness."

He leaned back in the chair and raised a brow. "You believe that is possible?"

His mother laughed. "I have changed, have I not? Perhaps not all the *ton* will, but those you associate with most frequently will come around to your way of thinking."

"Thank you, Mother." He smiled at her.

She stood and moved toward the door. "She will make a marvelous marchioness." His mother flicked her brows up before quitting the room and closing the door behind her.

She was right. He could not picture anyone else as the next marchioness. But more importantly, he could not imagine anyone else as his wife. He need only convince Marjie of that.

CHAPTER THIRTY-THREE

Arawn paced the length of the Lesser Hall, waiting for Marjie to appear. Her headache had kept her in her chambers since they returned from church the morning before. All his plans had come to nothing. The guests would begin arriving for dinner at any moment, and he still had not asked for her hand.

What if Mr. Pugh tried to engage her for a carriage ride or turn for the following day while at the party tonight? What excuse had she to turn him down?

He had wanted to use this party as a way of announcing their engagement. But unless he could secret Marjie away before dinner was announced, it seemed an unlikely situation.

And drat it all, his mother had planned for dancing and cards after dinner. He and Marjie were much more likely to be missed during a dance than something like a musicale. And it was not as if he could be called away on urgent business again.

He swore under his breath. This was not how he had planned things at all.

"Am I interrupting, my lord?" Marjie's voice brought an

instant smile to Arawn's lips. Just knowing she was there released much of the tension in his neck and shoulders.

He turned toward her. "*Noswaith dda,* Marjie."

She grinned. "Good evening, Arawn." She took a step closer, her head tilting to the side. "What is the matter? Your brow is furrowed, and your lips are pursed. You look completely out of sorts."

He lifted a hand and ran the back of his finger down her cheek. "I was worried you may not feel up to coming tonight."

She leaned into his touch, and he was tempted to pull her to him, allowing him to touch more than just her cheek. His arms nearly ached to hold her.

"I would not miss attending for anything," she said.

As much as he wanted her with him, he did not wish for her to come if she was still unwell. "Are you certain you are feeling well enough?"

She nodded. "It is why I stayed in bed for the whole of the day. I did not wish to miss dinner."

"I had hoped to speak with you before the guests arrive." It was not the ideal situation, to ask her here in the hall. He would much rather ask her in the garden or the abbey. But he felt an almost urgent need to ask her in that very moment.

But as he opened his mouth to continue, Havard opened the door and the first guests arrived. Mr. and Mrs. Griffiths and their daughter stood in the anteroom.

"Thunder and turf," Arawn growled. "Is it not proper to be late to social functions?"

"The evening will be over soon enough. We shall have plenty of time to talk then." Marjie grinned but wrapped her hand around his arm. "Hopefully tonight is the night we will discover Miss Penry's involvement in Ane's death."

If she says anything incriminating, Arawn thought with a scowl.

His mother glided through the door from the parlor and Great Hall. "Ah, Arawn, there you are." She smiled. "And Marjorie, I am pleased to see you are able to join us tonight."

"The hall looks lovely, my lady." Marjie smiled at his mother.

"Indeed, it does," Mrs. Griffiths chimed in as she came to stand beside Marjie.

Marjie moved to pull her hand from Arawn's arm, but he placed his hand on top of hers, holding it firmly in place. He was not above announcing his intention in that fashion. Indeed, he wanted the other men attending to know that Marjie would soon be engaged.

Although, he did not even know if she would accept him. He lightened his hold. Perhaps it would be better if he held back on publicly displaying his affections for her until she had accepted his offer.

"Come, let us adjourn to the parlor while we wait for the other guests." His mother led the way through the Lesser Hall and into the small parlor that had once been a part of the Great Hall.

Before long, every seat in the parlor was occupied and many of the men stood about the perimeter of the room, chatting amiably.

"I have not seen you much of late. I had thought once you put off mourning, that might change," Seren sipped at his drink. "Although, seeing you look at a certain young lady, I am no longer curious as to why."

Arawn pulled his gaze back to his friend. He could not dispute the accusation. He had hardly taken his eyes off Marjie. In part, it was to make certain Mr. Pugh did not speak to her, nor Miss Penry, for that matter. But in truth, it was mostly because he simply could not help but look at her. His gaze drifted to her of its own accord. "She is handsome, is she not?"

"Very," Seren said and Arawn raised a brow at him. His friend did not think to set his sights on her, did he? "But I believe there must be more to her than a handsome face if she has bewitched you so thoroughly."

Arawn smiled. "I've never met another like her."

"I am happy for you, my friend. Shall I expect the banns soon?"

Arawn nodded. "I had hoped to make the announcement tonight, but a headache kept her in her chambers since church." He could not help the slight pout in his voice.

Seren gripped Arawn's shoulder. "I believe you have time. Did you not say she and her mother were staying on through Twelfth Night?"

Arawn nodded, but his gaze flicked over to Mr. Pugh. He stood on the other side of the room, speaking to Miss Penry, of all people. But Arawn did not miss the frequent flick of his gaze in Marjie's direction.

He didn't like it. Not because he was jealous, although he was, but because he could not shake the unsettled feeling in his stomach whenever he saw the man. "Mr. Pugh seemed to take an interest in her at church yesterday."

"That is hardly surprising. He is always ready to entertain a pretty face." Seren sighed. "Nor am I surprised by your irritation. Pugh has never been among your favorite people."

"Favorite? I should not list him even among my unfavorite. I hold him in that little regard."

Seren rubbed his chin. "Why is that? I know you have told me the story before. But I cannot for the life of me remember it."

Arawn only took his gaze off Mr. Pugh for a moment. "Do you not recall what he did to Ane's rabbit?"

Seren's brow creased before remembrance dawned in his eyes. "Oh, yes. He killed it, did he not?"

"He did not just kill it. He tortured the poor creature first."

Seren nodded. "He was just a boy. He certainly has grown out of his meanness."

"I don't believe it." Arawn folded his arms, shifting his weight. "I believe he simply learned to hide it better."

"What have you seen to know that?" Seren now scrutinized Mr. Pugh as intently as Arawn.

"It is just a feeling."

∽⁓

Marjie sat down on the sofa and leaned against the arm. Her headache had not completely subsided, and the brightly lit dining room had slowly increased its intensity. The Great Hall lighting was only slightly less bright, and the noise that dancing would cause surely would not help the matter.

The chairs in the Great Hall had been moved to the sides leaving the center open for dancing. Several tables sat at each end for those wishing to participate in card games instead.

Marjie frowned. She was not particularly fond of cards, but she disliked balls and assemblies even more. She was proficient enough in her dance steps. But she was often left in want of a partner. If only Arawn could dance every dance with her.

"What has you in such a state?" Miss Penry sat down next to her.

Marjie looked over and tried for a convincing smile. But it was difficult knowing that this woman was likely the cause of Ane's death. "A state? I'm in no state."

"You looked positively fierce just now," she prettily arranged her skirt.

Marjie shook her head. "My apologies if I looked unfriendly. Since being thrown from the horse just after my

339

arrival, I have suffered with frequent headaches. This one seems to have a rather tight hold."

Miss Penry flinched, but quickly recovered. "Your accident?"

"Did you not hear of it? I was thrown from one of Lord Angle's horses while we were out riding."

"I hope he has rid himself of the beast." Miss Penry smiled but it looked tight and forced. "I understand he still keeps the horse that killed his sister."

Marjie shook her head. "I believe he was considering ridding himself of both the horses. Fortunately, it was discovered that a nail had been placed beneath the saddle. It seems it was not the horse's fault after all." Marjie leaned in as if she were sharing a great secret. Although, from the pale look on Miss Penry's face, Marjie felt certain the young lady had played a role in Ane's death. "And from the looks of it, it had been there so long it was surely the reason Lady Ane was thrown from her horse."

"She did it, did she not?" Ane hissed in Marjie's ear. "She is the one responsible. Look at her face. An innocent person would not look so guilty."

Marjie tried not to react to Ane's angry mutterings.

Miss Penry coughed and sputtered. "It is a pity Lord Angle doesn't have better help in his stables. My father would not tolerate something such as a nail working its way loose in *his* stables."

Marjie lifted her shoulder. "That is what is so troubling. The nail had been purposely placed where it might cause more discomfort. There was no other reason for it to be where it was."

Miss Griffiths leaned forward, and Marjie only then realized the girl had heard most of the conversation. "But that would mean someone purposely killed Lady Ane."

Marjie nodded, a serious look on her face. "It would seem so."

Miss Penry released a slightly crazed sounding laugh. "Perhaps it was only meant to hurt her. I do not think we can assume the person thought to kill her. How could you know their intentions if you do not even know who did it?" She flicked wide eyes to Marjie. "You have not discovered who did it, have you?"

Marjie shook her head.

Miss Griffith's brows rose.

"There," Ane pointed her finger at Miss Penry. "Is that not an admission? She very nearly said she did it. Not to kill me, but to hurt me." She snapped her mouth shut. "But why would she wish to hurt me?"

The men entered the room and Marjie locked eyes with Arawn. She slightly nodded her head and tipped it toward Miss Penry.

Arawn's brows hitched up.

Mr. Pugh hurried past Arawn and stood behind the sofa. "Miss Fitzroy, I wondered if you would consent to be my partner for the first set?"

Marjie glanced at Arawn, who scowled. While she did not wish to partner with Mr. Pugh, if she refused him, she could not dance with Arawn. And she desired that above all else. "It would be my pleasure." She said with little enthusiasm.

The man sneered at Arawn as if he had just won an argument.

Arawn turned to Miss Griffiths. "Miss Griffiths, is your first set claimed?"

She shook her head.

"Then I shall claim it for myself."

A smile stretched across her face.

"I suppose that leaves you stuck with me, Miss Penry," Seren bowed.

Miss Penry glared daggers at the young lady.

"I shall fetch us a drink before we start." Mr. Pugh bowed to Marjie before setting off across the room to the table of refreshments and large bowls of lemonade.

"I cannot believe you are simply going to dance as if there is not a murderer in the castle. Why do you not tell Miss Penry that you know what she did? Send someone for the constable." Ane moved in front of Marjie, her hands resting on her hips and her mouth set in a tight line.

"We have no proof," Marjie hissed.

"Mistress, th're is nay proof gainst th fiendish maiden," Gwen said as if she could convince Ane to calm down.

Mr. Pugh appeared and handed a glass of lemonade to Marjie and one to Miss Penry. Why had be brought one to her?

Marjie's nose wrinkled slightly. They had put too much mint in the lemonade. Usually, she was not opposed to the addition. It added a delightful twist to simple lemonade. But what she held in her hand smelled more like a little lemon in her mintade.

She smiled at Mr. Pugh. "Thank you, sir."

He grinned widely and gave a little swish of his hand. "Drink up. I require a lively dance partner."

Miss Penry put the glass to her lips, while Marjie only pretended to drink. The intense smell of mint made her head throb even more. "Where is your glass, sir?"

"I drank it at the table." Mr. Pugh licked his lips. "I saw no need to bring it all the way over here."

Gilford flew to a stop next to Ane. "Refuse the nectar, mistress. 'Tis tainted." He leaned over and put out a hand to push the glass away from Marjie's lips, but his hand went straight through. "Curse my spectral form!"

Marjie lowered the glass. "I beg your pardon?"

Mr. Pugh looked around in confusion. "I simply said I enjoy a lively dance."

Marjie looked at Arawn as he dipped his head to Miss Griffiths and extended his hand to her.

Marjie's eyes widened. "I'm sorry, but the footman must have put too much mint in the lemonade. It is too strong to drink, and Gilford advises against it." She emphasized the last words, hoping Arawn would understand.

Arawn excused himself from Miss Griffiths and took the glass from Marjie's hand. He sniffed it. "That does not smell like mint—" he looked over the glass at Mr. Pugh.

Mr. Pugh's eyes widened, and he glanced at the door.

Arawn shoved the glass in Seren's hands and grasped hold of Mr. Pugh. "I believe we need to have a little chat, Pugh," he spat out the man's name.

"I have nothing to chat with you about," Mr. Pugh sputtered.

Seren sniffed. He raised his brows as he held the glass at arm's length. "That smells of pennyroyal mint. At such a strength, I believe it would be quite lethal."

Miss Penry, spit a mouthful of lemonade back into her glass, coughing and choking.

"Blame your servants. It is not my fault they are quite inept." His nose curled. "I believe several of them are in from the stables."

"Put thy faith not in that fellow. He, verily, hath tainted the vessel with venom." Gilford swished a finger in front of Mr. Pugh's face.

Marjie pushed off the sofa. "Perhaps this conversation would be better had away from the party." Several people had stopped their conversations and stared over at them. It was no wonder the way Mr. Pugh carried on.

Lady Angle and Marjie's mother tried valiantly to keep the other guest's attention by instructing the music to begin playing.

Miss Penry, however, was quite the opposite of Mr. Pugh. Her mouth stayed pinched as her eyes flicked around the small group and she slowly backed away.

"No, I wish to speak here," Mr. Pugh demanded.

Arawn smiled mirthlessly. "Very well. I have no qualms telling everyone here that you put a lethal amount of pennyroyal in Miss Fitzroy's lemonade." He cast a glance around. "It is about time they knew your true character."

"They will not believe you." Mr. Pugh lifted his chin.

"Oh? You believe they will take your word over mine?"

Mr. Pugh's eyes squinted, his decision flitting across his face as he looked out over the crowd of people. Most of them looked away when he caught their gaze. "Very well, let us take this some place more private."

Arawn propelled him toward the door.

Marjie and Seren followed Arawn out of the Great Hall. She noticed Miss Penry seemed content to stay seated, but she watched them leave with a grim look on her pale face.

Ane, Gwen, and Gilford floated behind along with several footmen who took up positions at each doorway.

Mr. Pugh shrugged Arawn off once they were out of the room. "Unhand me," he sneered.

Arawn released the man but did not take his eyes off him as he spoke to Dafydd who was currently dressed in livery and acting as a footman. "Please, go fetch my mother, Mr. Davies, and Miss Penry. I believe they all should be present for this."

Dafydd nodded and hurried back through the parlor door.

"And see that the portcullis is ready if it is needed," Arawn called after Dafydd.

Marjie raised her brows. That felt a bit excessive. But in a sense, she supposed the castle *was* under attack.

"You are making quite a spectacle of yourself, Angle." Mr. Pugh yanked down his coats. "Portcullis, indeed"

Arawn gave Mr. Pugh a lazy-eyed shrug. "Why have it if you never use it. Especially to keep vermin like you from escaping."

"Vermin," Mr. Pugh's eyes rounded. "I do not know what you think you know, but I can assure you, it is false."

In a matter of minutes, Dafydd appeared with the two wide-eyed ladies and the bewildered-looking constable. He dipped his head at Arawn. Marjie assumed that was to mean he had taken care of all Arawn's requests.

"What is the meaning of this, Angle? I had a winning hand in there." Mr. Davies grumbled.

"I thought you should be present to hear this man's confession." Arawn leveled his gaze at Mr. Pugh.

"Confession?" He laughed a bit too loudly for it to be genuine. "What do I have to confess?"

"He tried to poison Miss Fitzroy with pennyroyal." He glanced at Seren. "Give Mr. Davies the glass."

Mr. Davies lifted the glass Seren offered to his nose and breathed in. His brows shot up. "I concur with your conclusion. There is pennyroyal in the lemonade, but how can you be certain Mr. Pugh put it in the glass?"

"Yes. It is just as I said. You know nothing." Mr. Pugh glanced toward the door where Baglan stood guard.

Arawn looked indignantly at the constable. "He is the one who brought it to her. Who else would have done it?"

"It was one of your shay-brained servants. They accidentally added too much," he looked haughtily around the room.

The constable shrugged. "Perhaps it is as he said. One of your servants accidently added too much."

"That might be a possibility," Arawn tapped his finger to his lip. "If we were, indeed, adding pennyroyal to the lemonade. How would they have accidently added something we do not have?"

"Maybe one of them has it in for Miss Fitzroy," Mr. Pugh glared at her.

"Inspect yond sir's pocket," Gilford said. "Yonder thee shall discover the evidence."

Marjie leaned toward the constable. "If you check his pockets, perhaps you might find your proof."

The constable stepped forward, "I beg your pardon, Mr. Pugh. But do turn out your pockets."

Mr. Pugh's face turned purple. "I shall do no such thing," he roared.

Mr. Davies raised a brow. "If you do not turn out your pockets, I shall be forced to accept the accusations leveled at you as truth. Come now, if you did not do it, there is no reason to object."

Marjie caught sight of Miss Penry from the corner of her eye. The woman looked ready to flee the room.

Marjie took several steps closer to her. "You need not worry that he will harm you, Miss Penry. I know Arawn would not let harm befall you while you are in Hywel."

She looked at Marjie, her eyes large and frightened. "Did he not bring me tainted lemonade also? You obviously do not know Mr. Pugh well." She twisted her fingertips.

Mr. Pugh stood, the debate in his head displaying across his features. He was caught, and he knew it. The only question was what he thought to do about it.

"Why did he do it?" Ane asked.

Marjie studied the man. Something was off. Why had he tried to kill both her and Miss Penry. Unless... "Perhaps if he tells us why he killed Ane and tried to kill me, his punishment might not be so harsh?" Marjie looked at Arawn, willing him to relent so they might have answers.

Arawn nodded, but then his head jerked back as her words played through his mind. "He killed Ane?"

Margie shrugged. "Or he helped to do it. That must be why he tried to poison Miss Penry also. She is the only witness. Perhaps if he explains himself, you will not see him hanged."

"I will consider it," Arawn's eye ticked as he started at her pensively. He was not going to agree.

"I did not kill Lady Ane." Mr. Pugh flicked a sneer at Miss Penry. "Fanny took care of that."

"It was your idea," Miss Penry lurched at Mr. Pugh, but Mr. Davies reached out and caught her before she reached the man. "You said it would only hurt her. Then I could come and visit. Those visits would allow Lord Angle to see me as a suitable wife. You promised I would become a marchioness."

Marjie stared. Ane had died as a ploy to gain Arawn's favor? She had no words for the sick emptiness she felt.

"You wanted a title and did not care how you came to get it." Mr. Pugh smirked at Miss Penry. Then he turned vacant eyes on Marjie. How had she never noticed the coldness there? Or perhaps she had but had not realized what it was.

"I have no qualms with Miss Fitzroy, per se. Other than her association with you." He looked back to Arawn. "I have waited for years to destroy you. I thought for a time that the death of your sister might do it, but in recent months you seemed to rally. No other plan presented itself until I observed you together in church." His face lit. "It was then I realized the best way to kill you would be to kill the woman you loved. So close upon the heels of losing your sister, I knew it would be your undoing."

A cold chill ran up Marjie's spine. How was such a man to be punished?

Mr. Davies stared between Mr. Pugh and Miss Penry, his mouth open. But no sound escaped.

"Saints above," Lady Angle whispered.

Mr. Davies finally came to his senses and motioned to Dafydd. "Please secure that one. She looks as if she might try to flee."

The constable took Mr. Pugh from Arawn and gave him a shake. "I had a winning hand, you know." He shook his head and muttered. "Trying to kill young ladies and disrupting a card game. I would not have thought it of you, Pugh." He patted the man's coat, shoving his hand inside he withdrew a small, corked vial. Mr. Davies' head continued to shake.

"Marjie?" Ane's voice called out from the doorway behind them. "Marjie, something is wrong. I feel different."

Marjie spun around. "What is happening? Ane, I can barely see you."

"I think it's happening. I think I'm leaving."

Marjie waved to Lady Angle. "I think she's leaving for good."

Ane reached out. "Tell my mother and Ari I love them."

Tears filled Lady Angle's eyes. "But I want her to stay. I just got her back."

"Ane?" Arawn hurried over and stood between Marjie and his mother.

"She said she loves you." It felt like a hollow reassurance.

Arawn sniffed and scrubbed his palm over his eyes.

Only a slight haze remained where Ane had been. "Thank you, Marjie," her faint voice could barely be heard above the noise in the Great Hall. "Thank you for giving me more time with them. And thank you for making Ari happy." The last words floated to Marjie, almost as if they were simply a breeze.

Marjie wiped her eyes, wondering if it was the tears making Ane impossible to see or if she was truly gone. Her presence had become so much a part of Marjie's life. What would she do without her?

Marjie looked around. Had they all disappeared?

Gilford and Gwen stood close together near the window. "Tis as the maiden desired. Perchance, anon the lady shall beest content." Gwen looked almost sad to see Ane leave.

"What is happening?" Lady Angle held onto Arawn's arm as if she were too weak to stand on her own. Marjie understood the feeling.

"She's gone," Marjie whispered past the lump in her throat.

Lady Angle broke down, deep sobs heaving out of her.

Marjie looked up at Arawn. His face was drawn, but he did not look as distraught as his mother.

"I'm sorry," Marjie whispered. "I should never have told you I could see her. I've only brought you more pain."

Lady Angle's gaze jerked up. "No. You are our greatest blessing. You gave us more time with her." She pulled a hand-kerchief from her sleeve and dabbed at her eyes. "I've suspected this day would come and have prepared myself. I will be well soon enough." Her shoulders heaved and shook as a fresh batch of tears fell down her cheeks.

Marjie did not think she had ever seen someone so forlorn.

Arawn led his mother over to a settee and helped her sit. Walking over to Marjie, he pulled her to him, wrapping his arms around her. His quiet, steady breathing was the only sound she could hear. It calmed her.

But then a deep, guttural yell sounded from the next room.

Arawn pulled away and in that moment, something crashed into her, sending her sprawling into the table behind her.

She drew in a breath as everything went black.

CHAPTER THIRTY-FOUR

Arawn paced outside Marjie's door. It had been two days since Mr. Pugh attacked her. Two days since she had opened her eyes and looked on him. Two days since he'd held her. And two days since he'd done anything but pace the stairs outside her chambers. His legs ached from the exercise.

He fisted his hands at his side. If he ever saw Mr. Pugh again—. For the first time in his life, Arawn wished the dungeons were still functional. The thought of seeing Pugh chained to the dungeon wall brought a heady sense of joy to Arawn's heart.

But seeing him in such a state...seeing him at all hardly seemed possible. At the very least Mr. Pugh would be transported—if he was not hanged first. But for now, he had been taken to Cardiff Gaol to await his trial.

Susanna, Marjie's maid, stepped out onto the stairs.

Arawn stopped pacing. "Is she awake?" The maid must surely have tired of the same question every time she stepped from the room. But Arawn did not care. He wanted to know the moment she woke up. Because she would wake up. She had too. No matter what Dr. Wells said.

Susanna smiled. "She just awakened, my lord. I am fetching her some broth as we speak."

Arawn's chest tightened. She had awakened. Surely that meant she would be well. Although, he would not fully believe it until he saw her with his own eyes.

He knocked on the door and a weak voice called out to him. He swung the door open and stared.

Marjie lay in bed, her lovely red hair splayed out on the pillow beneath her head. Her face still looked pale, but compared to the night Mr. Pugh attacked, she looked rather well. Every impulse inside him shouted for him to race over and take her in his arms, never letting her go. But he used every bit of restraint to hold himself back. He could not risk hurting her more. "Susanna said you had awakened."

Her mother sat on the edge of the bed. She eyed him, but the grin on her lips told Arawn she did not wholly object to his presence. If he had just been able to propose to her before the dinner party, this situation would be completely different. He might be welcomed at her bedside.

Marjie's smile was instantaneous, even as she pulled the counterpane up to her chin.

"I simply had to see it for myself to fully believe it."

"As you see, I am awake and well."

His heart pounded in his chest. He physically ached to touch her and feel the warmth of her skin beneath his. That was the only thing that would convince him she was truly well.

But it was not his right. While he wanted nothing more than to marry her on the spot, before anything else could prevent it from happening, he knew that his wishes and desires were not the only ones in consideration. And Marjie had yet to express her feelings to him. He hoped the delay was only because she had not been conscious, not because she didn't feel the same.

Two days was a long time to think and ponder. It was long enough to make him doubt what he thought he knew about her feelings. Especially those she felt toward him. The only thing that would set him at ease would be to hear her say she loved him.

Lud, he hated feeling so vulnerable. He wasn't sure what he would do if she didn't love him. Especially now, after losing Ane again. Could it be that Pugh would get his wish?

"Arawn?" Marjie's voice penetrated his thoughts.

He blinked rapidly at her. "Yes?"

"May we have tea together this afternoon?" There was a hopefulness in her voice that he shared wholeheartedly.

"I should like nothing more." He nodded like an idiot. "Are you able to walk? If not, I shall carry you to the parlor."

"I believe I can help her to the parlor," her mother said.

She smiled. "I'm certain I have not forgotten how to walk. But I appreciate your kind offer."

He sighed. Lud, he had missed her these past few days. He'd had no one to speak to and take walks with. Seren had stopped by several times to ask after her, but Arawn had not been in the mood to entertain him.

And his mother was still mourning Ane. Not that Arawn wasn't. But it was different this time. It had not been so sudden. Besides, he'd had Marjie to worry about.

Arawn had taken to speaking to Ane in the dark of night, even though he knew she was no longer there to hear him. Perhaps that made it easier.

Susanna nudged her way past him with a tray in her hands. "Begging your pardon, my lord."

Arawn grudgingly took a step onto the staircase. He should leave her to her mother and her maid. But he could not seem to make his legs move. He just wanted to watch her. Ensure that she was safe.

Lady Mariane stood from the bed and walked over to the door. She had a teasing glint in her eyes. "Thank you for checking on Marjie, my lord. But I do not think this entirely proper. Once she is dressed, I will help her downstairs so you might see her." She placed a hand on his arm. "Just give her some time." And then she closed the door on him.

He stood staring at the deep aged wood for several heartbeats, simply nodding at it. With a sigh, he made his way across the wall-walk and down the stairs toward his study.

At the bottom of the stairs, he bumped into his mother. "*Bore da*, Mother. I did not expect to see you out of your chambers."

"*Bora da*, Arawn," She smiled but looked more worn than Arawn had seen her since Ane died. "I understand Marjorie has awakened?"

Arawn nodded. "Yes, just this morning."

"Have you seen her?"

"Only from her doorway. But it was enough to see she looks well. Still a bit pale, but her eyes seemed bright."

His mother put a hand to her chest. "Thank the heavens. I've been so worried."

Arawn raised a brow. He was not certain his mother had been capable of worrying about anyone for the last few days.

She twitched her lips to the side. "Do not give me that look, Arawn. I may have been mourning Ane, but that does not mean I could not worry after Marjorie also." Her lips quivered slightly and Arawn braced himself for the tears. There had been so many tears. "I think on her almost as my own daughter." She straightened and the moisture all but disappeared. "You could make her my daughter if you would quit dilly-dallying and ask for her hand already."

"I quite agree and plan to remedy the situation as soon as I am able," Arawn grinned. "It seems you have put off your mourning, Mother?"

She sighed. "I shall never stop mourning. But life moves on whether we choose to or not. I should like to move on with it."

Arawn clasped his hands behind his back, and they strolled through the inner bailey, walking past his study door. "If you had it to do over, would you wish to know she was there? Or has the new grief been too much?" He knew she told Marjie that she was grateful for the time, but he wondered if she had been in earnest.

"How could I wish it away?" She pulled a crumpled paper from the cuff of her sleeve. "I should not have my letters to remember her by, if not for those extra weeks."

Arawn knew what she meant. He had pulled out his letter from Ane on several occasions. When he read it, he heard her voice again. It was comforting. "Yes, and we do still have Gwen and Gilford. That is something."

His mother shrugged. "While I bear them no ill will, if Ane is not here, I do not care to speak to the others." She suddenly rubbed her hands down her arms. "Lawkes, it is growing colder."

"I thought it a lovely day." He smiled, wondering if it had been the weather or just an angry Gwen.

Marjie walked cautiously on her mother's arm down the stairs of her tower. While she wanted to take the stairs two at a time, so as not to wait any longer than necessary to see Arawn, she knew she would end up in a heap at the bottom if she was not careful. It had already taken a great deal of coaxing for her mother to agree to this outing in the first place. She need not fall and end her bouts of freedom before they even started.

Her mother led her, supporting her with an arm around her waist and the other clutching the iron handrail. "Just a few more steps, Poppet."

Marjie nearly shook with anticipation. While she could not say she had felt the passing of time while she slept, she did feel as if she had not seen Arawn in ages. Only the short glimpse she had seen of him as he perched in her doorway earlier that morning. And it had not been nearly enough. She felt parched and that drinking in of him had not satisfied her thirst.

Dr. Wells had proclaimed her recovered, although he could not promise that the headaches would not continue. That was disheartening. But she was alive and on her way to see Arawn, so she would dwell on that instead.

They entered the Lesser Hall and Marjie's gaze immediately searched the room for Ane. Her heart squeezed when she remembered Ane was no longer there. If it hurt her that much, she could only imagine what Lady Angle and Arawn must be feeling. "The gold sofa will do nicely, Mama."

Her mother led her over and helped her sit. "Shall I ring for tea?"

Marjie shook her head. "No. I shall wait for Arawn to arrive. I do not want the water to be cold."

Her mother nodded and went to the settee where her sewing basket sat in the corner. She settled in and set to work on the sampler.

Marjie picked up her book that still rested on the side table where she had left it. But when she opened the cover, the words swam before her eyes, and her head throbbed. Perhaps reading would have to wait.

She looked around, wondering where Gwen and Gilford were. She had not seen a single ghost since she awakened. Not that she usually saw them in her bed chambers. She had put a stop to that immediately upon discovering she could see them. They had been respectful of her wishes. Well, everyone except Ane. She had come whenever she wished to speak to Marjie. Which had been often. Marjie would miss their conversations.

"*Prynhawn da*, Marjie," Arawn said as he entered the room.

"*Prynhawn da*, Arawn." She could not take her eyes off him. He looked tired, but that was understandable under the circumstances. But even tired, he was the most handsome sight Marjie had ever seen.

He came and sat next to her on the sofa, his hand clasped in his lap. "How are you feeling?"

She felt marvelous at that moment. Indeed, she felt as if she could do almost anything if Arawn was there with her. She grinned. "I feel a bit tired. Although, how that can be, I have no notion."

He released a stuttering laugh and her chest swelled. "It is rather baffling how you slept for two days and still feel fatigued."

He sat quietly, his gaze flicking to her mother and then back to his hands. Finally, he sighed and twisted toward her. "Marjie, I have wanted to speak to you since church the other day. But the time was never right."

She nodded. "Yes, headaches and unconsciousness. They are bothersome, are they not?"

Her mother stood up and cleared her throat. "I have not seen Sable today. Perhaps I will check on her."

Arawn's shoulders relaxed as he stood up and bowed. "Good day, Lady Mariane."

Once the door closed, he turned back to Marjie. "I had planned to do this in the garden, but I do not wish to wait until you are able for that activity." He ran a hand along the back of his neck. "Marjie, I have an offer for your consideration."

She tipped her head to the side. "Oh? What kind of offer?" She hoped she knew what it was, but would not allow herself to consider it too deeply, lest she was wrong.

"You told me once that you would consider living in Wales if an offer came from the right Welshman."

She smiled so widely that her cheeks hurt. "Yes, I did say that." But then remembered. It was not to be. No matter how much she had convinced herself that it would work, it could not.

"I should like to propose that I would like to be that Welshman. Let me prove that I am right for you—that I am the only man right for you."

She reached out to him, cupping his cheek in her hand. Tears filled her eyes, making it hard for her to see him clearly. "You don't know how much I have wanted to hear you say that. And as much as I want it, I know I cannot. Society will never allow it. My family connections—"

"Hang society. I almost lost you twice in one night and it nearly killed me." He sighed. "One of the things Ane told me in her letter was that she regretted allowing society to tell her who she could love." He reached out and ran a finger softly down her cheek. "I do not intend to make the same mistake. I'm a marquess, and I intend to act like one. No one tells me what I can and cannot do."

"But if you come to regret it? Regret me?"

"My only regrets will be if I do not follow my heart."

She pushed back the doubts plaguing her mind. If Arawn could follow his heart, could she not do the same?

"Please," he whispered. "Let me prove I am the only man— Welsh or otherwise—that is right for you."

Marjie's eyes blurred even more with a sheen of tears, and she bit the side of her cheek to keep from throwing her arms around him. "I might be agreeable to such an offer."

"Does that mean you'll marry this not old curmudgeon? I cannot picture Hywel without you." His gaze looked hopeful, yet vulnerable. "I cannot picture my life without you."

"Do you think it would please Gwilym and Rhys to have a relative living in the castle again?"

"While I respect your relatives, I am not asking for your hand because of them. I'm asking because I love you."

Marjie launched toward him, surprising herself with the energy she expelled, and wrapped her arms around his neck. "*Hir yw'r dydd arosaf am fy Arawn.*" She pulled back. "Long is the day I wait for *my* Arawn. I will wait for you every day of my life."

He held her close, and she could feel the rumble of laughter bubbling up in his chest. "My intention is to never make you wait, because I do not foresee you leaving my side. You are my other half." He pulled her slightly away from him, but only so he could look down into her eyes before he dropped his lips to hers.

She scooted closer, wrapping her arms tighter around him.

"*Dyna ferch dda,*" he whispered against her lips.

Never had Marjie felt so loved in her life as she did with Arawn. While his kisses made her toes nearly curl, it was the look of sheer adoration she saw in his eyes that made her know she was right where she belonged.

EPILOGUE

Marjie stood in the inner bailey, waiting for Arawn and their mothers to join her. She ran a hand up her arms, warming her already chilled skin. The warmth of September had given way fully to the cold of October. Especially in the evening once the sun dropped below the horizon.

She looked around, hoping to see Gwen or Gilford. She would even be happy if it was the one in a tunic that she could not understand. But the ward was empty, as was the castle. Or at least it was to her eyes. She had not seen a single ghost since awakening after Mr. Pugh's attack.

While she had spent much of her time utterly vexed by the ghosts and their demand for her attention, she missed them and wondered why she had wished them away. Why had she seen her gift as a burden? She frowned. It was too late to change her mind. The fates had made the decision for her.

"What is that look about, *fy nghalon*?" Arawn slipped his arm around her waist and tugged her to him.

She smiled at him. They had been married less than a fortnight, but she still swooned when he called her 'my heart'. She had never felt so loved as she did with Arawn.

"I thought you were anticipating *Nos Galan Graef*."

She nodded. "I am. I was just lamenting the irony that tonight of all nights, I cannot see or speak to Gilford or Gwen. Not to any of them." She sighed. "Because I know they are here, somewhere. I'm simply sad they cannot enjoy the evening with us."

"Ah, but I think you are wrong," Arawn twisted his head to the side. "They are enjoying it with us. I am certain of that. Their joy is just silent to our ears."

"Do you really believe that or are you simply trying to cheer me?" She tilted her head to the side.

"Does it follow it cannot be both?" He dropped his forehead to hers. "The difference now from years past, *fy nghalon, is* when we see the flutter of leaves or the flicker of a flame, we know who is doing it. I believe we shall enjoy *Nos Galan Graef* with them for the rest of our lives."

As if to confirm his words, Marjie's dress fluttered, and a deep chill ran from her head to her toes.

"Thank you, Arawn." She looked around her. "And thank you, Gwen or Gilford. I feel much better." She turned and tugged on Arawn's cravat. "This is your holiday, is it not? Does not the legend say you will be out with your dogs tonight?"

He stood up taller. "The dogs will have to mind themselves. I am otherwise engaged." He dipped his head and brushed his lips over hers. "Dogs are terrible company compared to you."

"If there are to be any stones left, we must leave at once," Dowager Lady Angle bustled out the door of the Stockhouse Tower with Marjie's mother close behind.

"Stones?" Marjie turned questioning eyes on him.

"It is tradition to scratch your name on a stone and throw it in the bonfire. In the morning, if your stone is still there, you shall have a prosperous year."

Marjie squinted. "And if your stone is not there?"

Arawn grimaced. "Then you shall die within the year."

It seemed a rather gruesome game to play especially so soon after Ane had left them.

As if reading her thoughts, Arawn leaned toward her. "Ane found her rock last year. I do not put stock in such things," he whispered.

The sadness Marjie had seen in Arawn's eyes when she first arrived at Hywel was no longer there. He could speak of his sister without the cloud of sorrow marring his very handsome face. She reached up and placed her hand on his cheek. "Perhaps we should focus our attentions on the apple bobbing."

He grinned down at her. "A very sound plan, indeed."

While Lady Angle had understandably been a bit of a watering pot after Ane left, it had only lasted a few days before she was back to smiling and laughing. "*Hir yw'r dydd, Arawn,*" she said as her head shook with impatience.

He lifted his arm for Marjie to take. "Shall we, *fy nghalon?*"

Marjie tucked her hand in the crook of his arm, curling her fingers so she might keep a tight hold on him. "I thought you'd never ask."

The four of them left the looming castle walls behind and headed for the village square to join all the festivities *Nos Galan Graef* had to offer. And while she could not see them, Marjie knew Gwen, Gilford and the other ghosts were surely walking with them—enjoying all their night had to offer.

AUTHOR NOTES

Dear Reader,

Thank you much for reading Charming the Recluse. This book was so much fun to write! But also so much work and stress because I knew I had to get it just right, or it would never work. I think I got it right.

Hywel Castle is based on Conwy Castle, also located in Wales. Many of the stories attributed to Hywel are actual stories from Conwy Castle with a few exception. First, the nun beheaded by Henry XIII was actually known as the Nun of Kent. Her story is true, jester location was changed. Second, the story of Arawn's ancestor that intervened with the Parliamentarians to save the castle was purely a product of my imagination. As are the ghosts that haunt the castle.

I hope you loved this book as much as I do!

Don't forget to read the Rest of the Castles and Courtship Series

An Amiable Foe by Jennie Goutet

To Know Miss May by Deborah M. Hathaway

A Heart to Keep by Ashtyn Newbold

A Noble Inheritance by Kasey Stockton

The Rules of Matchmaking by Rebecca Connolly

A Suitable Arrangement by Martha Keyes

An Engagement with the Enemy by Sally Britton

Happy Reading!

If you enjoyed this book, please leave a review on your favorite book retail site.

ACKNOWLEDGMENTS

To Cara Seger and Brandalyn Seaman, my fabulous editors who make sure my stories are complete and that I sound like I'm partially literate.

For my great writers' group: Sally, Laura, Anneka and Laura! Thank you for helps me mold my sometimes scattered thoughts into cohesive beginnings!

To my great ARC team. Thank you for all you do to help me be successful! I couldn't do it without you guys.

And last and most importantly, for my boys. Oh, deadlines and editing fatigue are real. Thanks for putting up with the long hours and missed story times. Thanks for reading over my shoulder and telling me you think my story sounds 'really good.' And thanks for encouraging me—and saying you're proud of me. I love you, tons! Especially to Christopher for supporting and helping me push through when it just feels too hard. For seeing I have the tools I need to make me successful. You are my greatest cheerleader! I couldn't do this without your support! LY

ABOUT THE AUTHOR

Mindy loves all things history and love, which makes writing romance right up her alley. Since she was a little girl playing in her closet "elevator," she has always had stories running through her mind. But it wasn't until she was well into adulthood that she realized she could write those stories down.

Now they occupy her dreams and most every quiet moment she has.

Her kids are used to being called names they have never heard and they use words like 'vexed' and 'chagrined'.

When she isn't living in her alternate realities, she is married to her real-life Mr. Darcy and trying to raise five proper boys. They live happily in the beautiful mountains of Utah.

Want more? Sign up for Mindy's newsletter here to receive updates, deals, and new releases. f you want to listen to the audio books you can find them on my Youtube Channel: https://www.youtube.com/@mindyburbidgestrunk7846   Or your preferred audiobook retailer.

You can connect with her on her website mindyburbidgestrunk.com.